LOVIN Mrs. Jones

A Novel

Edward Dean Arnold

LOVIN Mrs. Jones

A Novel

For information, please visit our Web site at
www.pendiumpublishing.com

PENDIUM Publishing and its logo
are registered trademarks.

Lovin Mrs. Jones: A Novel
By Edward Dean Arnold

ISBN: 0-9724586-0-3

PUBLISHER'S NOTE

Table of Contents

For anyone who has ever been in love . . .
at the wrong time.

MR. AND MRS. THEODORE ERNEST ANDREWS
REQUEST THE HONOUR OF YOUR PRESENCE
AT THE MARRIAGE OF THEIR DAUGHTER

Tracee Denise Andrews

TO

Gabriel Emmanuel Washington

SATURDAY, THE TWENTY SECOND OF APRIL
AT FIVE O'CLOCK IN THE EVENING

MOUNT OLIVE BAPTIST CHURCH
ODENTON, MARYLAND

RECEPTION TO FOLLOW

CHAPTER ONE

The Middle of It All

Baltimore-Washington Int'l Airport

"I could kill you right now for doing this to me," she said, with gritted teeth, her tone as serious as a heart attack. "And all you have to say is that you're sorry. Are you serious? You must be crazy."

She let out a small, barely noticeable, psychotic smirk of disbelief. She took only a quick second to break her stare of pure disgust directed at the man standing before her. Gazing off into the distance, she tried to come to terms with what was taking place here but doing so was too much to take in all at once.

"This can't be happening," she mumbled, to herself. "I gotta be having a bad dream. This is not happening to me. It can't be."

She turned back towards him, shook her head at him like 'you've gotta be freaking kidding me'. But his silence confirmed that he was for real, as he broke his eye contact with her for only a second.

Slowly turning his attention back in her direction, he met her right hand coming down on his face like a bolt of lightning that strikes without warning. The sting of her anger coupled with the sound of flesh on flesh was felt by nearby onlookers, who had paused briefly in their hastily strides to search for a clue as to what the commotion between the two was all about.

The assaulted man stood frozen in front of his angry assailant as if he deserved what had been dealt to him. The sympathetic look in his eyes, coupled with his unprotected stance revealed that he fully understood why this seemingly sane-looking woman was livid, choosing him as the sole target of her pain.

Still with fire in her eyes, she stared at him deeply as if searching for an answer for her heartache. In what now appeared as the calm after the storm, she purposely dropped his carry-on bag from her left hand and to the floor, as if she had just released the last bit of dead weight and surrendered her fight.

Without another word, she turned to walk away from him and from this.

In a weak attempt to stop her, he tried to grab her arm to keep her from prematurely leaving this unfinished scene playing out in the middle of the airport with an unintended audience.

"Don't touch me! Get off me!" she shouted, pointing her finger directly into his face. "Don't you ever touch me again! Ever!"

She violently yanked away from his grasp, and quickly took a few steps to again try to escape from his apologetic stare and silent plea of forgiveness. He knew not to try touching her again and took a step back to give her space to walk away.

Watching her leave, he took a deep sigh of uncertainty, slowly picked up his bags and after a beat, he eventually began walking in the opposite direction without looking back at the wreckage left behind.

Raleigh-Durham Int'l Airport – (Three hours earlier)

A love story is the last thing I expect to hear as Gabriel Washington and I—best friends, fraternity brothers, and fellow writers—await his 10:45 a.m. flight call to Maryland. We have a little time to spare. We've arrived over an hour early, with plans of me taking a later flight with my family. You see, Gabriel is getting married tomorrow. I am his best man. And, you would think that on the eve of such an important occasion, we would have plenty to talk about. Instead, we've been sitting silently for awhile now in the waiting area positioned right before reaching the security check. I assume that Gabriel, like most men in the same situation, needs a little mental space to come to terms with the next twenty-four hours.

As a heavy wind tosses sheets of rain against the airport windows, I aimlessly flip through pages of the latest issue of Black Enterprise while Gabriel answers yet another call from his fiancée. Sitting shoulder to shoulder with my friend, I can hear pretty clearly Tracee's one-sided dialogue, although I pretend as if I hear nothing. Seemingly, things aren't going as planned with last minute wedding details. Gabriel holds the phone to his ear, but does not utter a word as Tracee continues.

"Gabe, are you listening to me?" I heard Tracee ask.

"What?" Gabriel replied, suddenly shaking out of his trance. Wiping the dampness from his forehead and then lowering his head into the palm of his hand,

Gabriel tried to refocus and return his thoughts to their conversation. He expelled a deep, impatient breath as he listened carefully for an opportunity to interject a response to her endless questioning.

Sensing the tension, I glance over at him covertly, taking note of his perplexed expression, his increasingly annoyed tone as he responded to her questions in monosyllables. "Yes. No."

Finally, as if trying to find an out, in seemingly more ways than one, he finally stated, "Look. I really need to get off the phone. The battery is about to die. I will see you when I get there. Everything will be fine. Tomorrow will be perfect."

With another glance my way, he finally breaks free from the conversation and clicks off, emitting a ragged sigh of relief and withdrawing into silence. In our eleven years of friendship, I have never seen this guy like this. I might be tempted to write it off as pre-nuptial jitters if it were anyone other than Gabriel.

I bite back the urge to ask, "Are you nervous about the wedding or something?" But I know he would reply without hesitation, "A man nervous about his own wedding is a man who isn't sure about what he's doing." At least, I think I know him well enough to believe that's what he'd say.

The distracted expression on his face intrigues me. I know he and Tracee oftentimes argue about the whole bank exec versus his dream of quitting his job and being a writer. If I remember correctly from what he's told me she's said before, passion doesn't always pay the bills according to her. But today, I sense what is happening here with him is something different and not related to writing at all. I think to myself, well there's only one way to know what a brotha is thinking and that's to ask him.

"Hey, is everything okay, man?" I cautiously question, noticing a distant, unfamiliar look in his eyes.

He sits there in a trance, and I wonder if he even heard me. Gabriel eventually nods, but he doesn't take his eyes off the cell phone clinched in his right hand.

Finally, Gabe looks up. His eyes meet mine, and what I see there makes me uneasy, but I wait for the confession I sense he is about to make. Determined to suspend judgment, I meet his steady gaze. Then, as if some heavy weight has been lifted, he lets out a deep moan.

"Actually, Ed . . . everything's not okay."

"What's up?"

With that, he begins to tell me a story. I watch him carefully as he speaks, waiting for an easy laugh, a punch line that this is a joke or a tale created solely for my amusement. It never comes. Instead, Gabe tells me the sobering truth about a man and a woman who have fallen for one another. I ask no questions. I only listen and wonder. Why is he sitting here, eyes brimming, relating this tortuous love story in the middle of RDU airport as if it happened to him? Even the best of writers have never made a story live so clearly and visually in my mind as the one my friend is telling me. What he says reminds me of fateful stories pretended in movies, read in novels, or that I've watched 'by accident' on Lifetime network. I am completely drawn in.

Suddenly, he falters and begins to well up. What is going on here? I try to appear unaffected. Now that he has started talking, I don't want him to stop. I need to hear how it all ends. I dare not interrupt.

Then, all of a sudden, Gabriel smiles. My mind races to catch up with his words. I begin to slowly discern that the story is no story at all. He is telling me, on the eve of his wedding, that he is the man in the story, and the woman is not the woman he is due to marry tomorrow. I have a thousand questions. I wait for the answers that I hope will come. Gabriel, eventually, answers most of those questions in my mind as if I had actually spoken them aloud. Then he answers one more. Yes, he's fallen for her, but it can never be. Everything and nothing has changed.

This is what he told me.

CHAPTER TWO

The Beginning of It All

"That was Boyz II Men with 'Let It Snow,' and that's exactly what we're gonna do. It's a cold day in the Triangle with a chance of light snowfall for the remainder of the morning and into the afternoon. The time is 7:02 a.m. and it's currently forty-seven chilly degrees out there, so make sure you bundle up warm and find that special someone to snuggle up with tonight as we head into the Christmas holiday."

Alexandria exhaled slowly. The deep, soothing voice of her favorite DJ was a small compensation for being stuck in the early morning traffic jam she had hoped to avoid. *Thank God for Ty Blackwell*, she thought. Her original plan was to be home in time to watch the morning rerun of *Oprah*. Instead, here she was fidgeting impatiently in the driver's seat of her Infiniti, brought to a standstill by more ill-timed road construction on the inner-beltline. The road ahead resembled a parking lot. Unbelievable.

"Why didn't I just go through town?" she moaned, anticipating the time that would be eaten up by her decision to take what was usually the quickest way home from the gym.

Her exit was still more than two miles away according to a road sign up ahead that she could just make out. *At this rate, two miles might as well be thirty,* she thought, as the cars ahead of her inched forward, jockeying for space where construction vehicles had narrowed four lanes of highway to one. Her plans for catching this morning's show featuring Art Smith, Ms. Winfrey's personal chef, were definitely out the window. *No chance of picking up a new recipe to make for Lionel.*

Just as quickly as the thought invaded her mind, her eyes began to well. For a fleeting moment, she had forgotten, or at least wanted to, but then the pain of her recent separation came flooding back. She wouldn't be fixing supper for her husband tonight or any other night. *Where are you God when I'm hurting like this?* she thought, while pressing her hands against her face in an attempt to push back any oncoming tears. She took a deep breath to calm herself, but it was not enough to prevent the recollection of that day just months ago. It was all still very fresh for her.

"I SAID GET OUT!" she had screamed at the top of her lungs, furious.

"At least let me explain," Lionel pleaded while following closely behind Alex in desperation, like a man about to lose everything sacred to him.

"No! You have to go! Right now!" she insisted, finger pointing to the front door, not wanting to hear any of it. "I can't believe you even thought you could come back here."

"Alex, don't . . ."

"I'm not going to tell you again to get out," she

asserted angrily, interrupting. "If you don't leave now I'll have the police escort you out. Try me. I am dead serious."

"What? How can you say that to me like you don't even know me? I'm your husband. This is my house, too." Lionel's facial expression was one of genuine confusion and bewilderment.

"After something like this, I don't know you," she uttered coldly.

"Don't say that," he murmured, shaking his head.

Pacing heavily, she said, "It's the truth. But liars don't know anything about the truth. You're a liar, Lionel. I never thought I would say that about you, but you're a liar. I can't trust you, in or out of my sight. And I can't be with you."

"Sweetie, please. Can you stop for a minute so we can talk about this?" he begged. "It's not what it seems. You gotta believe me."

"I don't want to hear anything you have to say. And what do you think you could possibly tell me that would be worth listening to? Huh? More lies, Lionel? Is that what you want to tell me? I already know the truth. I know what you did. Everyone knows what you did, who you are. It's in the paper. On TV. The radio. How could you?"

He dropped his head in shame, realizing he had failed. The pain in her eyes was so evident, and hurting her was hurting him. After a brief moment, he said, "I'm sorry."

"Yes, you are," she smirked, in disgust. "About the sorriest I've ever seen. And sad. You're not the man I thought I was marrying."

Lionel let out a heavy sigh.

"I really messed up, I know it," he added, as if he was confessing to something.

"You're right, you did," she said sharply. "I was good to you, Lionel. I've never given you a reason to do something like this to me. Never. I don't deserve this. If you weren't happy at home, then . . ."

"It's not that."

"What is wrong with you? And with a tra . . ."

He interrupted before she could finish, and said, "I don't know. I mean, nothing. It's not like that. I'm not like that."

"You need to go. You're sick." Her face was serious. "And the more I think about it, it's making me sick. I literally feel like I'm going to throw up."

"Oh God, help me. Babe. Please. I don't want to lose you," Lionel said.

"Don't you get it . . . you already have. I can't be with you." Her facial expression displayed pure disgust when she said the words. "And honestly, it's taking everything in me not to put a bullet in your behind right now. That's the place you've taken me to."

Lionel suddenly realized she was serious. Never having seen her like this, the look in her eyes had him cautious.

"I'm really hating myself right now."

"Not more than I am towards you," Alex replied. She took a breath. "Why won't you just leave? Why are you still standing here? Do you want me to shoot you?"

Lionel's departure was Alexandria's only concern at this point. She needed him out of this house and out of her life before she did something she would regret. But he didn't move. It was like he thought he was going to change things.

"Babe?"

"You know what . . . keep standing there," Alex said.

She brushed by him, seething with rage as she bolted from one room to another looking for where she had placed her cordless phone. "I'm calling the police. They're real sympathetic to black men in domestic situations, especially ones with an already pending case for something else."

"Don't do this to us. Please," he begged, walking right on her heels.

Now with phone in hand, she quickly turned around to him enraged. Pointing her index finger directly in his face, she said sternly, "You did this! Don't you dare try to turn this around on me! Don't you dare. So just stop it. I'm tired and I don't have the strength to do this with you anymore. Do you realize what you've done?! You can't fix this. There's no fixing it. No matter what you say, or try to do, you can't. Your lawyers might be able to make it go away, but your money can't fix us. I just don't want you anymore. I shouldn't have married you. You are the worst mistake of my life!"

"Please," he continued to beg, his voice even more pitiful than before.

"I thought you were different. You're not. You are so much worse."

"Babe?"

Lionel attempted to reach out to embrace Alexandria. Before he could succeed, she turned on him in a fury. "Boy, don't touch me!" she yelled and, before she knew it, she had hit him hard against the side of his head with the phone, missing her intended aim for his face.

Lionel was frozen in surprise, eyes blinking repeatedly from the unexpected blow. It was obvious the hit hurt like hell from the explicit word that fell from his mouth. Then, before he could utter another word, and for good measure, Alexandria hit him a second time, this one landing across the right side of his cheek – hindering any form of composure on his part. Lionel looked at her directly in her eyes, his eyes almost to the point of welling up. He was now standing there as if he was asking to be hit if it would make her feel any better.

"You deserve much worse, and you know it," she said, coldly.

"We're gonna keep our songs of the season going just a little bit longer with one of my personal favorites: "This Christmas" by Donny Hathaway. Hopefully, it'll keep us all in that holiday spirit and add just a bit of warmth to everyone's day," Ty announced over the opening bars of the song in his buttery voice, interrupting Alexandria's flashback and inviting her to tune back into his radio program.

"Where are you God when I'm hurting like this?" she muttered.

Determined to clear her thoughts of Lionel, she reached forward and turned the volume up a notch as the song began. "It's gonna be okay," she told herself, as the music seeped into her weary mind. "Just gotta get through the holidays. You can do it, girl."

" *. . . this Christmas . . . and as we trim the tree . . .*" Alex sang along softly with Donny's uplifting lyrics. This song did her soul good. It was definitely a small part of what she needed right now.

Only a minute had passed, and out of the corner of her eye, she noticed that traffic in the next lane beside her was beginning to creep forward. The make and model of a car that she had not seen before was now positioned to her left, and the curiosity of what it was caught her attention. *Sweet*, she thought, glancing away and then quickly turning back for a second look at who was driving. From what she could make out, a young brotha was behind the wheel, dressed in a suit from what she could gather. To her surprise, his lips were moving in sync with the song she was listening to on her radio.

"*Fireside blazing bright . . . we're caroling through the night . . . and this Christmas . . .*" she sang with the stranger in the car next to hers. Oblivious to the traffic jam around her, she watched his head sway with the music, his strong jaw working the words, brow lifting and lowering, completely unaware of his audience in the car over. As his fingers tapped the song's beat on the steering wheel, Alexandria suddenly realized how much she was enjoying his performance.

She smiled to herself.

The sharp bleat of a car horn startled her and brought her attention back to the road ahead. Although cars were now creeping forward, traffic appeared to be going from bad to worse. The congestion was thickening, fed by more hapless commuters merging in from new entrance ramps.

With a deep sigh, Alex turned her attention back to the entertainer. *Might as well enjoy the show while I'm here*, she thought as a smile tickled the corners of her mouth. It had been a very long time since something so simple had amused her so much.

"*And as I look around . . . your eyes outshine the town . . .*" the lyrics flowed from his lips as well as hers, while she continued studying his profile and imagining the sound of his voice as Donny hit the high notes. Could the stranger hit them, as well? She'd like to think he had a good voice.

She took a quick inventory of his features, those that she could make out from the distance.

"Mmmm, definitely very nice," she told herself as she watched . . . and watched . . . and watched some more. Then she giggled quietly to herself, completely taken with both the gentleman and the moment.

The stranger continued singing, but then, all of sudden, he leaned forward and turned in her direction as if drawn by an unseen force. By surprise, he caught Alexandria in her unabashed fascination. And just as quickly as he did, his lips immediately stopped moving at the sight of her.

Her face hot with embarrassment, she ceased singing and quickly turned away.

"Oh-my-goodness. Did he just see me watching him?" she mumbled under her breath, just barely able to restrain herself from laying her head on the steering wheel to hide her humiliation. The thought of now being the one observed made her uncomfortable.

Seconds quickly ticked past. Still flushed with embarrassment, Alexandria stared directly ahead, resisting the urge to glance over just in case he was still looking her way. But curiosity soon took hold, and she slid her eyes sideways, only to find him staring right back at her with a slight smile on his face.

"Okay, he saw me," she admitted aloud, speaking through clenched teeth. She dredged up a smile in return, and his smile broadened even more, as he apparently explored what could be seen of her. He took inventory of everything he could make out.

They both looked away. He looked back at her. Then she cautiously looked back at him, only to catch the remnants of his glance as he focused ahead. She looked away again, just as he allowed himself a glimpse in her direction. A visual Ping-Pong match was in progress.

Alexandria was about to take her turn in the match underway when the insistent blast of another car horn made her abandon the prospect. She inched her car forward, closing the gap between herself and the car in front.

Traffic was finally starting to flow, with drivers in both lanes aggressively edging their cars towards the one open lane ahead. As she neared the 'left lane closed/merge right' sign, she could see the stranger's car pull up next to hers. He gazed in her direction with another warm smile that accented his kind features even more. Flirtatiously, she smiled back and then waved him on to take the position in front of her. Their eyes met briefly as he pulled into her lane, giving her a friendly wave of thanks. She figured it was the least she could do, since he had entertained her for a brief period in this awful mess this morning. She waved at his rearview mirror just as she nuzzled her car up close to his, satisfying her earlier curiosity on the make and model of his ride.

Letting out a slow breath, Alexandria relaxed her grip on the steering wheel and forced herself to focus once again on the silken voice of Ty Blackwell leading listeners into a commercial break. Crawling by the construction zone, she checked her rearview mirror and, revving her Infiniti's powerful engine, she pulled out from behind him.

Without another glance, but not that she didn't want to, she zipped by him towards her exit. As her car moved up the long ramp, she caught a final glimpse of his vehicle gliding along the now wide-open highway. Silly as it seemed, she was almost disappointed that he hadn't followed her. She smiled again over the innocent encounter, and then winced as she realized that the short time she had spent in this man's company, even at a distance, might very well turn out to be the best part of her day.

CHAPTER THREE

Alexandria Jones

Taking a much needed aspirin for an oncoming headache and chasing it down with a glass of water, Alex slowly made her route from the kitchen to upstairs, past unpacked boxes. Although she had been in this house since her recent separation, she had very little motivation to do anything when it came to putting things in their proper place. The disorganization in her new home reflected the upset in her life for the past several months. As she maneuvered around boxes in her path, she tried to resist the urge to shuffle through the stack of tapes scattered about the floor. In the back of her mind, she knew that amidst the pile lay her wedding video, a painful reminder of a beginning that she thought would never end.

Watching this video was a willful act of self-torture on Alexandria's part. It grieved her deeply to sit and watch Lionel's face, to hear his voice and see the two of them together on a day that resembled a fairytale wedding. Yet, every now and then, she found herself pulling it out to revisit a happier time, what now seemed like a life that belonged to someone other than herself. Watching the blissful moments captured between her and Lionel angered her as she grappled with the reality of their separation and pending divorce. Rage was her new companion. She laid awake at night going over every single detail of their relationship. The barrage of questions that raced through her mind sounded like a self-inflicted interrogation of what, why, and how long. The only thing she was certain of was that the hurt from Lionel's betrayal left her bitter and without a sense of direction for her future. Feeling out of control was not a familiar place for Alex, and she struggled with the unpredictable chain of emotions that raided her mind without warning.

Today she again sat studying Lionel and herself as if she were looking for clues, some hint of the train wreck that awaited them. There they stood, their bodies intertwined, smiling and laughing with their guests at a beautifully decorated outdoor wedding reception. She raised the television volume so she could clearly hear each guest offer personal commentary about them as a newly-married couple. Phrases like 'they fit perfectly together' and 'I couldn't think of two individuals better suited for one another' now all sounded like scripted lies delivered on cue. Did he pay these people? Nothing in her life seemed authentic anymore. Her husband was a liar, among other things, and she was naive for believing he was different than the many disheartening stories she heard from close friends about their failed relationships. He had proven he was the same as all the others, if not worse. She just happened to get swept away by this one and it burned her inside to think she could have ever believed in the whole 'happily ever after' nonsense.

Alex sat locked in disbelief as she watched herself glide in the arms of her strikingly handsome, new husband. Dressed in an elegant, custom-tailored Armani tuxedo, Lionel resembled a cover model on an issue of GQ Magazine. She had always told him that he could put Denzel Washington to shame any day of the week. His strikingly handsome facial features complimented his strong, statuesque build, and his chivalrous demeanor.

At 6-foot-7, he was her knight. His chiseled physique was the result of his athleticism from years of playing professional baseball. Much of his career had been spent with the New York Mets until a leg injury took him permanently out of playing the game. He was a good player, making a name for himself as one of the most feared sluggers who was also known for his prodigious home runs and dominant presence in the field.

Determined to not let an injury interfere with his love for sports, he eventually started his own sports management company. Successful, his work kept him away for weeks at a time. No matter how hard he tried to balance the demands of his travel schedule with family obligations, their marriage suffered when he had to choose. Still, Alex understood his work made him happy in spite of her dissatisfaction with her 'backseat' status as his wife and partner. She liked being Mrs. Lionel Jones and did her best to appear understanding when, more often than she preferred, his choices called for sacrifices in their married life.

As she reflected on the early days of their courtship, she remembered that even her mother had wholeheartedly approved of Lionel, a rare honor for any man dating Margaret Robertson's baby girl. On occasion, Alexandria had even jokingly accused her mother of loving Lionel more than she loved her, her own daughter. But her mother always quickly reassured Alex that her adoration for Lionel was purely based on the kind of man he was. She had completely trusted Lionel with her daughter's well-being, and Lionel had earned both Margaret's trust and her daughter's heart. Alex's relationship with Lionel caused her mother to reminisce about the wonderful 30 years of marriage she shared with Alex's dad, a marriage that abruptly ended when her father was killed in a car accident from being hit head on by a drunk driver. Alex was a senior in college when the accident happened and the tragedy took its toll on the entire family, especially Alex's mom. The matriarch of their family was broken and her mother suffered with severe depression after her father's death. Alex, always the dutiful daughter, pushed past her own grief to take care of her mother and to bring some normalcy back to their lives. Putting off graduation, she left school in her final semester to make sure her mom received treatment. After returning to school, she graduated with honors just the way her dad would have wanted her to finish what she started.

Not a day passed without Alex thinking of her father. His absence was felt, especially when she made her way down the aisle on her wedding day. Her younger brother Omar was there to give her away, but it still didn't remove the fact that something special was missing. After her father died, Alex knew the void left in her heart could never be filled by any man in her life. She reserved a hidden place in her heart for the love she shared with him. Her dad's death, and watching powerlessly as her mom battled severe depression, proved to be the most difficult time in her life. Back then her faith grew stronger and anchored her. But this upheaval in her marriage was a new place of brokenness, leaving her feeling bitter and uncertain about her future.

As she continued to listen to the video relay the good wishes of family and friends, she slowly raised her head to look at the faces on the television screen. What she saw instead was a quick turn of the camera towards the dance floor underneath the massive tent. There, in the center of the floor, she stood wearing an off-the-shoulder, satin-trimmed wedding gown that accentuated her hourglass frame. Her dress was a fine adornment to her natural beauty and she stared on in silence as her new husband joined her for their very first dance. It had been their moment and, gracefully, they rocked slowly in each other's arms to the melodious sounds. She recalled him whispering in her ear, "I am loving myself some Mrs. Jones."

As she continued watching herself move about the reception, she remembered something the camera had not been able to catch on tape. For one all too brief moment, she had surprisingly caught Lionel watching her with an expression of total adoration on his face. He stood across the crowded room completely oblivious to anything but her. Despite the bombardment of a constant stream of well-meaning family and friends repeatedly congratulating him, he gazed at her with a deeply satisfied stare. For one split second, Alexandria had turned her attention away from him to continue greeting family members. To her amazement, when she looked back, he was still standing there with his eyes locked on her and a sly grin growing across his face as if he was more than pleased. Curious as to what he was thinking, she subtly mouthed to him, "What?" Lionel's smile widened, and then he replied with the smoothest motion that consisted of a quick toss back of his head as if to say in street lingo, *"Whatsup?"* Alexandria imitated the same head gesture, with a blushing smile, as they shared a private moment in the midst of the reception chaos. They both knew what awaited them, as their stares resembled two individuals counting down the minutes to when they would be able to make love as husband and wife. And their lovemaking was going to be intense tonight, given their long courtship and Alexandria's insistence on waiting to have sex until marriage. Lionel never pressured her to reconsider, although he confessed to her his struggles to suppress his urge to have her completely. He understood that having her in his life meant waiting and he accepted that she wanted to do things differently in their relationship. While a young Alexandria had made past mistakes in relationships, when she and Lionel met she was stronger in her faith and more focused on being a woman of spiritual integrity. It wasn't easy to abstain as her feelings grew stronger for Lionel. But the two agreed, it was worth the wait and neither wanted to risk losing possibly their greatest blessing.

As Alexandria continued to watch and listen, the band struck up the sounds of Pure Soul's "We Must Be in Love." Seductive women began leading their dates onto the outdoor dance floor. With her eyes glued on the television screen, Alex watched Lionel hold her close while they danced and stared into each other's eyes, lost in the depths of one another. Things couldn't be more perfect.

Although the video didn't capture the sound of their words, looking at their mouths move Alex recalled what they both had said. She now repeated the words, mouthing them to herself.

"Just you and me?" she asked him, as if only they mattered. "Just you and me," was the reply she received.

She placed her hands on his face, then pulled him towards her and gave him an affectionate and passionate kiss on the mouth. This moment was right, so she believed.

After this long and fervent kiss, she rested her head on her man's chest. Facing the direction of where her mother sat, Margaret gave Alex an admiring and loving glance and a subtle nod of approval. Alex smiled back, agreeing with her mother.

The focus of the wedding video suddenly shifted to an unruly gathering of women and men laughing, doing old school dances and beginning to form a Soul Train line. The band then suddenly switched the music to a more upbeat tempo, and the Soul Train line went off in full motion. Alexandria turned up the volume at the sound of the guests clapping loudly as Lionel and her headed down the line, pumping them up and chanting, "Go, go, go, go, go." Lionel danced behind her, his hands waving in the air and shoulders bouncing to the beat. As usual, he was completely off-rhythm, unlike his grooving wife who rocked her body effortlessly to the beat as if the music lived inside her. Lionel had always told Alex she made him look good on the dance floor. It was true.

Alexandria carefully looked on as Lionel slipped away from all the dance mania into a quiet area to talk directly into the camera. Still slightly out of breath and with his clothes disheveled from the dancing, he peered directly into the lens of the camcorder and happily raised his drink to toast his new bride.

"I just wanna say to my beautiful wife that I am the lucky one here today." He paused to clear his throat. "I honestly can't remember a day before you stepped into my life, babe. I love you so much, Alex. I really do." Choking up, he paused only briefly. "Ummm . . . you are my heart, my entire world, and I look forward to waking up with you every morning and growin' old with you. You make this thing called life worth livin' and I wouldn't have it any other way than with you, babe. You are the best, and I just love you. I promise to be true to you and treasure you everyday of our lives together. You and me forever and always, I promise." Lionel raised his glass in a toast to a day well done and finished it off in one swallow.

"All lies," Alex mumbled in disgust, while raising herself up from her bed. "Enough," she said, abruptly switching over from video to TV and landing directly into the news.

"*. . . and more expected snowfall tonight and tomorrow, more than what was originally predicted,*" Howie McMillan, the local weather guy finished his report and handed the spotlight back over to Tracee Andrews, the lead anchorwoman. *"Now, back over to you Tracee."*

"Thanks, Howie," the anchorwoman replied back. *"And in other news today . . ."*

Alexandria muted the TV, sighed heavily, let out a yell, and then fell flat on her back, oblivious to the comfort of the goose-feather mattress, pillows, and pristine white bed linens. She stared unseeingly into the recesses of the white ceiling above her head. "I hate him," she mumbled angrily under her breath while surveying her surroundings. Her pain was reflected in this room, which she now kept constantly dark and tightly shut against the outside world.

Finally, she shook her head as if to shake free of the confusion, then slowly stood to her feet, slid into a pair of furry, black slippers and dragged herself into the bathroom. A now lukewarm bubble bath she had run earlier, before being interrupted by an earlier phone call from her mother, awaited her. She began to undress slowly, staring at her reflection in an oval mirror above the double vanity sink. As she removed her sweats, letting them fall to the floor, she turned to the cheval mirror. Alexandria was a stunning woman, small-framed but with a full bosom and backside that was all proportioned. She had long auburn-tinted hair and dark brown eyes that drew you in.

Stripped bare before the mirror, she observed the fragility of her frame. The pain of her ordeal had taken its toll on her strength and she could see a weakness in her stance. Having always been naturally athletic—a cheerleader, a track star, and a pretty decent basketball player, according to her brother, she had never done much else to stay in shape. Now, she looked at herself as if seeing her naked form for the first time and wondered how much longer she could go on this way without losing all of herself.

Suddenly, the phone rang again, bringing Alex's trance to an abrupt end. She headed back into her bedroom to pick up the cordless phone on the bed. She hesitated and allowed it to ring once more in the hope that perhaps her voicemail would pickup before she did. She really was not in the mood for a lot of conversation today. However, as she quickly glanced at the caller ID screen, she noticed it was her best friend Jaz.

Alex answered, relieved that she could be herself and not have to put up a front for the caller.

"Hey, Jaz."

"Hey, girl. What'cha doing?" Jaz asked in an upbeat, playful voice, like always.

"Nothing. About to take a bath."

"Everything okay?"

"Yeah. I'm fine," Alex replied, somberly. "Just one of those days."

"I know," Jaz's voice softened with understanding. "Did you at least make it to the gym this morning?"

"Yes and no. I got there when they opened and sat in the parking lot for about twenty minutes, starring at everyone through the glass windows, and then I came home after running an errand. I tried."

"You're gonna be okay, sweetie. Hey, you've been to hell and back in the last six months. It takes time to find yourself, right?" Jaz stated, out of deep concern.

"Yeah, I guess." Alex sounded doubtful. "What's up?"

"Nothing. I was just headed to the mall in the next hour or so and wanted to know if you wanted me to come by and scoop you up to do a lil' last minute, real quick like Christmas shopping with a sistah?"

"Ummm . . . I'm not really feelin' it today, Jaz. I don't think I'm even gonna get dressed again after my bath, to be honest with you."

"Ah, Alex. I could really use your company. Y'know how I hate mall shopping without you. And you know how we love ourselves some sales," Jaz added, enticingly.

"Is it still snowing?" Alex asked, suddenly changing the subject.

"Just some light flurries right now, so you can't use that as an excuse."

"I'm sorry, Jaz. I really don't feel like being around a lot of people, especially at a mall."

"Okay," Jaz sighed, "but I know those boots you were checkin' out last time we were at Saks are probably half off today."

"Have you called Theresa?" Alex asked, trying to give Jaz the alternative of asking another one of their girlfriends.

"No, I called you and only you."

"Oh," Alex replied, in a lifeless tone.

"I don't like the way you've been sounding lately and we just need to get you out and doing some stuff to take your mind off things. So, I'm not taking no for an answer. I'll give you a couple of hours to do whatever you need to, and I'll be by so get ready."

"Jaz, don't do this," Alex pleaded.

"Sorry."

Alex loved Jaz and usually spending time with her was nothing but fun, but today was different. Alex wanted to be alone with her memories and her pain. Jaz was an upbeat, no-nonsense, straight-talking girlfriend. She was a hairstylist and a business manager with two beauty shops, "A Touch of Jaz" and "A Touch of Jaz Again." Her shops were both full-service salons catering to the Triangle's most well-to-do black clientele. Always firmly in her corner, Jaz and she had been the best of friends since childhood and had been practically inseparable since they met in eighth grade. The two were often mistaken for sisters because of their physical likenesses. Both were slim with mocha-colored complexions, but they were total opposites when it came to personality.

Alex was the soft-spoken one, and Jaz was a loud and boisterous sistah with a lot of attitude. Maybe that's part of the reason why in their earlier school years, before they actually became friends, neither was very fond of the other. Alex thought Jaz talked too much. Jaz thought Alex acted as if she knew everything. So much so, that they occasionally had fights after school because their personalities clashed. To ask either how they became the best of friends in the midst of all that, neither probably could say exactly. It just happened.

At present, Alex knew her sanity would have dissolved by now had it not been for her girlfriend's undivided, loving attention. When she just couldn't sleep, Jaz had packed a bag and stayed with her for a full two weeks solid. It had been tough in the beginning, but Alex never felt totally alone, thanks to all the attention from Jaz. Sometimes they would stay up late, until 4 in the morning, and Jaz would patiently listen to Alex recite every detail leading up to the breakup over and over again. Jaz was always there, no questions asked, refusing to allow Alex or anyone else in her presence to sulk for too long. But Alex also knew Jaz would not take no for an answer like she had said.

"Tell me it's gonna be okay, Jaz. I need to hear that it's going to be okay," Alex sighed.

"It's gonna be more than okay, sweetie. I'm going to help make sure of it."

Alex had always leaned on Jaz when it came to heartaches and frustrations. Jaz's carefree outlook on life and her unstoppable sense of humor always left Alex with a sense of calmness and a lot of laughter, even when it hurt to laugh. These two dear friends had a deeply rooted understanding of each other's needs.

Over the past twenty-plus years, they had shared their deepest hurts, greatest triumphs and all the little stuff in between, usually over a gallon of Haagen-Dazs ice cream topped off with crushed Oreos. Everything from their first sexual encounter, their first true love, their worst breakup, Alexandria's wedding day, and now a looming divorce.

Jaz knew the kind of relationship that Alex and Lionel had shared as if they were characters living in a romance novel, destined to live out their happy ending together. No one saw this coming. Lionel had seemed to be honest and trustworthy, but today wasn't about Lionel. It was about getting her girl back on her feet, which was going to take time and a lot of it. Jaz refused to give up. Her bulldog attitude about life had gotten them through tough times before, and she wasn't about to stop trying now.

"What do you think about spending Christmas with me and my family? Because I refuse to let you sit up in this new house and do nothing but mope. I'm spending it at my Aunt Elsa's, so you gotta come over. She is too excited about finally introducing us to this Thurman fella she's been dating. Can you believe her? She's what, almost seventy? And still tryin' to find my grown-tail cousins a daddy as if they are nine years old or something," Jaz laughed.

Alex smiled, but didn't answer.

Jaz continued, "She has a Christmas present under her tree for you too, so you gotta get that even if it's just for the laugh. We both know it's something extremely tacky. I keep telling her to stay out of the As Seen On TV section of the store. No one wants a Clapper anymore."

"She is too funny."

"Indeed."

Alex smiled. "You know mama's probably expecting me to spend Christmas over at my Aunt Catherine's with her and . . ."

Jaz interjected, "And your mama can come, too. Dang, her and Aunt Elsa only live two blocks from each other and it'll give them the opportunity to talk about their good ol' days of raising us two rambunctious girls and all the hell we put them through."

"I never put my mama through hell," Alex insisted. "It was you, always wanting to fight me after school for no reason."

"For no reason," Jaz replied, sarcastically.

"Yes, for no reason. I was stupid for allowing you to push my buttons," Alex contended, her spirits seemingly picking up a bit. "This scar on my forehead is because of you."

Jaz looked at Alex's forehead. "What scar? You can't even see that."

"Still. After twenty some years, I know it's there. It's internal."

"It's a paper cut at best."

"Why were you such an angry eighth grader, always wanting to fight?" Alex asked, not expecting an answer.

"Growing up poor can do that to you. But look at us now . . . the best of friends."

Alexandria smiled big, thinking about their journey together.

"How in the world did the best friends thang happen?"

"I know right? Look. I'll call your mom and invite her to Aunt Elsa's lil get together and tell her that you plan to join us . . . okay?"

Alex didn't respond.

"Okay?" Jaz repeated, waiting for an answer.

"Okay," Alex finally replied, touched by her friend's authentic love and relentless concern for her well-being.

"We'll eat and chill out. We'll ring in the New Year with music, family and friends the way it should be, y'know? We'll rent some of our favorite movies. *Coming to America, Soul Food, Love and Basketball, Love Jones* . . . all the good stuff. And you know you love yo'self some Larenz Tate in *Love Jones* with his fine lil' self."

Alexandria smiled and said, "You know that's one of my all-time favorites."

"Yes, I do know and I also know we're gonna have a good time. I don't do it any other way."

"Remind me again why I let you hang around with me?" Alex asked, jokingly.

"I know, I know. I'm very honored."

Alex smiled to herself at Jaz's banter. Suddenly, she remembered that although her day had begun badly, the little encounter she had in traffic earlier this morning had made her smile as well. She made a mental note to make sure she told Jaz about it later. Even though it was nothing but a *funny*, she thought her girlfriend would enjoy it.

"Thank you, Jaz," Alex whispered.

"For what?" Jaz curiously asked.

"For nothing . . . and everything," she replied.

CHAPTER FOUR

Gabriel Washington

Every store in the mall was filled with holiday mayhem, with shoppers, music, sale signs, and kids taking pictures with Santa Claus near a majestic Christmas tree. The sights and sounds indicated that the Christmas shopping frenzy was well underway. Gabriel and his sister Kenya walked casually amidst all the hustle and bustle weaving in and around anxious last minute shoppers. Quality time for the two siblings was a rare occurrence with Kenya's busy schedule as she finished her last year in graduate school and Gabriel's demanding career along with his pending nuptials. Although only 8 years separated in age, Gabriel consistently imposed his unsolicited wisdom on the impetuous Kenya. And as far back as Gabriel could remember, his sister resisted doing things her big brother's way or any man's way for that matter. While she stood only 5 feet 4 inches, Kenya was a fireball. A fast-talking, au naturale-looking diva with a strong sense of self, she left even the most confident suitor speechless. Her brother understood her outwardly tough exterior, yet he knew deep inside her beat the fragile heart of a young girl still looking up to her big brother every once and awhile for guidance.

Lately, she tried flipping roles with Gabriel, offering her big bro some of her own homespun advice regarding his relationship with Tracee. Gabriel's happiness mattered to his sister and lately she sensed there were some unspoken reservations regarding the wedding, and maybe even the bride-to-be. When she tried to broach the subject with Gabriel, he became very guarded and quickly dismissed her unwelcomed psychoanalysis of his relationship.

However, today wasn't intended for any heavy topics of discussion for Gabriel and Kenya, unless the door opened itself to it that is.

"You hungry?" Kenya asked.

"Not starving, but I could eat," Gabriel replied, as they walked side by side.

"Cheesecake Factory good with you?"

"Sounds good to me."

"Didn't you say you wanted to stop by the bookstore?" she asked, pointing towards Barnes & Noble only a few feet away.

"Yeah, I do. Thanks for reminding me."

"Do you want to stop now or after we eat?"

"Um, now is fine since we're right here."

"I'm gonna wait for you out here. I need to send a quick text to a friend."

"Okay, I'll be back out in a minute," he said, as he walked away and stepped out of the chaos of the mall and into the quietness of the bookstore.

Kenya took a seat on a bench right outside the store. She placed her bags on the floor and pulled her phone from her handbag with the intentions of sending a quick text message.

Nearby, Jaz and Alexandria walked out of the Starbucks laughing, moving through the crowd of mall shoppers, both enjoying a mocha latte.

"So is it love?" Alexandria asked, smiling at her friend.

"Girl, please. Far from it. More like a free trip to Jamaica."

"Now which one is Willis, anyway?"

"You remember, the one I met at the gym? I told you about him," Jaz explained.

"Him? The one that's six three and wears a size eight shoe? That Willis?!"

Jaz hesitantly nodded "yes."

"What sideshow do you find these men at?" Alexandria continued.

"What? He's cool."

"He may be, but you do know in all honesty that there's really something unnatural about a man that tall with feet that small? That's someone that belongs in a traveling circus or something."

"You so mean," Jaz laughed.

"I'm playing but I'm for real," Alex shot back, their laugh eventually tapering off. "Let me stop. I could be bashing your future husband."

"What'eva. You crazy like that glue for even going there and saying such nonsense."

Alexandria looked at her girlfriend, shook her head and smiled.

Walking in silence for a few moments, Jaz eventually asked, "So you decided what you're gonna do about the job yet?"

"I have, I'm gonna do it when I go back. It's time."

"Yayyy. Good for you. Go Alex."

"I appreciate your support."

"Always. I'm proud of you," Jaz replied, happy for her girlfriend's decision to make a huge career move at the start of the New Year. "And how are things going with the lawyer?"

"Girl, let me tell you, she does not play. I feel good that if things do get messy, which I pray not, that she can handle it. I just want to be done with the whole thing and put this chapter of my life behind. I don't want anything other than my share of what's mine. I'm not looking for anything extra or anything that will keep him and I tied together in any form or fashion."

"I know that's right," Jaz replied. "And you're sure you don't want me to get Ray Ray and them to pay him a visit?"

"Girl, no. I don't wish him any harm."

"They'll make it look like an accident."

Alex wasn't sure whether Jaz was playing or for real. She sounded for real, but surely she was being comical, that's just who she was.

"Jaz, no," Alex stated.

"Now is your no really a yes? Or are you really saying no?"

"No. My no is really a no."

"Okay, well let me know if you change your mind. I got Ray Ray on speed dial. He's in the business of kicking butts and the butt kicking business is good right now, according to him."

"Girl, you need Jesus. You and Ray Ray."

"I know. Keep us in your prayers." A familiar face seated on one of the mall benches suddenly caught Jaz's eye. "Hold up, I see someone I know."

"Don't you always," Alex replied, following close

behind Jaz.

Just as Kenya began typing her text, she thought she heard her name being called.

"Kenya?" the voice repeated.

Kenya looked up to see the face attached to the voice, and smiled when she recognized her friend.

"Heyyyyy, Jaz." Kenya stood, and both ladies gave each other a friendly hug.

"I thought that was you."

"Merry Christmas," Kenya said, as they both released their embrace.

"Merry Christmas to you, too. What are you up to?"

"Having a lunch date with my brother and doing some last minute shopping. I tell myself every year I'm not going to do this. And every year I find myself out here in this mall madness. You know what I mean?" Kenya smiled and noticed an attractive woman standing just a few inches to the right of Jaz.

"Alex, this is Kenya, my cousin Tre's girlfriend," Jaz said, turning to Alex to introduce the two women. "Kenya, this is my girlfriend Alex."

Alex stepped forward and the two ladies greeted with a smile and hellos.

"I love your hair," Alex said.

"Jaz hooked it up," Kenya replied, as she touched Jaz's arm.

"What can I say, I'm good at what I do," Jaz chuckled.

"Even when she's bragging, she's being sincere," Alex joked.

"Ha-ha," Jaz sarcastically responded. "So true."

Kenya smiled.

"Jaz, I need to stop in and get some more of your

Shea Butter from you, too. That stuff is awesome. I love it."

"Didn't I tell you that you would?"

"You did."

"Anytime. Just let me know when, and I'll set some aside for you. Not a problem."

"You're the best."

The three ladies chatted for a minute more, until finally saying their goodbyes. Just as Jaz and Alex began to leave, Gabriel exited the bookstore with an extra bag in hand, catching only a glimpse of the two ladies from behind as they walked away from his sister.

"Hey, you ready?" Gabriel asked Kenya.

"I am," she replied, dropping her phone back into her bag and putting her text message off until later.

"Who was that you were talking to?" Gabriel inquired.

"Oh. That was just Tre's cousin and one of her girlfriends. She was nice."

"Oh, okay, cool."

They moved through the mall, made a stop by Dillard's next, and then finally reached the restaurant where a crowd of hungry people were waiting to be seated. Making their way to the hostess stand, Gabriel was kindly told it would be at least a 15 to 30 minute wait.

"You wanna stick it out?" Gabriel turned to Kenya and asked.

"Hey, we're here. Might as well," she replied. "It's probably a wait everywhere else."

Gabriel turned back to the hostess.

"Okay. Two. Last name's Washington."

The hostess jotted the name down and then handed him a pager. Gabriel and Kenya then moved to an open floor space where they stood in silence for only a brief moment, with the chatter of others who were waiting to be seated around them.

"What did you buy at the bookstore?" Kenya asked.

"Oh. A book on how to sell your first screenplay. Eddie recommended it, said it was good."

"How's he doing anyway?"

"Ed's good. Still writing, too."

"Cool. And how's your writing coming along for you?" she asked.

"It's coming. Sometimes I don't know where it's going, but hey . . . I'm not giving up. Got writers block like a mug right now, though. Trying to remain inspired."

"Really?"

"Yes."

"Sometimes the best thing to do is step away from it all and then come back to it. It works for me," Kenya explained.

"Yeah, you might be right. Almost done with the screenplay, though. Now what to do with it after I've finished writing it."

"Just don't give up. You're good. Sometimes blessings are right around the corner. Things can change with just one phone call from the right agent that recognizes real talent. It only takes one yes."

Gabriel smiled. "I appreciate that, sis. That's what I keep telling Tracee."

Kenya made a face that expressed a slight distaste for the name being mentioned.

"Ah. Tracee."

They stood in awkward silence for a few moments. Since the door was partly open for asking a question or two about his bride-to-be, Kenya could not resist a chance to pry for a glimpse of what was really going on between her brother and Tracee behind-the-scenes.

"So what's up with that?"

"What's up with what?"

"Is she supporting your dream?"

"Ohh, here we go," Gabriel replied, as if he knew it was coming, hating that he even mentioned his fiancée's name in the presence of his sister. He took a deep sigh, knowing his sister was on the hunt for a sign of discontentment with his bride-to-be.

"What?" Kenya responded, pretending to not know what her brother was implying.

"Nothing. It's all good."

"Riiiight," she replied, not totally believing it.

A beat of silence lasted between the two, until Gabriel felt the need to release a thought.

"I really wish you two had more love for one another."

"What makes you think that I don't?" she asked, turning towards her brother.

"Kenya? Come on now." Gabriel said, shooting her a look as if to say "be for real."

"She alright. That's bout all I can give you."

"She's a good woman."

"That's nice," Kenya replied, with zero emotion behind the remark.

"If you took the time to get to know her you would find that out for yourself."

"Are you serious?"

"Yes, I'm serious."

"I'm not taking applications for new friends right now," Kenya said, waving the very thought off.

"Don't be like that," Gabriel said.

"I'm just telling you, I'm not."

"Kenya."

"You two have been dating since forever, and if it ain't happen by now then it is what it is."

"It doesn't have to be like that though. You two really do have a lot in common."

"Like what?" Kenya quickly shot back, with a wrinkled forehead.

"Umm." Gabriel was thinking hard. "Let me get back with you on that."

"I thought so. I won't wait on it."

"See. That's not nice."

"You two still new house shopping?" Kenya asked, trying to move on from the subject of her and Tracee bonding.

"We're working on it."

Kenya took a deep sigh, trying to contain her thoughts from coming out of her mouth and her words being taken the wrong way. It took a lot for her to do that, and most of the time it didn't work out.

"Can I be honest and tell you what my issue is with her?" she asked, not wanting to hold her tongue.

"Huh?" Gabriel was slightly taken aback. "Yeah, sure."

Kenya gave it further thought before speaking. She then changed her mind.

"Nevermind."

"No. Don't do that. You've put it out there now, so say what's on your mind."

With a sigh, Kenya then said, "I don't mean to bring up the past, but she just did you wrong. You're such a good guy and I just hate to see someone take advantage of that, especially when they say they love you."

"What are you talking about?"

"Nothing. Forget it," Kenya said, waving it off. "I gotta learn to be quiet."

"Kenya?" Gabriel's voice now serious. "What?"

"She hurt you. In a way I've never seen you before."

Gabriel looked slightly defeated, now knowing what his sister was referring to. He quickly tried to gather his composure. It was evident that there was still some hurt present, perhaps it had been pushed deep down. He tried to stop his mind from going backwards, but he couldn't help but to take a moment to reflect.

"Gabriel stop!" a half dressed Tracee screamed, crying, scared out of her mind of what was taking place before her in this apartment that showed evidence that an intense brawl had taken place. "Please stop! I'm sorry!"

Paying no attention to her plea, Gabriel slammed the badly bruised fella into the wall and then immediately threw him across the room like a rag doll onto the glass coffee table, breaking it into pieces. With fist balled, face red like fire, almost unrecognizable from the man he is presently, Gabriel began walking towards the guy to finish kicking his butt without mercy.

His stride over was briefly halted by the pull on his arm from Tracee.

"Gabriel, I'm sorry," she said, doing her best to slow him down and bring him to his senses before he killed this dude or did something that landed him in jail for life.

He turned to her in a fury, and looked her dead in her eyes. "How could you do this to me? Huh?! And with him," Gabriel responded, the pain evident in his eyes. "And let go of my arm," he added intensely, violently yanking his arm from her grasp.

"Gabe, please forgive me." Her eyes were heavy with tears, voice shaky.

"How long Tracee? Huh?"

The sound of his sister's voice immediately brought Gabriel back.

"Gabe, I'm sorry. It's not my place to go there," she apologized.

There was a beat of silence before Gabriel responded.

"I forgave her for that. That was a long time ago. We're different people now. And I know you would like to think I'm perfect, but I've made mistakes too. Every relationship has its up and downs, Kenya. It's a personal choice if you decide to stay and stick it out or give it up and get on."

"I know," Kenya sighed, hating she had taken her brother back to a place she probably shouldn't have, even if only for a moment. She just knew that Tracee's betrayal broke his heart, to the point where he didn't eat or sleep well for months. Regardless of how long ago it was, Kenya just wasn't as forgiving as her brother. It wasn't just about this, but about anything. She could hold a grudge like no one could. You do her wrong, and she's done with you. And Tracee hurting her brother so deeply back in the day fit right into that category. She took it personal. Adding to the sting was the fact that David was one of Gabriel's fraternity brothers. He was a dog in every sense of the word.

Not wanting to sour the rest of their day together, Kenya searched for something to bring the good mood back to their time together.

"I'm thinking I may invite Tre over for Christmas dinner with us," Kenya said, referencing the new guy she had been dating for awhile.

"Really?" Gabriel responded, trying to break from his somber state.

"Thinking about it."

"Must be getting serious then."

"He's a good guy. Puts up with my mess," she replied. "No matter what I shoot at him, he keeps coming back. I think he likes it."

"Takes a special guy."

"For real. You know me."

"Well, you better prepare him for meeting Uncle Arthur. That will be the true test of how long he'll be around."

"I know right. Uncle Arthur be tripping."

"He just loves you, wants the best for you that's all. I don't think he'll ever think anyone is good enough for you."

Kenya smiled.

"Like I said, I'm thinking about it. It's not set in stone yet. It's only been six months, I'm not ready to run him off just yet. I gotta birthday coming up."

"Funny," Gabriel replied. "Should be a very interesting dinner, if you do. Gonna make some good book material."

"Ha-ha," Kenya sarcastically replied.

The pager in Gabriel's hand suddenly lit up, letting them know their table was ready.

"Finally," Kenya said, as they both made their way to the hostess waiting for them with menus in hand.

"So you think Unc is gonna have him in a full-nelson or a headlock by the end of dinner."

"Oh, you got jokes. You ain't funny," Kenya playfully replied. "Maybe I should wait. Tre needs to prepare himself mentally for Uncle Arthur. I don't think he's quite there yet."

As they both made way to their table, Gabriel quietly chuckled to himself at his sister's sudden reluctance. As he took his seat, Kenya placed her bags down and excused herself to the ladies room to check her makeup and wash her hands. When she walked through the door, Alex, a familiar face that Kenya had just come to know was surprisingly inside drying her hands.

"Hey, small world," Kenya said, slightly surprised, with a smile.

"Hey, more like small mall," Alex replied.

"Yeah, that sounds more like it."

Standing side by side at the sink, Kenya pulled a paper towel, placing it down on the countertop so she could sit her handbag on top of it. Alexandria took notice.

"Nice bag," Alex stated.

"Oh. Thank you."

"Y'know, I do that same thing, with the paper towel," Alex said.

"Oh, in a public restroom it's a must."

"I know that's right," Alex laughed.

"And I'm like the biggest germaphobe when it comes to public places. I touch nothing."

"I'm the same way. You are not alone."

"My brother gets on me all the time when we go out to eat because I always ask for my drink in a plastic cup and replace the silverware with plastic."

"See. I'm gonna have to start doing that myself. Not a bad idea."

"Yeah, I cannot drink outta something I know a stranger has been drinking out of or eat off utensils someone else has had in their mouth at one time."

"That is nasty when you think about it."

"What if the dishwasher had an off day or something, back there washing everything in cold water and not giving a flip."

Alex laughed, both ladies staring at the other's reflection in the mirror as they continued talking.

"Right. You never know. There aren't too many places I even eat at anymore, to be honest with you," Alex said.

"You ever eaten at Ramona's?"

"Ramona's?"

"Yes."

"Never heard of it."

"Oh, it is the best. You have to go to Ramona's. My brother and I eat there all the time. And if you go once, you're hooked, I lie to you not. Best spot in downtown."

"Cool. Good food?" Alex questioned.

"Great food. The best. I promise you would love it. I don't know if you like salmon . . ."

"I do," Alex interjected.

". . . but theirs on their lunch menu is to die for," Kenya added. "And the sanitation grade is always a hundred plus. The cooks wear gloves and the owner is meticulous about cleanliness, from what I read in an article."

"That's definitely a plus. Where exactly is this place?"

Continuing their chat, Kenya gave Alex a quick route to finding Ramona's, with Alex finishing with a kind, "I'm glad I met you." The two eventually parted ways and headed back to their individual tables to enjoy a nice meal, Alex with her best friend Jaz and Kenya with her brother Gabriel.

CHAPTER FIVE

Breathe Again

A delicate morning air clung above the snow-dusted buildings, making a picture postcard of the usually bustling city. While driving, Alexandria smiled at the sight of snow flurries that lightly swirled in her path, dancing with the translucent wind, then blanketing the ground in serenity. With the car window partially cracked, she could hear a soft, hollow breeze whistling through the bare pine trees as a few frail barren branches swayed. Tentative rays of sunlight brought the promise of sunshine. The scene reflected a pure sense of godly order, the new day dawning, a rebirth, a chance to begin again.

"Today's going to be a beautiful day for Alexandria," she told herself as she pulled into a parking space at the North Raleigh office complex. Grabbing her leather briefcase from the passenger seat, she stepped out of her car, looking every bit the successful, professional woman in her favorite black Chanel suit. She pressed her keyless remote and the car alarm system barked back as the doors locked.

Moving gracefully towards her building, heels lightly tapping the pavement, she was determined to make it through the entire day without a single breakdown. Today was the day she planned to begin her life again, making major changes, both personal and professional. She had begun to believe that somehow she would regain some semblance of normalcy again.

Stepping into the elevator, she searched her mind for the right words to let her boss, Bentley, know she was resigning today. She hadn't been with his company very long, taking the job only after relocating back to North Carolina from Dallas where she and Lionel had resided. Back in Texas she had worked under a much larger agency, so coming here was a total change from what she was used to. Starting over where she grew up allowed Alex to not only leave Lionel behind but also be closer to her mother who now resided in an assistant living facility.

Alex had always felt the pull to start her own agency, and she felt with the start of a new year the timing was now or never. She appreciated Bentley for taking a chance on her, but she now realized that her own fear was one of the main reasons she hadn't yet stepped out to do her thing. She enjoyed the work—making clients happy and experiencing the joy of seeing people find just the right home for their families was incredibly rewarding to her. But even a great agent needed a completely different skill set to run a business, and that's what frightened Alex. She knew how to close a deal, the biggest of deals, and she was known among her peers as an aggressive and a politically tactful agent. She knew she had what it takes to run a profitable business with integrity, but she also knew she would have to overcome her fear of failure by taking that first step and that meant walking out of this place and not thinking the worst when it came to any part of her life.

As she entered the office suite, she changed her mind about heading to her office first and immediately redirected her steps towards Bentley's corner office instead.

"There's no need to wait. What have I got to lose?" she mumbled to herself while mentally refocusing on her primary reason for returning to work at all, which was to resign.

Just walking towards Bentley's office was enough to make her feel sick all over again. Although Alex got along with him okay, he was not very likable by most in the office, to say the least. And the smell of his cologne was always so strong and overpowering that you could smell it long before entering his office.

Outside his door sat his secretary, Bettina, a tall full-figured black woman with short twisted hair. She was always sharp, dressed as if she had just left Sunday service. She was on the phone, so Alex gave her a polite smile and a little wave, then tapped softly on Bentley's door before walking in.

Bentley looked up briefly before returning his gaze to his computer. "Mrs. Jones. Good morning. What can I do for you," he said, in his best pseudo-sincere voice.

"You gotta sec?" she asked.

"I do," he said, never looking up. "Have a seat. I need to finish this up real quick, and I'll be with you in about half a minute."

She seated herself directly across from him in a leather upholstered armchair. She placed her briefcase on the floor next to the chair and surveyed his office. The south wall was crammed full of pictures of horses and bulls running down the prairie depicting scenes from the Old West encased in cheap frames. His file folders were piled on the floor next to his desk where a solitary photo of his wife had been placed by the phone. Alexandria studied the picture. Linda had a beautiful face and an incandescent smile. Alex wondered how such a delightful woman, or any woman for that matter, would settle down with someone as distasteful and unpleasant as Bentley. It took a special woman for sure.

Alexandria continued to scan the office while Bentley hastily glanced over a printout.

"Numbers this month aren't too good, Alex." He clicked his computer's mouse a few more times. "You know what I always say—your timc is my money."

"Bentley . . ." Alex interrupted, noticing that, as usual, the conversation was all about him.

He continued, talking as if he hadn't heard her. "Luckily for you, I forwarded a potentially big deal your way this morning. Check with Bettina on your way out for the paperwork. I believe they should be here around nine, so make sure you free up your schedule for as long as it takes. They're buyers, and they're not going to be an easy win, so I really need you to put on the charm this morning," Bentley said. He hardly made any eye contact with Alexandria.

"Bentley?"

He continued, "By the way, I didn't even know that you were taking additional days off during the holiday. Most of us were back in here the day after Christmas."

As he droned on, Alexandria sat quietly, maintaining a neutral expression, in the hope he would feel like an idiot and notice that he hadn't allowed her to say more than two words since she came in.

"I left messages," she interjected. "You were on the phone each time I called. Bettina said she would make sure you got them. And you could have called me if it were a problem."

"I didn't know Bettina hung up the phone long enough from her personal calls to take messages," he said, trying to get in a quick joke.

Alexandria was still waiting for him to make eye contact with her for more than a fleeting second. Her facial expression remained stern and emotionless as she stared intently at him.

He went on, "Alex, I know you've had some personal things going on, and I know everyone needs a little time off now and then, but . . ."

"I'm resigning, Bentley," she interrupted.

Bentley continued to talk as if he hadn't even heard her voice, " . . . right now I have more clients than I have agents. So I really need you to stay on top of your game here. For the most part, business is good and things are continuously picking up with the market, but . . ."

Alexandria raised her voice this time to make sure he heard her, "Did you hear what I just said?"

"No, I didn't. What?"

"I'm resigning."

The firmness of her voice finally got his attention. As Bentley stared at Alexandria in the face, she could see she now had his full attention by the way he appeared completely caught off guard and more than unpleasantly surprised by her news.

"Excuse me?" he sputtered. "I don't understand."

"Resigning. Quitting," she stated calmly, a small

smile peeking through her grim facial expression.

He cleared his throat just before speaking.

"What seems to be the problem?" Bentley searched her face for some clue of why she would want to leave.

"I just feel it's the right thing," she said.

"You're kiddin', right?" Bentley asked.

"No, I'm not," she quickly replied.

"Okay, then what's going on?"

"I'm just ready to call it quits, here at least. I know I've only been here a short time, but I think I've served my purpose. And honestly, I haven't been very happy here since I started. It's nothing personal, just as simple as that. I don't think I should take on any additional clients and I'll successfully tie up any loose ends, so don't worry. But I think I'm going to try this on my own."

Taking a breath in disbelief, Bentley stood up and walked around his desk towards his office door. As he did, Alexandria's eyes immediately glanced down at the snake-skinned cowboy boots that he often wore to give him a few extra inches of height. When he closed his door, Alexandria looked back at him and noticed that he had a perplexed look on his face. He paused next to her chair for a moment, his eyes focused on the floor while pondering what to say next.

He eventually took a seat directly beside her in the open chair, and said, "Alex, indeed your contract with us doesn't prohibit you from moving out on your own. But if you need more time for anything, a couple more days off just to think about things, by all means take it. But don't make any hasty life-altering decisions like this. Please think about what you're doing here. Seriously."

Before Alex could speak, she made a slightly

distorted facial expression as if a stench had hit her nose unexpectedly. OMG, his breath was kicking! Bentley didn't have halitosis, he had hellitosis. It was bad enough to make you wanna cuss.

Alex mustered up the strength to speak in spite of attempting to hold her breath when possible.

"This isn't a hasty decision. I probably should have done it before now. I accept responsibility for that."

"So that's it . . . the student is already thinking she can become the teacher, I see. Wow." Bentley sat up straight in his chair and stared down and over the rim of his eyeglasses at Alexandria. Leaning in closer to her, he said, "Alex, not to discourage you and with all due respect for what you're trying to do, but starting your own agency is a risky endeavor. Do you really think you're ready to go into the market alone? I mean it's tough, take it from someone with firsthand experience. You know, if I were you, I would definitely wait until the economy improved even more. You make great money here. I don't know your financial situation, but . . ."

"That's right, you don't. And my finances are more than fine," she asserted. Alexandria knew he would try to discourage her, mainly because he'd fear the competition. But he didn't realize that he had a fight coming because Alex had prepared herself to combat his negative comments and not allow what he said to influence her decision.

"I'm just sayin' that I want you to make sure that walking away from your job here is really what you want to do and that you've really thought this thing through. You're a good agent, one of the best I had come thru here in a long time. I'll admit, I would hate to lose you. Are you absolutely sure about this?"

"Indeed," Alexandria replied, with no hesitation. "Now I hope this isn't about Bentley Flack being scared of a little competition," she added with an air of cockiness.

Bentley chuckled and said, "Ha! I welcome it, Mrs. Jones. You're good, but it takes more than that."

"I know exactly what it takes," Alexandria said. "I was doing this long before I started working for you. This isn't my first job, let me remind you."

He sighed, then stood and walked to the other side of his desk. As he did, Alex exhaled, glad to have him from talking directly in front of her face. Bentley turned and gazed out his window. He remained silent for a brief moment, as if thinking of his next thing to say.

"Okay. It's your decision. I'm not one to talk anybody into staying where they don't want to be."

As he continued, suddenly feeling disrespected by the fact he was not looking at her, Alex said with a hint of attitude, "Could you not talk with your back to me, please?"

He turned, and just as he was about to start with his next point, Bettina buzzed in over his phone's intercom.

"Bentley," she called.

"Yeah, what is it?!" Bentley shouted directly into his speakerphone.

"Alex's morning appointment is here with . . ." Bentley abruptly picked up the phone receiver and placed it to his ear, taking Bettina quickly off the speaker before she could reveal who was waiting in the lobby, " . . . Ms. Tracee Andrews and Mr. Gabriel Washington. Should I have them wait until you two are finished or send them on in?" Bettina asked.

"No," Bentley spoke directly into the receiver, "go

ahead and send them over to Amanda so they won't have to wait. She will be handling them instead of Alex. Just buzz her office and give her a heads-up before you do and tell her I'll join their meeting momentarily. Make sure she's aware these are important clients. They're not sold on using us just yet." He hung up the phone and, as he did, his wife, Linda, opened the door and walked in unannounced.

For Alexandria, Linda couldn't have walked in at a better time. Alexandria stood up and greeted Linda warmly.

"Hi, Linda. Nice to see you."

"Good to see you, as well, Alex. I hope you had a good Christmas."

"It was well, thank you. And yours?"

"Very good. I'm sorry to interrupt, but I need a second of my husband's time to get his signature on something," Linda said, politely.

"Please, go ahead. I'm just heading out the door, anyway. I think Bentley and I are all done." Alex turned to Bentley and said, "I'll have my formal letter to you by close of business today."

Picking up her briefcase, Alexandria headed out of the office. As she made her way, she suddenly felt invigorated and weightless, something she really needed for herself. She felt empowered, in control of her destiny, and more motivated than ever before.

The office lobby was completely empty when Alex reentered the suite. Knowing that Bettina had probably overheard most of the conversation, if not all, she exchanged a quick high-five with her as she passed the desk. Alexandria smiled and made her way to her office, taking confident and long strides with her head held high. Without taking a look, she passed Amanda's office and overheard her speaking with the two seated clients inside about the benefits of signing with the company for their home search.

In the distance, she could hear Bentley's voice instructing Bettina to hold all his calls as he hurriedly walked towards Amanda's office to join the meeting. Alexandria didn't look back, but headed straight to her office instead, closing the door behind her. After she sat down behind her mahogany desk, she turned to face her office window and exhaled a long-awaited sigh of relief at her faint reflection smiling back at her.

CHAPTER SIX

Directions

New Year's had passed, and the days after proved to be profitable and busy enough for Jaz to reopen the hair salon. She had actually planned to keep it closed for at least a week after the New Year, but desperate calls from regular clients were mounting. Her staff at "A Touch of Jaz" wasn't complaining. They expected that business would pick up in the first weeks as women searched for that special, new look to jumpstart the New Year. Alexandria was one of the first to try a change.

Jaz's salon was spacious and easily accommodated the five other hair stylists and two nail technicians who were busily working on their clients. In Raleigh and Durham, "A Touch of Jaz" was one of the most popular spots for getting that do done, and Jaz's expertise in original and funky hair designs and unbelievable weaves was well-known throughout the area. Customers were pampered with complimentary herbal tea along with occasional tidbits, such as Moravian tea cookies. Jaz was truly the creative and daring self-starter, who had indeed built an empire of success, beauty and class and the crowded salon only made it more evident.

Alexandria peeped in the mirror and examined the way her new hairstyle was taking shape as her makeover began to spring forth. While she carefully looked at her new do in the mirror, she noticed the salon door open and was surprised to see Tracee Andrews entering the establishment, moving with the stride of a runway model. As she walked, she removed her black lambskin jacket, leather gloves and merino wool scarf, then dropped them in a lobby chair. Wearing a gray, cashmere fitted sweater and tapered black pants, her curvaceous body moved gracefully to the desk in front.

"I didn't know Tracee Andrews came here," Alex whispered.

"Yeah. Ms. Thing has been coming here for awhile now," Jaz said, concealing the movement of her lips as she waved to the new arrival, receiving a half-smile from Tracee.

"Sit tight for a minute, I'll be right back."

"Okay."

Jaz walked towards Tracee to say "hello" and welcome her back to the salon. Tracee was glancing at her watch when Jaz said, "Ms. Andrews, so pleased to see you today."

"Hi. I have a manicure and pedicure appointment scheduled for 1:00 p.m. and it's very important that I be out of here within an hour, hour and a half at the latest, Jazmine," Tracee said.

"Well, we'll definitely try to get you outta here way before then. Roberta's finishing up with a client and will be with you in about five minutes," Jaz calmly replied with a smile.

"Perfect. Thank you."

"Can I get you somethin' to relax you? Herbal tea, maybe?" Jaz offered.

"That would be nice. Yes, please."

"Okay. I'll be right back. Oh, and you should try our new cranberry scones. They're delicious, and not too fattening."

"Sure, okay. Thank you," Tracee replied, taking her seat in the lobby area.

Jaz headed over to her receptionist, Toni, who had just returned from lunch and was busily answering the phone and scheduling appointments. Jaz politely interrupted, "Toni, could you get Tracee a cranberry scone and a cup of herbal tea as soon as you get a chance, please?"

Toni, phone cradled between her ear and shoulder, nodded "yes."

Jaz looked back at Tracee and smiled, then headed back to Alex. "Alex, did you want something else to nibble on or anything else to drink, sweetie? We'll burn it off when we go to the gym."

"No, I'm fine. She ain't giving you a hard time is she?" Alexandria inquired, referring to Tracee.

"She's cool today. I can handle her. She has those moments when she comes in here thinkin' she's some movie star or somethin' and we're supposed to drop everything. But I run the show in here. You ought to see the way my staff cringes at the sight of her walking through the door." Jaz motioned to the other side of the salon. "Check out the way Melissa over there is looking at her."

Alexandria glanced over at Melissa, one of the other

stylists, who was doing a client's hair and occasionally peeping at Tracee out of the corner of her eye. Melissa smirked and just shook her head at Tracee whose demeanor reeked of self-importance.

"Girl, she's looking at her like she hate a sistah," Alex said.

"Melissa knows that I've told her about that." Jaz was referring to Melissa's cold stare at Tracee. "I think most of the girls in here don't even watch or care about the local news, so they're not the least bit impressed by her." Jaz leaned closer to Alexandria and whispered, "I heard she's getting married soon."

"To whom?" Alex inquired.

"I have no idea, but pray for the brotha whoever he is. I wonder if he knows how much Tracee Andrews loves Tracee Andrews." Jaz laughed and walked off, requesting more tea for her best friend. Alexandria carried on watching Tracee through the mirror, admiring the woman she had so often seen just on television.

Jaz had returned to Tracee's seat and asked, "So, how are the wedding plans going?"

"Everything's going great, thank you for asking."

"Absolutely," Jaz responded.

Tracee's face beamed with excitement. "Only three more months to go," she added.

"It'll be here before you know it."

"I know, right."

"You need anything else?" Jaz asked.

"Nope. I think I'm okay."

"Well, holler if you need me. Roberta's almost done," Jaz said.

"She seems nice," Alex told Jaz as she returned.

"Honestly, she's not that bad. She just has some

ways about her that are easily misunderstood, I guess. But who doesn't, right?"

When Jaz finally finished styling Alexandria's hair with her fingers, she sprayed on a little spritz. "There! Check out your new do girlfriend. You look good, girl!" Jaz announced.

Glancing in the mirror, Alexandria appraised her new look. Her hair was shorter than before in the back, but Jaz had layered it nicely to give it more body and bounce. It looked sophisticated.

"I love it!" she happily exclaimed as she used the hand mirror to examine it all over again.

"I knew you would. Now, I'm sorry to have to put you through this, honey, but you're gonna have to sit next to the princess if you're gettin' your nails and toes done today," Jaz said, making a slight head motion in Tracee's direction.

"Oh, no problem." Grabbing her handbag from off the counter, Alexandria walked over to the other side of the salon towards the nail technicians' area.

"Hello, dear," Roberta, Jaz's longtime manicure and pedicure specialist, said as she escorted Tracee to her workstation. Tracee nodded and reluctantly smiled, but she was clearly agitated by the wait. Tracee and Alex smiled and nodded as they passed each other.

"It's a full house today," Roberta remarked, attempting to make small talk with Tracee.

Placing her bag on the floor, Alexandria seated herself at the booth next to Roberta's and waited for Sandy to come over and freshen up her French manicure.

Minutes ticked by without a word, until Alex's ring finger caught Tracee's attention. Breaking the silence, Tracee pointed at her finger and commented on her wedding ring with genuine interest and a hint of excitement in her voice. "Excuse me, but did you get your ring from Jafon's Jewelers?" she asked.

Caught off guard that Tracee's words were directed towards her, Alex murmured with confusion, "Hmh?"

"Your ring," she pointed. "I asked if you got it from Jafon's?"

"Why yes. Yes, I did." She immediately glanced over at Tracee's engagement ring and was pleasantly surprised to see an obvious Jafon's original—specially designed with a 3-carat emerald-cut diamond, his signature.

"I knew it," Tracee said proudly. "I know his trademark work anywhere."

"I guess we both have the same taste in jewelers," Alex said.

Tracee noticed her handbag as well and said, "Looks like in jewelers and handbags. I love that, girl. Where did you get it?"

"That old thing? It was actually a Christmas gift from Jaz over there."

"Nice," Tracee smiled. "Forgive me for being rude. I'm Tracee Andrews, by the way."

"Yes, I know. Your station is the only one I watch for my news."

"Well, that's good to hear. Thank you."

"I'm Alexandria. Alexandria Jones."

The two exchanged a "nice to meet you."

"That's a beautiful engagement ring. When's your wedding?" Alex asked.

"In April," Tracee replied.

"Sweet."

"How long have you been married, Alexandria?" Tracee asked.

"To be honest with you, I'm separated," Alex confessed.

"Oh, I'm sorry to hear that."

"No. Don't be. Just one of those things, y'know?"

"Yeah."

"Mr. Right just turned out to be Mr. Wrong in every way imaginable." Alexandria's eyes glazed over against her will at the mere mention of the word "separation," letting this stranger know her grief over the ordeal was still very present. She managed to mask her trembling voice and said, "You're going to make a beautiful bride."

"Thank you. We're both really excited. Everything is moving so fast. Everyone keeps telling me that April will be here before I know it. It's all I'm able to think about."

"I know. I was the same way." Alex smiled, reminiscing about her wedding, but quickly brushing it out of her mind. "I was nervous. I was so afraid that I was going to trip in front of everyone in church, or that some other major disaster would happen like my breast would pop out of my wedding dress. Oh, I tell you, I was a mess."

"That's the same kinda stuff I'm worrying about, and I'm the type of person that freaks out if everything isn't absolutely perfect."

"How long have the two of you been together?" Alex asked.

"We're actually college sweethearts."

"Oh, how nice. That's gotta be a beautiful feeling."

"It is. He's a great guy."

The two women continued talking, puzzling Jaz who peeped covertly at them from across the room.

"You'll be fine. It's your day and everyone is just there to see you and to share in your special moment," Alex reassured Tracee. "You gotta remember that," she added.

"You're right. I . . ." Tracee's cell phone suddenly rang, interrupting their conversation. She excused herself for a moment as she grabbed it from inside her handbag with her free hand while Roberta continued to work on the other. Tracee looked at the display to see who was calling.

"We must've talked him up."

Alexandria smiled.

Tracee then flipped her phone open and answered, "Hey, sweetie. No, I stepped out of the station for a bit. I'm getting my nails done at the moment. Where are you? Oh. Well, have a good lunch. Tell Eddie I said hi."

Jaz, noticing Tracee was now on her cell, took the moment to step over to Alex.

"Things okay over here?" Jaz asked Alex.

Alexandria responded, "Oh, we're fine, Jaz. Tracee and I have been over here talkin' about wedding jitters."

"Oh, okay."

As Tracee's continued with her phone conversation, Jaz, in a hushed tone said, "By the way, Alex, I forgot to tell you. You remember Eric Turner?"

"Nope," she quickly replied, without taking the time to search her memory bank to see if she really did. As of late, anytime Jaz brought up a man's name by starting with do you remember mostly meant she was attempting to hook her up.

"Yes, you do."

Alex thought for a second. "The one everybody used to call ET. Ol' big head Eric Turner?"

"Girl, that was high school. He's grown into his head . . . a little."

"Okay, good for him. What about him?"

"I ran into him the other day."

"And?"

"Remember when I mentioned I had to go to the Raleigh Entrepreneurs' gathering?"

"Right."

"Well, he asked about you. He was like, hey how's your girlfriend Alexandria doing. I heard she was back in town," Jaz explained, using a bad male voice, as if she were pretending to talk like the person she was telling Alex about.

"He sounded like that? He sounds terrible."

"Just listen."

"Uh-huh." Alex knew were Jaz was headed with this.

"Anyway, he asked me for your number and . . ."

"I know you didn't give him my number," Alex interjected, with a slight raise of her voice, giving Jaz a stern look.

"Of course not. I know homey don't play that," Jaz replied, mocking an infamous line from the TV show *In Living Color*. "But, he did give me his number to pass along to you."

Jaz tried to hand a piece of folder paper to Alexandria.

"No, thank you." She pushed the paper back, still in Jaz's hand.

"Oh, just take it. I'll put it right here." Jaz took the paper and slipped it into Alex's bag.

"You really want to get hit in the head with a loaded sock, dont'cha?" Alex joked.

"No, Homey, I don't," Jaz chuckled.

"Now you know where that slip of paper is going to end up, don't you?"

"I just don't want to have to lie when he asked if I gave it to you. I did. What you do with it afterwards, I have no control over." Jaz pointed, and added, "But the trashcan is over there."

"You're a real trip, and I think you know it," Alex said, shaking her head to herself as Jaz walked off. At the same time, Alex took note that Tracee was still on the phone.

"Hold on a sec, sweetie. My mom's calling." Tracee clicked over. "Hellooo. Hey you. Yeah. Whatsup?" Tracee's tone suddenly became discreet. "Okay. How long are you in town? Um-hm. Where are you staying? Okay. Tonight? When do you have to be back in Maryland? Sure, I can come by." Tracee smiled hard. "Can I call you back? My mom's on the other line. Okay." She quietly laughed. "Boy, you're so silly. I'll call you back. It won't be long. Bye, David."

David? Alex sat still but cut her eyes briefly in Tracee's direction, letting nothing in her body language express that she knew that Tracee had obviously just lied to both parties on the line. But it wasn't Alex's business to ponder on why.

Tracee clicked back over, her voice returning to normal. "I'm back, sweetie. I'm sorry to have kept you on hold. My mother told me to tell you 'hi'," she lied, biting the bottom corner of her lip. It was something she often did when telling an untruth.

"Are you going to have time to go by the printer's

to pick up some paper samples?" She paused, listened. "Um-hm. Yeah. Not sure what street it's on. They're a fairly new business so I'm not sure you'll be able to map it or not. Have you updated your GPS yet? I didn't think so. I told you to take care of that. I believe they're near West Hodges, but I'm not sure. It's called Trademark Printing."

Alex started. Tracee put the phone on her shoulder.

"Do you know where that is?" she asked Alex.

"Yeah," Alex said. "I do. I got my business cards done there."

"Oh, great. Would it be too much trouble for you to give my fiancé directions?"

"No, not at all. I would be happy to."

Tracee placed her cell phone back to her ear. "Sweetie, I have someone here that can give you directions. Hold on."

Tracee handed Alex her cell phone.

"Hi," Alex said. "It's really easy to find. Where will you be coming from? Okay. South Wilmington Street. Okay. Do you know where Lenoir Street is? Okay. If you turn left there . . ." Alex mapped out a quick route for him, finishing with, "Trademark Printing will be on your left. It's the big blue building. You can't miss it. Um-hm. Oh, you're very welcome. Glad I could help." Alex smiled at something he said. "I know, me too. Yeah. Okay, here's Tracee. Take care."

She handed Tracee back her cell phone.

"Got it, sweetie? Good. Okay, I'll give you a ring when I get back at work. Smooches."

Tracee closed her flip and dropped the phone back into her bag. She took a deep sigh while shaking her head to herself and said, "I appreciate that."

"Oh, you're welcome. Not a problem."

The two women continued talking and laughing for about thirty minutes or more, surprisingly finding out they were both members of the same sorority and traveled in some of the same social circles.

"I can't believe those two are actually getting along." Toni discreetly peeped over at Alex and Tracee as she and Jaz examined the appointment book.

"You know Alex. She can spark up a conversation with just about anyone," Jaz quietly reminded Toni while taking notice of Alex writing something on the back of one of her business cards and then passing it to Tracee, who casually placed it inside of her purse.

Jaz focused back on her appointment book.

"Yeah, she can," Toni stated, just as Tracee let out an annoying laugh that resonated through the salon seemingly followed by a remark from Alex. "Ms. Prissy laughs like a hyena," Toni added in a mocking tone.

"I know, but be nice," Jaz snickered.

"Well, she does."

Peeping back over at her girlfriend, Jaz was kind of shocked herself. Usually, she and Alex shared the same opinions about people, especially women. They could spot a phony a hundred miles away, and Tracee definitely fit the bill. But this was different. Alex seemed genuinely able to get along with Tracee, and Tracee seemed to like Alex. As Jaz shrugged her shoulders, she heard Tracee's laugh echoing annoyingly through the salon once again.

"Okay, we need to get her on outta here," she told Toni.

CHAPTER SEVEN

Do We Know Each Other?

"Have a good day, sir. And thank you for visiting Ramona's," said the smiling, bow-tied server as he passed Kenneth Young, a handsome, well-dressed man in his early 40's.

"Thank you," Kenneth Young replied with a nod as he retrieved his car keys from his coat pocket before heading out into the warm, midday sun, a sure sign the seasons had changed. Alex had suggested meeting her new client for lunch here rather than his studio apartment as he had originally suggested. Alex made it a policy to always meet her clients, particularly single men, in a public place. Besides, Ramona's was her favorite restaurant. Kenneth Young's place of business was problematic in this case, since the software design consultant worked out of his downtown apartment. This morning's meeting had proven successful for Mr. Young, as well as Alexandria. Alex had much more of a feel for what the bachelor was looking for in a house, and was sure she knew of at least three possibilities off the bat. They said their good-byes with Alexandria promising to follow up in a couple of days. Alex remained at the table, taking the time to enjoy her cappuccino and think about the rest of her day.

Glancing at her wrist, she realized that in her hurry to get to Ramona's early she had left her watch on the nightstand. As she surveyed the room, she realized there wasn't a clock in sight nor did any of the waiters and waitresses appear to be wearing watches. She smiled at the thought that this might somehow be deliberate, a means of calming the rushed minds of patrons. It was nice to imagine that Ramona's was a place of refuge from the inflexible boundaries of time and schedules.

In contrast to the downtown congestion that surged outside its doors, Ramona's was a quaint, neighborhood Italian eatery catering to the requests of customers in a tranquil manner. Cherubs wreathed the ceiling above and antique glass and brass chandeliers filled the room with a warm and inviting light. Tiffany lampshades hung low just above each table, providing a dimly-lit and cozy atmosphere. Fresh-cut flowers adorned each table. The waiters and waitresses, many of them Italian, exuded such warmth, you'd think the place belonged to them.

As she sat at a corner table far away from the constant movement of people coming and going, Alex flipped through her client's paperwork, making notes ever so often. She casually reached for her cell phone, fumbling inside her bag until she came up with it. Eyes still fixed on the paperwork, she flipped open the phone to check her voicemail.

Only one. She paused to listen: "Hi, Alex. This is Tracee. Tracee Andrews. I met you at the salon awhile back. Well, I found your business card at the bottom of my bag. You have to forgive me. I just looked at it and realized you were a Realtor. The reason why I'm calling is because my fiancé and I are very much in the market for a new home. So, it may have been *fate* that I met you. I went to your website, very nice. Like what I read there. Maybe we can get together after I return from the honeymoon. I'm heading to Maryland on Monday to prepare for the wedding next weekend, so I'll call you back, if that's okay, sometime after my return and maybe we can do lunch or something."

Tracee rambled on a bit more, until the voicemail cut her off mid-sentence. Alexandria was excited at the prospect of having yet another high-profile client. Things were going really well in the short space of time since she'd started her own company. Three closings in three months, hefty commissions, and she didn't owe a dime of those earnings to anyone else other than Uncle Sam. Now to top it off, Tracee Andrews might be a potential client. That could really beef up business, if she found her a home. Alex needed to share the news. She dialed Jaz, waiting anxiously for an answer.

"Hello," Jaz answered with a scratchy voice.

"Wake up, sleepy head," Alex said.

"Hey, girl," she coughed.

"You feeling any better?" Alex asked.

"I'm feelin' a lil' bit better. This sudden change in the weather is about to take me outta here. Cold one minute, hot the next."

"It's called spring. Have you eaten anything? Need me to drop off something?"

"No, I'm okay. Aunt Elsa stopped by with some of

her famous chicken stew yesterday. I'm still eating off of that."

"Well, if you should need anything just let me know, big baby. A Pacifier. A Rattle. Doesn't matter."

"Oh, you got jokes. Wanna play when a sista feeling her worst, I see."

"Always."

"What's going on with you?" Jaz asked.

"I've got some news." Alex almost sang the sentence.

"What?" Jaz asked. "I need some, as long as it's good."

"Guess who called me."

"Oprah? I don't know. Who?"

"Tracee," she said sarcastically, knowing Jaz was not Tracee's biggest fan.

"Morgan? From 30 Rock?"

"Tracy Morgan? Them meds got you talking out your head. No, silly. Tracee Andrews."

"Tracee Andrews? I know you didn't wake me to tell me that," Jaz said, in a disappointed tone. "Call me if you get a ring from Tracy Morgan instead. That's news."

"Don't be like that. Listen. She left me a voicemail saying she and her fiancé are in the market for a new home and she's gonna need an agent."

"Okay, and . . ." Jaz said in a monotonous voice, struggling to sound happy for Alex's sake, and wanting to find out where this was going.

"She's thinking of yours truly."

As Alex chatted with Jaz, she looked up to see a familiar face entering the establishment, but it was one she couldn't immediately place. He adjusted his cufflinks, scanned the place while he stood waiting. Eventually, the hostess appeared and showed him to a nearby table. Alex knew she'd seen him before, but she just couldn't remember where from.

"Here you are, Mr. Washington," said the hostess as she set a cup of espresso on the table in front of him. The man nodded his 'thanks' and settled into his seat, glancing over the menu. He seemed in no hurry.

Curious, Alex thought his elegant suit made him a pretty high-powered banker or lawyer or something to that degree.

Eventually, he noticed her too. But whenever Alex would glance over, the gentleman would lower his gaze to give the impression that he was only admiring the place. This went on for a while until, inevitably, their eyes met, and they exchanged small smiles with one another.

"Um-hm. Right," Alex occasionally responded to let Jaz know she was still listening, but she wasn't really. Her attention was focused off and in the stranger's direction whenever she could sneak a peek. Feeling a little silly at this point, she turned away and glanced out the window and into the square. To her surprise, she could see a faint reflection of the man's face looking in her direction. Starting to feel a bit uncomfortable with his attention, she tried to refocus her attention, but it was fast becoming apparent to Jaz that Alex's mind was elsewhere.

"Did you hear me?" Jaz asked, letting out another cough.

"Hmh?" Alex murmured.

"Earth to Alex, are you there? You ain't listening girl, what's up?"

"Sorry. I . . . I was just thinking about something."

"What?"

"Umm . . . nothing."

"Nothing is always something with you. What's up?"

"Well . . . I'm sorry girl, but this guy," Alexandria whispered into the phone as she glanced at her papers, pretending not to notice the man who was now staring at her. "This man keeps looking at me, and I don't know . . ."

"You got mace?" Jaz interjected.

"Yes, but it's nothing like that."

"Okay. Talk to me. Who is he?" Jaz demanded.

"I don't know. He kinda looks familiar, but I can't place him," Alexandria whispered, through clenched teeth. "You know how it is when you've seen someone before but have no idea where?"

"Oh yeah," Jaz replied.

"What does he look like? Maybe it's someone we went to school with?"

"Possibly. I didn't think about that."

"Give me a visual."

"He's . . . I can't really say," she whispered, fearful the stranger could somehow read lips and decipher her conversation. "Nice looking guy. Well-groomed."

"Okay, is he tall?" Jaz asked.

"Fairly tall, yes."

"How's he dressed? Casual? Sporty? In a suit?"

"No, no, yes." Alex was starting to have fun with Jaz's Q&A.

"Do you see a wedding ring?"

"Umm . . . no," Alex replied, briefly glancing at her own.

"No, you can't see one? Or no, he doesn't have one on?"

"The latter, from what I can tell," Alex answered,

emphatically.

"How's the body?"

"Yes, from what I can tell he's been drinking his milk by the gallon."

"Hmmm, it does do the body good. Now does his suit look like a custom-fit or one of those two-for-one deals? Two-for-one, sure sign of a budget brotha."

"Definitely custom. It's laying on him just right. I would say maybe it's Brooks Brothers or something close."

"Ummm, a classy brotha. Is he still taking looks over at you?"

Alex cut her eyes discreetly in the gentleman's direction.

"Not right now," she told Jaz.

"Now for the most important thing. Can you see his grill? Cause ain't nothing worse than a pretty man with a tore up grill, looking like Jerome in the mouth."

"No, I can't see his grill. I haven't gotten all up in the man's mouth, though."

Jaz had more questions, as they chatted for a little bit longer.

Eventually, Alex said, "But look, I'm gonna have to cut this game short. I have some errands I need to run before my next appointment, so I need to get outta here now or I'm going to be late."

"Alex, don't you dare hang up this phone when this *thing* is just getting good," Jaz pleaded. Her curiosity was piqued, and she needed to know more about the tall, handsome, unmarried stranger with the custom-fitted suit that was apparently showing interest in her girlfriend.

"Alright, Ms. Childs, we're going to have to talk later," Alex quietly chuckled, switching to a more professional tone. "And I'll definitely keep you informed on how all that pans out. Take care now."

"Alex, don't make me come down there," Jaz threatened. "You know I will. I will get out of my sick bed, in house slippers, robe, curlers and all, and be there before you can reach the exit door."

"Talk to you soon, okay? Bye-bye now," Alex smiled, flipping her phone closed and ending their conversation.

Still smiling to herself at the thought of Jaz, sitting phone in hand without all the details, Alex took a final glance over in the man's direction as she prepared herself to leave. A waiter taking his order blocked her view. She gathered her papers and placed them inside her briefcase. She checked the time on her phone and quickly put in a call to her next appointment as she stood and made her way to the exit. Her client's answering machine picked up just as she opened the door to leave.

"Hi. Mr. Donovan. This is Mrs. Jones. I was calling to see if it is possible for us to reschedule our . . . ." There was a quick break in her message as she held the door for someone that suddenly appeared directly behind her, "appointment at Ramona's today to one-thirty on Monday instead, same location. Please give me a call and let me know if that works for you. Thanks now. Bye." She closed her phone shut.

"Thank you," the male voice behind her said as they stepped out of Ramona's and into the warm April sun.

"No problem," she replied, without looking back and taking notice it was the familiar stranger from inside. She stopped in her stride to check one other thing on her phone before she continued her route.

While she did, the male stranger hesitated for a moment, as if waiting for the right moment and searching for the right words. And when he finally thought he had them, he said,

"Umm, excuse me. Miss?"

Alex didn't answer because she didn't hear him at first.

He didn't know whether he was being ignored, but decided to try one more time at getting her attention.

"Miss?" he called again, taking a few steps in her direction.

Alex heard the voice, and turned towards him.

"Yes?" she answered, surprise to see who it was.

"Hi."

"Hello." Her stance was a bit cautious.

"I apologize for bothering you . . ."

"Um-hm."

He continued, " . . . but since I first saw you inside I've been wracking my brain trying to remember where else have I seen you before. Do we know each other?"

Jaz would wholeheartedly approve, Alex thought as she searched the man's face for a clue. It was a nice face, and she liked it. She studied his teeth. Perfect.

"Hmh?"

"I was just thinking that I think I've seen you somewhere before, but . . ." He paused as Alex took a couple of cautious steps back. Speaking in a soft voice, he went on, "I'm not sure. And if I can't remember where I've seen you, it'll be on my mind all day and eventually drive me crazy, that's all."

"I'm sorry, I really don't know," Alex replied, not sure whether she liked where this whole scenario was headed, but not sure she didn't like it. "You do look kinda familiar."

"Maybe I have you confused with someone else,"

he said, beginning to sound less sure of himself. "I don't know."

"I'm not sure, either. I'm sorry."

"Well, I apologize for bot . . ."

Then, as if lightning had struck, it seemingly hit Alex. She was almost sure of who he was and where they knew each other now.

"Oh my." Alex smiled. "You're . . . of course. I remember you."

"You do?" He smiled a little, embarrassed by her excitement and unsure where this was headed now. He still couldn't place her, but she apparently knew him and even seemed happy to remember. This was a good thing.

He was still trying to figure out who she was. His mind was racing continuously trying to recall where they had met before.

"We went to college together."

"We did? Okay." He nodded. "I think maybe you're right."

"Yeah, I think we might have even had a class or two together."

"Okay. Yeah." He nodded in agreement. "I believe we did. That was you?"

"Yes."

"Okay. It's coming to me now, I think."

"Looks like you've been taking good care of yourself," she said. "My memory can be so bad sometimes. Please forgive me. It's been awhile though, hasn't it?"

He stammered out, "Yes, it has."

Nothing more came to him as he waited for her to give him a bit more info. He was still piecing things together.

"Truly. This is so wild. I knew you looked familiar, but, y'know, sometimes you don't want to make a fool out of yourself just in case you're wrong," she said, with a small chuckle.

"Exactly. Same here. I almost didn't say anything for that same reason."

"Funny."

He began to relax a bit as the tension lifted from their conversation. "It was like I knew I had seen you somewhere, but I didn't know exactly where. I kept looking at you in there and whatnot, and I wasn't gonna say anything, but . . ." he rambled, as he simultaneously tried to recall her name.

She nodded in agreement, anxious to get a word in. "So how have you been?" she interjected, touching him briefly on the arm as she searched her memory bank for his name.

"I'm good, real good," he said, smiling broadly at her friendly touch.

"So, what's been going on?" she asked.

"Nothing, really. Just working hard, y'know?" He stared intently into her eyes, not even daring to blink for fear he might miss his clue as to who she was.

"I know exactly what you mean," she said. "This is so funny because I just ran into Anthony Tucker about a month ago—you remember him. And now, I bump into you. How funny is that?" She smiled, proud to have puzzled out the stranger's identity.

"Yeah. Anthony Tucker? Really?" His left brow rose as he now searched his memory for an Anthony Tucker. Maybe he was the key. "So how's he doing?" he asked.

"He seems to be doing really well for himself."

"Great."

"He actually works here downtown."

"Really?" he nodded.

"Yeah. We three should do lunch sometime. It would be great to catch up with you guys."

"Sounds good. Absolutely. I'm down."

Seemingly reassured by her recognition of him, she continued, "Hey, how's ummm . . . what is his name? Brown-skinned fella you used to hang with? His name starts with an E. Gosh, it's on the tip of my tongue. You know who I'm talkin' about—your boy."

He was looking her directly in the eyes, searching for every clue imaginable. "Who?"

"Ummm . . ." Snapping her fingers, she was thinking hard while trying to recall.

He took a chance and guessed. "You talkin' about Eddie?"

"Eddie? Yeah," she said, a little unsure. "I guess that's his name. I really thought it was something more like Ellis, but maybe it is Eddie. Anyway, how's he doing? You two still tight?"

"Yeah, most definitely. That's my ace right there. He's good. Actually, I just saw him the other . . . how do you know . . ." His mind was having some difficulty comprehending how in the world did she know his best friend.

"So you two are still together, then?"

"Together?" He was totally thrown off guard by that question. "Yeah, we still hang," he answered.

"Wow, you both have been together more than some people stay married," she chuckled.

"Huh?" He was completely lost. It took him a moment to decipher her statement.

"Is life partners more of the politically correct

term?" she asked.

"Life partners?"

"Um-hm," she nodded.

He froze for a second, then began waving his hands frantically, before he signaled for a time-out.

"Hold up a sec." He began speaking slowly, "I'm not any *dude's* life partner. I'm not sure what we're talking about here."

Alex's face switched from joy to bewilderment. She stood frozen for a moment herself, then tried again. "You're Warren Stevens, right?"

"Who?"

"Warren Stevens," she said, nodding yes, waiting for him to confirm.

As she nodded yes, he shook his head no. With a smile, he softly said, "I'm not."

There was a beat of pure awkward silence.

"Are you sure?" she asked.

"Yes, I'm sure. Without a doubt," he replied.

She covered her mouth, face hot with embarrassment, and said, "Oh, I am so sorry. I'm rambling like I know you and—please forgive me. I thought you were someone I went to college with. I apologize." She quickly searched his face in more detail, but came up empty. "Then who are you?" she asked in defeat.

"I'm . . ." Chuckling quietly to himself over the confusion, he paused and said, "Look . . . I'm sorry. This is all just a harmless case of mistaken identity. I honestly thought we knew each other and whatnot, but . . . I'm sorry to have bothered you. I probably just confused you with someone else. Please forgive me."

"It's okay," she replied, slightly disconcerted over the moment. "Forgive me."

"I do. Enjoy your day."

"You do the same."

He flashed her one last smile before slowly turning away. As he did, Alex caught a glimpse of his profile and in the passing of a few seconds, it finally dawned on her where she had seen him before. No, it couldn't be. Was it? The handsome commuter, singing "This Christmas" at the top of his lungs in traffic months ago. It was definitely him. She was now sure of herself and his identity. A huge smile crossed her face. If he hadn't been standing in reach, she wouldn't have believed it was him.

She took a few steps towards him, then jokingly asked, "Hey, have you gotten a record deal, yet?"

At the sound of her voice, he stopped, then turned back, clearly confused, and said, "Excuse me?"

"This is really wild," she said. "I really can't believe this. It just dawned on me who you are."

"What," he replied, still lost.

"I remember you."

To clear up the confusion, Alex revealed to him where they both had crossed paths before. It was a surreal moment, in a sense.

"That's where it was," he said, remembering now. "Wow. That was you. No record deal, yet," he chuckled, "and it may be awhile because you've hit on the problem. No fan base. I'm only allowed to sing in the shower and my car. Alone."

She blushed and looked into his dark eyes, illuminated with something she was not yet able to describe. A sweet awkwardness engulfed them. She apologized repeatedly for the mistaken identity she had assigned to him. He reassured her that it was okay and that he was just glad she remembered their initial encounter. It really was driving him crazy. They both laughed, and then they became suddenly silent, but it was a comfortable silence. It was as if both had found an old and familiar friend in a new and unexpected place.

Still fully engulfed and helplessly frozen in the face of her beauty, he remained silent and hopeful that she would be the next one to speak. Shy, he never had been. Usually, he was assertive, witty, and always knew what to say, especially to beautiful women. But this was no ordinary woman. She possessed a timeless beauty. There was something extraordinary about her, something that made you want to get to know her. The depths of his attraction to her went far beyond her external beauty. His spirit and tongue were both being held captive by her essence. He was a submissive prisoner to it. He had always been a great conversationalist who had never worried about finding the right words. Because of his profession, he was accustomed to speaking in front of hypercritical and scrutinizing audiences' day in and day out. But now, he stood paralyzed, infatuated by this woman's presence with absolutely nothing to say. But his eyes said it all. His fixed stare was penetrating, yet outwardly he appeared fully engaged and alert. After only a few brief minutes, he was amazed at the instant attraction he felt.

He simply nodded and smiled at their new discovery.

Alex was aware that some short span of time had passed, but for some inexplicable reason, she didn't care if she had places to go or people to see. She was anchored to this spot. What is this holding them both captive and unable to move? Alex continued smiling at his smile, simultaneously realizing the absurdity of falling for an attractive face. She didn't know this guy. She didn't even know his name. He was just someone she had seen in passing and now here he was in passing again.

She had to be honest with herself, though. He was beautiful with a hypnotizing smile and the prettiest white teeth she'd ever seen on a man. She quickly studied him, taking another mental photograph up close, although she knew that it would be impossible for her to forget anything about him. She absorbed anything else she could—his smell, his build, his everything. His moustache, goatee, and thick eyebrows all complimented one another in a way that she'd rarely seen before on any man. He was attractive, but not model type attractive. And although she had been in the presence of nice looking men before, it was something about his spirit that drew her quietly in.

To break the curious power that was engulfing her, she decided she'd have to reopen their conversation with some words or phrase that would invite further discussion. But what came out was a simple, "Well—okay, then."

She was hoping the words would prompt him into continuing their dialogue.

"Okay," he nodded.

She smiled and said, "Well, take care."

"Okay. You do the same," he replied without moving an inch, except to extend his hand.

She took his hand and shook it gently. She liked the feel of her hand inside his. His hand was strong, but soft to the touch. Even in their fleeting encounter, she had felt the warmth of his touch travel through her body and into her heart, almost making it skip a beat while sending a small chill down her spine. She forgot for a moment they were strangers and forgot to let go of his hand. He softly squeezed her hand a bit, and then flashed her one last smile before letting go.

"Have a good day," she said, giving him a final chance to ask her name or say something to prolong this *thing*.

"You, too," he said with a dazed look on his face.

"Well, good-bye," she said smiling, turning slowly, almost in slow motion, to walk away.

"Bye."

As she strode gracefully to her car, he stood there watching her go. He glanced down at his watch. It had only been eight minutes since they had stepped out of Ramona's and spoken.

As she disappeared into the crowd, he suddenly thought about the number one question he should have asked before she walked away. He looked as if he wanted to shout to her "What's your name?!" But instead, the reality of his present status fell from his lips.

"Let it go, man. You're getting married," he said, wiping his hand over his face in an attempt to shake free of the trance he had been left in.

CHAPTER EIGHT

Thinking About Her

Morning sunlight streamed through the tall windows of the old gymnasium. On Saturdays, Gabriel and his uncle, Arthur Washington, enjoyed a hard, yet friendly game of racquetball. Today they played on Court 1 overlooking the basketball court, where below a group of young men were engaged in an intense full-court basketball game. The thick acrylic walls failed as a noise buffer as the thunderous sounds of competitive play echoed throughout the gymnasium. Both Gabriel and his uncle Arthur looked the part of two players ready for a challenge, wearing protective eyewear, gloves and sporting top of the line racquets. Despite having just reached retirement age, Gabriel's uncle was in excellent health, moving with the agility of a much younger man. As usual, he was giving his favorite nephew a real workout. With his salt-and-pepper hair, neatly-trimmed beard, and well-maintained physique, Arthur still managed to catch the eye of young ladies every once and awhile and, to his great delight, he was often mistaken for Gabriel's older brother.

Still, this particular game left Arthur perspiring and struggling to catch his breath. His T-shirt was drenched and he seemed exhausted. The two had been playing nonstop for the last forty-five minutes, but just before Arthur called it quits, he managed to give the ball one last whack, tying the score between the two.

Arthur held up his hand. "Okay, I need to rest young buck. Just for a minute." He squatted on the floor for a moment, panting hard. "Whew, what's got you going so hard today?"

Gabriel slowly made his way over to his uncle. "Nothing. You're just getting old, Unc, whether you want to accept it or not." Gabriel grinned as he leaned and patted his uncle on the shoulder.

"I might be old, but what's your excuse?" Arthur shot back.

Gabriel laughed aloud at his uncle's quick wit. Arthur chuckled as he stood to his feet, holding onto Gabriel who stood several inches taller, offering his uncle his right hand for support.

"Let's take a breather and walk the track," Gabriel suggested.

Arthur grabbed his bottled water and took a swallow before burying his head in his towel, trying to cool down. "Man!" Arthur let out an exhausted sigh before taking a second swallow of water.

"You sure you're okay? Need some Ben Gay or something" Gabriel asked, still joking.

Arthur playfully grabbed Gabriel's neck and put him in a headlock. "Oh, you got jokes I see," he said, affectionately rubbing the top of his nephew's head.

"Y'know I love ya', old man," Gabriel replied, finally breaking loose from his uncle's playful, vice-like grip.

"Love? Oh, is that what that is?"

They grabbed their things and headed out to the indoor track. Walking slowly, they continued to talk, sometimes having to raise their voices over the enthusiastic shouts emanating from the basketball courts below.

"So how's the wedding stuff been comin' along?" Arthur asked.

"Good," Gabriel nodded.

"And how's the bride-to-be holding up?"

"She's good. She's excited. She's leaving for Maryland on Monday to see how things are coming along with the wedding planner. I've got a few things to wrap up at work, so I'll be heading out Friday morning. Oh, that reminds me. Don't forget to pick up your tux on Thursday. I've already paid for yours, so you don't need to do anything but try it on and go."

"Will do."

"Cool."

"Well, it looks like next Saturday is it for you then. One week to go and I will officially welcome you in as a member."

Gabriel turned to his uncle. "Member of what?" he asked, unsure of what he was referring to.

"Of the Married Man's Club!" Arthur said, picking up his pace, obviously feeling more rejuvenated after his brief rest.

"Oh. Yep, I guess so," Gabriel nodded. "If that's what you all call it. Sounds like a club with a lot of turnover. Divorce rate is high."

"It happens. Just gotta make sure it doesn't happen to you. So you're all set, huh?"

"Yeah, it seems so. As you said, next Saturday is it. As usual, Tracee has taken care of mostly everything. It's like she's the only one getting married next week. Seems all I have to do, basically, is show up."

Arthur chuckled. "Sally was the same way when we got married. It's just a woman's nature to want to be in control of such an important day, y'know?"

"Yeah, I guess so." There was a brief silence between the two until Gabriel felt compelled to ask a question. "You mind if I ask you somethin', Unc?"

Arthur turned, looked at Gabriel and said, "Sure. Shoot."

"How did you know Sally was the right one for you before you married her? I mean, out of all the women in this entire world, how did you know she was *the one* that you wanted to spend the rest of your life with?"

Pleased that his nephew always looked to him for guidance, the older man responded with a smile, "Dang boy, I thought you were gonna ask me something hard. Honestly, the only answer I can give to that question is that I just knew. And that's just how it is with any man that finds that right woman. You just know it, without a doubt. You honestly can't and don't want to remember any other woman in your life before her."

Arthur looked at his nephew who appeared to be waiting for something more. Arthur's eyes began to sparkle. He continued, "And the woman that's for you always has something extra special about her that no other woman has. Like my Sally, she's always had a few extra somethings that make her different from any other woman I've ever met, y'know?"

"Right," Gabriel agreed.

"I mean, the first time I laid eyes on her she made

me melt. Still does, y'know? After all this time. I mean, I look forward to going home knowing she's there."

"Yeah, you've definitely got one of the good ones, Unc," he nodded, enthusiastically. "You're definitely blessed. She's a good woman . . . with a beautiful heart that makes her even more beautiful. And she looks great for her age."

"You got that right," whispered Arthur.

"Um-hm."

"Boy, I tell you. Woo-ee, I mean . . ." Arthur chuckled out loud. "Just thinkin' bout her makes me want to rush to the house right now and . . ."

Gabriel interrupted, "C'mon, Unc. Don't take me there. I get the point." Gabriel shook his head in an attempt to dispel the mental image of his aging Uncle Arthur in a lusty tangle with Sally. His mind shuddered at the unwelcomed fleeting thought.

Arthur turned to him, his face serious. "Why you askin' me this, anyway? Sounds like the question somebody would ask that's not sure what they're gettin' themselves into next Saturday. Don't tell me you're getting cold feet 'cause the wedding's right round the corner? Ain't the time for that, young fella."

"No!" Gabriel let out an unconvincing laugh. "Tracee and I are cool. I'm cool. It's nothing like that. C'mon now, you know me. I'm cool. Always have been, always will be."

"Umm-hmm," Arthur murmured, not buying it.

An increasingly loud silence grew between them.

Clearing his throat, Gabriel continued, "It's just . . ."

Arthur unknowingly interrupted the younger man, "Look. Tracee is a nice girl. Got some *ways* about her that I haven't quite figured out yet, but I believe she's good people. You two been together for a long time, which is not a reason you should marry someone. You gotta know in your heart, in your spirit, that you can't live without her. You want to make sure you do this thang one time and one time only. That's the way God intended marriage to be . . . forever. So many young folks rush to the altar unprepared for the actual marriage part. Focusing too much on a thirty minute ceremony and the honeymoon can mess you up. Once the wedding's over, you've got a lifetime to live with this person and love them through the highs and the lows. This ain't for the faint of heart. There's a lot of give and take in a marriage. Sometimes one person is takin' more than giving and that ultimately doesn't work. Yeah, it's two people that are willing to give up their own selfish wants and meet somewhere in the middle."

"Um-hm," Gabriel murmured, his face adopting a perplexed, vacant expression as he tried to measure his pending nuptials against Uncle Arthur's wisdom.

"She does make you happy, right?" inquired Arthur abruptly.

"Who?" Gabriel asked with a blank look over his face, still distracted by the mental disturbance created by his uncle's commentary.

"Tracee. The woman you're going to marry."

"Oh. Um-hm, yeah. Most definitely," he nodded, looking unsure.

"Then why do you have that twisted look as if you've been eating a bag of prunes or your laxative just kicked in and there's not a toilet around?" Arthur questioned, with a bit of light humor in his voice.

Gabriel chuckled.

"I don't look like that. Believe me, I'm cool."

"Okay, I hear ya' 'Mr. I'm Cool'."

They remained in silence for a moment. But Gabriel's turbulent mind was anything but still. He glanced quickly at his uncle and spiritual mentor.

"I was just askin' you that question to navigate the waters, so to speak, with somebody that's already been there done that, like your old, tired self."

"Uh-huh." Arthur looked Gabriel over suspiciously. "You young people, I tell ya'. Times definitely do change."

Arthur began an entire story of how he and Sally had married young and yet their marriage had worked for all these years because they had trust, respect, and much love for one another. His uncle's voice droned on, but Gabriel's mind began to drift elsewhere. It was focused on the beautiful woman he had run into at Ramona's the day before. The encounter replayed frame by frame, over and over in his mind. It was an incident that he was unsure he should even mention to Arthur.

Searching keenly for Gabriel's reaction to his story, Arthur noticed the glazed expression on his nephew's face. Suddenly, Gabriel's mind awakened and he rejoined the conversation with his uncle.

"Yeah, that's special and whatnot. But look. This is gonna sound crazy, but . . . . like the weirdest thing happened. I met this woman yesterday—and, for some reason, I haven't been able to get her out of my head." The words tumbled from his mouth. Gabriel was relieved at being finally able to talk openly about these feelings that had consumed him for the past twenty-four hours.

Arthur's focus, however, was somewhere else. He

was still reflecting on his marriage. Arthur continued, oblivious to Gabriel's confession, "I mean, Sally and me, it was simpler times, good times. You got married and you stayed married. Y'know? No matter what. No matter how hard things got, nobody was leaving nobody. You just stuck that *thing* out and made it work. Simple as that. Divorce was not even something folks from our time even considered. You heard that old song by Betty White?" Arthur struggled to find the right tune to sing a bit of the song. "Goes something like . . . *don't blame Mr. Charlie. Mr. Charlie is just a man and heeee's doing the best he can*." Arthur hummed a bit more while laughing to himself.

"Betty Wright," Gabriel said, tuning back in only briefly to correct his uncle.

"What?" Arthur responded.

"Her name's Betty Wright, not Betty White. That's Golden Girls."

"White, Wright, all the same."

Refocusing entirely on his own thoughts, Gabriel couldn't quite figure out what to make of the whole scenario with this mystery woman. He continued, "I mean, when I say she was beautiful, Unc—I mean she was beautiful."

"Sally literally took my breath away when I first saw her. I had never seen such a *beautiful* woman," Arthur continued. "I tell ya' I wouldn't trade her for nothing in this world."

"God knows she had the sexiest lips," Gabriel continued, off in his own thoughts. "And those eyes of hers. My my my."

"Her *pretty eyes* and that smile is what first got me," Arthur added. "They've always brightened my day. I don't care what can be going wrong in the world, but when I come home and see that woman with that beautiful smile across her face, knowing that she loves me, it makes me realize that the world still has some good in it. And I know what you're thinking to yourself."

"I shouldn't be having these thoughts," Gabriel mused. "I shouldn't be thinking about her. I'm getting married in like seven days. But I am thinking about her and the harder I try not to think about her, the more I think about her. What do you think?" he shook his head and pulled his fingers through his hair.

"I mean, when I really think about it, no other woman had ever made me feel that way. I knew right then there was something *special* about her if she could do that to me. It took me awhile, but I finally realized that it was nothing but *love*."

"I mean, I *love* Tracee, don't get me wrong," Gabriel declared firmly. "And I've never stepped out on her and I don't have any intentions to. I believe in being faithful."

It was then that Arthur looked at Gabriel, and asked pointedly, "Who is she?"

"Huh?" Gabriel jumped slightly, now realizing his uncle had heard every word he had said. "Who?"

"The woman you've been talking about for almost five minutes now," Arthur sighed, patiently. They had reached the locker room. Listening attentively now, Arthur stopped and turned to his nephew for an answer.

"I honestly don't know. Not even her name. We just bumped into each other again."

"Again?"

"Yeah. It's wild, you wouldn't believe me if I told you, but . . . I don't know." Gabriel shook his head in disbelief. "Maybe it was just a coincidence."

"No such thing nephew. What's meant to happen, happens, never forget that. Did you talk to her?"

Gabriel could sense that he now had Arthur's full attention. "I did, and I didn't," he answered.

"Okay, what does that mean? You froze up or something?" Arthur fired at Gabriel. "Not 'Mr. I'm Cool'. Say it ain't so."

"For whatever reason, I just couldn't get my thoughts completely together. That's not even like me, y'know?"

"She was that bad, huh?"

"Yes," Gabriel stressed. "You would have to see her for yourself to believe it."

Gathering their belongings, they left the locker room and continued talking as they headed to the parking lot where Arthur's Chevy Malibu and Gabriel's silver Ducati 620 Sport were parked. As the two walked towards Arthur's 1979 family icon, Gabriel couldn't help feeling like a star-struck kid again.

"It's like I'm almost hoping I'll see her again. Is that wrong?"

Arthur chuckled as he opened the trunk of his car and placed their racquetball gear inside.

"That's one I'm gonna have to let you figure out for yourself. Just remember what I always say. Listen to your heart. Let your soul confirm what you hear."

"Right," Gabriel agreed, with a nod of his head.

"You know right from wrong, but those two things will always lead you in the right direction whenever you're unsure."

"True," Gabriel replied.

"Really think about it."

Arthur looked Gabriel straight in the eyes as he

closed his trunk and headed to the driver's side. He was giving his nephew that special look that Gabriel knew from years of experience. It was a look that said: "Prepare yourself, 'cause a good old lecture is coming your way any second now." Far from resenting his uncle's input, Gabriel knew that Arthur was the one person he could rely on when he really needed sensible advice. Sure, the advice was sometimes more than Gabriel wanted or cared to hear, but mostly, his uncle's long stories with their underlying moral lessons were usually right on target. Arthur was always there for Gabriel and his sister and loved them both like they were his own. Gabriel felt blessed to have him around.

Arthur began, "I am going to tell you this much, son. It's nothing new for a man to have his head turned by a beautiful woman just before he gets married. You start thinking about everything you're givin' up for that one woman, and every beautiful face that passes your way adds just a little more doubt and confusion as to what you're about to do. Life is funny like that. Just about every man goes through it. It's like that last final test or something. But if you really love Tracee," Arthur said, pointedly, "this will pass. So don't worry about it. I promise it'll blow over. You'll be at the altar next week and this whole thing will not even be an issue. Your focus will be on the woman before you."

"Yeah," Gabriel nodded, unconvinced.

"Even after you get married, same thing—if not worse. I'm propositioned constantly by these hot little things running around here, but the thought of hurting Sally and losing what we've got over nothing—oh hell no! Nothing's worth that. And once the fling is over, what are you left with? Guilt, I tell ya. And guilt is the mutha of all muthas," Arthur said. "Remember this, the guilt always outlast the pleasure. It's not worth it."

Lost in a whorl of thoughts, Gabriel felt he had to say something reassuring about his love for Tracee to his uncle. He spoke the words, emphasizing each one like an incantation. "I do love Tracee."

"I'm sure you do," Arthur replied with a chuckle, "but who are you trying to convince, me or yourself? Trust me, son, when I say that's a can of worms you don't want to open. A path you don't want to travel. You gotta let that go. You're getting married one week from today."

"Yeah, you're right."

"I know I am."

Moving towards his bike, Gabriel wondered why this wind of doubt had blown his way out of nowhere.

Arthur stepped inside his car and started the engine. He rolled down the window and changed the subject.

"Look. In exchange for my wisdom and if you have time between now and Monday, I'm gonna need you to come by and help me move that couch I was telling you about. Sally wants to put it in the basement to make room for the new one being delivered Tuesday. It shouldn't take any more than a few minutes. Okay?"

Gabriel never hesitated when it came to helping his Uncle.

"Yes, sir. Not a problem."

"And your sister's coming by after Sunday service tomorrow, bringing over this boyfriend of hers for us to finally meet. Thought I would have been introduced to him by now. You met this knucklehead she's been seeing?"

"Tre? Yeah."

"What's his story?"

"He's cool. Good guy. Got his head on straight."

"We'll see," Arthur replied, with an air of a man obviously protective over his niece.

"Don't give him a hard time. Kenya really likes him."

"Um-hm," Arthur replied, knowing he wouldn't be heeding to his nephew's advice. He had a certain way in which he could be intimidating to the fellas his niece introduced him to. Arthur only had her best interest at heart, just as if he were her father and screening any new love interest in his daughter's life.

As the two joked on how Arthur planned to put Kenya's new boyfriend through the ringer and how he would take the opportunity to definitely show the young fella his gun collection, Gabriel briefly managed to put aside the thoughts that were fast taking over his mind.

"Well, I'll talk to you later," Arthur said, putting the car into reverse. "If you and Tracee can make it after church tomorrow, you're more than welcome. I could use someone to play the good cop."

"Okay, we'll try." Gabriel chuckled. "Love ya, man."

"Love you, too. And be careful on that bike," Arthur requested, pointing at Gabriel's sports bike.

"Will do. Never taking it above ninety in the residential areas, I promise," Gabriel joked.

Arthur shook his head with a smile as he cut the steering wheel gracefully and pulled out of his park with ease, giving his nephew a final wave out the car window.

Today, like mostly every day, "A Touch of Jaz" hair salon was wall-to-wall with divas of all ages, shapes and sizes getting pampered for the weekend with a full day of beauty regimes from hair-dos to waxing to pedicures. Others, waiting patiently for their turn in the chair, perused the latest issues of *Essence, Vogue* and *O*, tapping their feet to the sound of a smooth jazz melody playing softly in the background. And some watched *The Young and the Restless* playing on a flat screen television that Jaz had mounted on the center wall of the salon. Stylists were busy taming their clients' hair, gossiping and laughing in a shop that was live today.

Jaz was listening intently to the rest of Alex's story about her recent chance meeting with the male stranger at Ramona's. Flipping through the pages of an *Essence* magazine, Alex was seated in Jaz's chair, although not for a hairdo today but for no other reason than to talk. Jaz had stopped anything she was doing. She smiled and looked at her best friend's reflection in the mirror as she proceeded with her story in a soft tone. Alex hadn't noticed Jaz's full attention on her, taking into account how she spoke of this man.

"Girl, I don't know anything about him. He's extremely attractive, though. It's just the way we met and then . . . it was crazy because even though it took me awhile to remember him, I was . . ."Alex suddenly lost her train of thought.

"What?" Jaz prompted.

"I . . . I just couldn't believe I actually remembered him, that's all."

"Right."

"You know how bad my memory is, right?" Alex explained.

"Um-hm," Jaz murmured with a nod. "Terrible," she added, listening carefully and closely watching Alex's facial expression change.

Alex flipped through the pages of her magazine as she continued talking, "And to think I would run into him again after all this time. It was weird, but it was like there was some kind of . . . I don't know. It was just nice." Alex looked up and into the huge wall mirror in front of her. She was about to continue, but paused when she discovered that Jaz was staring at her with a huge smile on her face. "What?" Alex asked, smiling back at Jaz's reflection.

"And that's it? That can't be it. There's got to be more to this story than what you're telling me, girlfriend."

"That's it," Alex replied, emphatically.

"Okay, let me get this straight. You're telling me you first saw this *fine* brotha, who was looking at you in Ramona's yesterday, like four months or so ago?"

"Yes."

"When you were stuck in traffic . . ."

"Yes."

"Singing Donny Mathis or Donny and Marie songs or something, right?"

"Donny Hathaway, silly."

"Right. You run into him again?"

"Yes."

"And this is all you have to report?"

"Yes."

"I don't believe it. You're concealin' information, my sistah."

"No. Honestly, that's it."

"I hear you," Jaz said, with an unbelieving tone. "That's a story that definitely won't make the evening news."

"I'm telling you that's all that happened and that's all there is to tell. I lie to you not," Alex smiled, and insistently declared.

Jaz gave Alex's reflection in the mirror a disbelieving look.

"See. This is exactly why I don't like tellin' you stuff, even though I do tell you everything. And I'm not concealing anything. Next time I'll just keep my little uninteresting story all to myself."

"Um-hm. I agree."

"Make me sick," Alex mumbled, under her breath, playfully.

"What was that?" Jaz asked sharply, holding a pair of scissors in her hand as if she would cut all of Alex's hair off if she answered incorrectly.

"Nothing. I see that angry eighth grader is resurfacing."

"That's exactly what I thought," Jaz said, with a smirk on her face. "How were his fingers?"

"His fingers?"

"Yes. They weren't too long, were they? There's something very effeminate about a man with long, skinny fingers. Stay away from 'em. Trust me, I had to learn the hard way. That's definitely a sign of a man being gay or very gay friendly," Jaz laughed.

"Girl, where do you come up with this stuff?" Alex chuckled. "You talking to me about fingers instead of feet, when you're dating someone with the same shoe size as you?"

Paying Alex's comment no mind, Jaz continued, "Listen. I know what I'm talking about. I was just as surprised as you are sitting here. Who knew? I'm telling you the truth is in the fingers."

"Ah, okay. Fingers and toes," Alex replied, with a comical facial expression.

"I'm trying to school you."

Changing the subject, Alex asked, "How do you think I would look with this type of do, Jaz? I'm thinking about going au naturale." She pointed to a picture in the magazine.

Jaz quickly glanced down at the photo. "That's cute. It's kinda how I hooked Kenya's hair up, but a little different."

"Kenya?"

"Remember my cousin Tre's girlfriend?"

"Oh. Yeah, right. It is kinda like that, if I remember correctly."

"It might be a nice look for you. You'll probably look a hundred times better than the chick in the magazine there. Her face is too round for that look. The stylist should know better."

"I might try it for the summer or something."

"Cool. I'll hook it up. Put a new twist on it, make it your own."

Alex continued, "Don't you think it's funny how we can cross paths with strangers everyday that we think we'll never see again?"

"What?" Jaz asked, not quite hearing her full statement.

"Nothing."

"No. What?"

"I just said *life* is funny, that's all." Alex stared off into space.

"Yeah-yeah-yeah. That's very profound and everything, but what's the brotha's name?"

"His name?" Alex thought for a second. "I don't

know," she answered.

"You mean to tell me, out of everything you just told me, which wasn't very much—that you didn't even get his name?"

"No, I didn't."

"Okay. Well, did you see if he at least had a nice booty? Did you check out the melons?"

Alexandria blushed, with a naughty grin.

"You are a trip. No I didn't, but I wouldn't doubt that he does."

CHAPTER NINE

What Am I Doing Here?

The Monday morning air was crisp and refreshing as early morning traffic in downtown Raleigh began to build into an endless stream of cars along Wilmington Avenue. Gabriel Washington had already arrived at his office, a 15-story high-rise in the heart of downtown. Dressed in a Corneliani pinstriped suit, tailored to his frame, Gabriel walked at a steady pace, his morning newspaper under one arm, cup of coffee in one hand, and his black leather Kenneth Cole briefcase in the other. As always, he gave the security guard a polite nod, stepped inside the elevator and headed to his office suite on the 14th floor.

Arriving early had advantages. The welcomed silence usually gave him time to organize his day. This morning, he also needed to think about how to tackle his growing to-do list before leaving for Maryland on Friday morning. But he was distracted. The conversation on Saturday with his Uncle Arthur was still echoing inside his head, as it had been for the entire weekend.

The elevator doors opened.

As Gabriel stepped out, he scanned the lavishly decorated executive suite. Taking a deep sigh, he stepped into his office, one of a few with a view of the city against the background of trees and a Carolina blue sky that went on as far as the eye could see. It was a captivating sight that never failed to draw compliments from clients and visitors. On the east wall stood floor-to-ceiling mahogany bookshelves filled with books and magazines on business-related subjects from finance to international commerce interspersed with a few pictures of family and friends. On the west wall hung a custom-framed portrait of the ten founders of his fraternity with "Kappa Alpha Psi" engraved on a brass plate at the bottom and his MBA diploma from Duke.

He slid his briefcase on top of the U-shaped mahogany desk at the center of it all and walked around, placing his coffee on the leather blotter. He sat down in his black, high back, leather armchair to begin the ritual that he faithfully performed each morning. He slipped his laptop out of his briefcase, placed it on his desk, then leaned back in his chair, clasping his hands behind his head. He suddenly noticed that his voicemail light was blinking. He picked up the phone and keyed in his code. Waited. Listened. Only one message.

"Hi, sweetie. It's Tracee. Just wanted to give you a quick call before my flight left and wish you a great day. I also wanted to make sure we were okay. You seemed kinda out of it last night, like you had a lot on your mind." She sighed. "Any who, I forgot to mention that I may have found a Realtor we both might be happy with. But we can talk about all of that later. I'll give you a call when I land. Love you. Okay, hun. Smooches."

Gabriel hung up, got up from his desk, paced, and then took a deep breath. After a moment, he looked at his watch. It was already time for the eleven o'clock staff meeting.

As he stepped into the hall, he could hear the usual morning routine getting underway: the familiar chords of computers logging on, desk drawers opening and closing, and the muffled laughter of coworkers debriefing each other on their weekend adventures.

The conference room was no more than ten strides from his office. En route, he passed the desk of his executive assistant, Ester, who resided over a well-organized and spacious workstation just outside his office. Gabriel often boasted about Ester to his co-workers. She was, after all, the most competent and pleasant assistant he'd ever had, a bit on the motherly side, but that was part of her charm. Although she didn't look a day over forty-five, she would proudly inform anyone who asked that she was actually fifty-six. She had beautiful dark skin, a compassionate smile that would melt the heart of the meanest client, and was undoubtedly the most knowledgeable assistant ever to grace the floors of the bank. And Gabriel was her biggest fan. And this morning, as normal, her desk was in order with a neat stack of files and a mug of steaming hazelnut decaf coffee, indicating she was somewhere nearby.

He entered the conference room, greeting other executives already seated. He was more than ready to get this meeting started and over with as soon as possible. He was mentally not here today, and already behind on a long list of chores. To add insult to injury, as the meeting got underway, Thomas Fields, the Senior VP of

Small Business Development and an all-round windbag full of hot air and little personality, rose to speak.

For several hours, Gabriel sat listening to Fields deliver a predictable and unoriginal presentation with his usual cockiness and know-it-all attitude. Gabriel tried hard to conceal his disinterest.

"I think that providing equity capital, long-term loans, along with debt-equity investments and management assistance to qualifying small businesses will allow us an opportunity to share in their success as they grow and prosper," Fields concluded, while Gabriel quietly sighed to himself.

Gabriel glanced at his watch and then around at the men gathered around the large beveled glass table. He had secretly hoped to find an ally who appeared equally numbed. He wondered what they might be thinking when they weren't listening.

In meetings like this, his mind often drifted toward more creative aspirations, which made him all the more aware of what he already knew. At times, he did more than just think. He would pretend to take notes, all the while discreetly jotting down a short poem or notes for the screenplay he had written almost six months ago. He was a creative soul and deep down, it bothered him that his script took a backseat to everything else going on in his life. He also wished that Tracee could be more supportive of his dream to become a writer. Unfortunately, the future Mrs. Gabriel Washington saw "wife of a successful banker" as a much more suitable role for herself than "wife of a writer wannabe." Her picture of the future had him framed as president of the bank, not a Tony-winning playwright.

Today's mental escape was different. Something

else had invaded his mind, offering a pleasing and enticing release from his present reality. Right now, against his better judgment and Uncle Arthur's advice, Gabriel found himself again playing back the warm encounter with the exquisite and unforgettable woman at Ramona's on Friday. He couldn't believe he hadn't been able to pull himself together long enough to even ask for her name.

Suddenly, in his playback, he recalled overhearing a small piece of her conversation when she held the door for him on their way out of the restaurant. She was talking on her cell phone and he believed he overheard her tell somebody something about meeting them at one-thirty today. He glanced at his watch again in the hope that he could possibly time his arrival at Ramona's to coincide with hers, if that so happened to be the case. He had no idea what he would do or even what he would say.

Time had slowly ticked by, but it was already nearing one-thirty. This morning's meeting had already gone longer than expected and each time it appeared that Fields was finally wrapping up his presentation, he would move on to something else. Gabriel nodded, giving the impression he was in complete agreement with what was, hopefully, Fields' closing point.

"How about you, Washington. What do you think?" Mr. Nelson, bank president, interrupted his reverie. He looked up to see that his colleagues were focused on him and waiting for a response. Gabriel needed to cover being caught off guard. He could hear his Uncle Arthur's advice: "When you just don't know—just look like you know." Gabriel took a moment, as if reflecting on the subject at hand, before speaking. In reality, he was slowly trying to recall the reason he had been sitting in this meeting and what had been said.

"Honestly, I think as long as we can maintain and increase our focus on investing in small businesses owned by entrepreneurs who are willing to relocate into economically distressed communities, while still exploring investments in manufacturing and service industries, then we should be fine. But, I think we also need to seek out small businesses with strong technological products or services because of the growth potential of such firms in this market."

"Um-hm," voices murmured in agreement.

"By investing more financial resources in under-resourced communities and industries, we can solidify and ultimately exceed our competitors," he continued. "In a nutshell, I think Mr. Fields and I are speaking the same language." Gabriel's eyes quickly glanced towards Fields who nodded in agreement, looking a bit wide-eyed. The other executives seated around the conference room table nodded enthusiastically.

"Excellent," Mr. Nelson said, then nodding to Fields added, "I suggest that you set up a meeting with Washington, perhaps some time in the next few weeks after he gets back in the office and devise a plan the two of you can work on together. I think we're on our way to unfolding some excellent profit potentials." Mr. Nelson placed his Mont Blanc pen on the table, a move that always signified the end of a meeting. "Thank you all for your time."

Many of the execs headed back to their offices. Mr. Nelson remained seated at the head of the boardroom table, sipping his morning coffee. He continued to scan his notes while the team noisily dispersed into the hallway.

"You free for lunch, Washington?" Mr. Nelson inquired as Gabriel stood up.

"Lunch?" Gabriel replied, knowing he needed to divert any company in his plans to head back to Ramona's.

"Actually, I have a wedding-related appointment my fiancée scheduled about a week ago that I need to get to first," Gabriel sighed aloud. "I'm sure you know how that goes."

"Believe me, I do," Mr. Nelson said with a hearty chuckle, "it does get better."

"I'm sure," Gabriel smiled. "See you when I get back, sir."

"Have a good one."

Gabriel left the boardroom and headed to his office to grab his coat and car keys. While standing at his desk, he noticed Ester coming out of the copy room with a handful of papers.

"Meeting over already?" she asked, poking her head in.

"Yes, thank God. It took everything in me to keep from stabbing myself in the neck with a pencil just to get through it this morning," Gabriel joked.

Ester snickered.

"Let me guess, Fields must've headed up the meeting again?"

"How'd you know?" Gabriel retorted.

"Just a gut feeling. That man could put a cup of coffee to sleep."

"Yes," Gabriel agreed, smiling at her comment.

She smiled. "You headin' out?"

"Yeah. I'm supposed to meet Eddie for lunch, and

then I have a quick errand to run. But I should be back in an hour or so."

"Okay, Boss Man. Oh by the way, I almost forgot. You had only one message when you were in your meeting this morning. Tracee called and said she had arrived safely in Maryland."

"Okay, great. Thank you," he said putting on his jacket.

"I told her you would probably be leaving for lunch soon. She said she would call back before five."

"Okay, cool."

"I also took the liberty of sending that financial report over to Mr. Covington for you."

"I had completely forgotten about that. My mind has been all over the place. Thank you, Ester, for always looking out for me."

"Somebody has to. Be safe now."

"Thank you," Gabriel replied.

Gabriel made his way to the parking garage with a thousand thoughts flooding his mind. He hit speed dial on his cell and waited patiently for an answer on the other end. Speaking aloud to himself, he said, "Okay, I'll call Eddie and reschedule lunch, and I'll just go by the travel agency to pick up the tickets when I get off work instead."

Suddenly, the voice of his best friend on the other end of the phone interrupted his mental conversation.

"Ed, what's up? This is Gabe," he said, as he got into his car. "Man, do you mind if we reschedule lunch? Nothing. I just need to take care of something and it may take a little longer than I expected. Um-hm. Yeah, that's cool. What? Oh yeah, I'm straight. I'm just running late for something that completely slipped my mind. But look, I'll hit you up later. Cool? Okay. Yeah. Later, man."

Within minutes, Gabriel found himself pulling up in front of Ramona's, slipping into the only available parking space on the street. He sat there for a moment. Took a deep breath. Thought about what he was doing here and whether it was right. He took another deep breath.

"Okay. I'm outta here," he stated firmly to the dashboard, as if it would respond.

He started the car. Just as he was about to shift to reverse, he thought for a minute. He turned the car back off. Thought about what he was doing. Started the car again. Turned the car back off again. "Okay, I'll just go in and grab something to eat, take it back to the office and that's it. A brotha gotta eat, right?" he reasoned aloud.

He got out of the car. Inside, he took a small table by the window and ordered his favorite dish, fettuccine alfredo. He quickly scanned the room in search of the familiar face etched in his memory. Instead, his eyes met the stares of two professional-looking black women who had been giddily whispering to each other from the moment that he had first walked into the restaurant. Gabriel exchanged a friendly smile with both ladies. He felt totally self-conscious after realizing that he was the subject of their whispers. He politely turned away and glanced at his watch. It was one-thirty.

As he waited for his to-go order, Gabriel quietly sipped on a cappuccino. After sitting for fifteen minutes, while watching for the woman he so desperately yearned to see, he became restless. He started fumbling with his car keys. Noticing his own nervousness, he placed his keys down on the table while his eyes continued to observe every patron who walked through the door. He glanced at his watch again. It was apparent that she was not coming. He sighed heavily as disappointment washed over him, thinking maybe he had overheard her wrong. It probably was for the best anyway.

But not yet ready to give up, he continued staring at the entrance, trying not to look obvious.

Finally, his waiter approached and said, "Here's your order, Mr. Washington." He handed Gabriel a carryout bag with Ramona's scripted elegantly on the outside.

"Thank you," he replied as he quickly glanced at the young waiter's badge to remind himself of his name, "Walter," he added.

With his hopes of another chance encounter dashed, he slowly headed outside into the downtown square, moved swiftly through the chaos of the lunch crowd to his parked car, then searched his pockets for his keys. They weren't there. After searching again and glancing through the car window to make sure he hadn't left them in the ignition, he finally realized where they were. He headed back.

Inside Ramona's, Alex had arrived, late for her one-thirty appointment. She was anxious, but it wasn't the client she was worried about missing. "What am I doing here?" Alex mumbled quietly, eyes eagerly searching Ramona's for the gentleman she'd crossed paths with just a few days ago. Only minutes ago, her client had canceled, but Alex came to the restaurant anyway, and she knew it wasn't just for lunch.

She sat down at a spot near the window, then noticed a set of car keys on the table. She looked around to see if a waiter was nearby, thinking she may have taken someone's seat. But, no glass was on the table, and as she looked around, it seemed that everyone was seated. She decided to tell the waiter when he arrived to take her order that the keys had been left behind.

Gabriel walked back through Ramona's doors and headed for the table where he had been seated. He was stunned to see her sitting there. His heart suddenly started beating faster, trying to figure out where she had come from so suddenly. He had only left less than five minutes ago. But there she was, picking up his car keys and about to hand them over to Walter, the waiter. He cautiously approached the table.

"They're mine," Gabriel said.

As their eyes met, Alex smiled at the sight of him.

"Hey."

"Hi."

"Are you following me?" she teased.

"I probably should be asking you that. You're the one who has my keys," he replied, playing along.

Walter glanced from one to the other. As the two shared a moment, Walter smiled and took his cue to leave them alone.

She took the keys and held them out to him, dangling them in midair on her finger. She observed his nervous hands when they touched during the exchange. There it was again. That electric tingle that shot through her entire being. What was that? Whatever it was, it felt good. It was something that was almost difficult to put into words. You would have to experience it for yourself to truly understand.

"Thank you. I wasn't going to get too far without these."

"No, you weren't. And I was two seconds from

having me a second car," she said, trying to ease the awkwardness with a funny.

He smiled.

"That's funny."

She smiled at his smile.

"Well. Umm . . . thanks again," he said, as he nervously jingled his keys in his hand.

She couldn't help but notice his deep, caramel-colored eyes. "You're welcome," she said.

He turned slowly to walk away. Alex didn't move a muscle nor did she take her eyes off him. As her eyes fell to his behind, she bit her bottom lip as if a naughty thought had jumped into her head. The melons were nice. And then, without warning, he suddenly stopped and turned back towards her. She quickly looked up to meet his gaze.

"Excuse me, again," he said, quickly walking back to her table.

"Yes?" she answered, with a wide-eyed look.

"I didn't take the opportunity to introduce myself last time amidst all the confusion, and here I am walking off without properly introducing myself to someone who just rescued me from having to take the bus home today." He extended his hand to her. "Warren Stevens," he said.

She laughed, remembering.

"Just joking, of course. Gabriel Washington," he said.

He had a sense of humor. She liked that. She took his hand.

"Hello again." She then introduced herself. "I'm Alexandria Jones."

They released hands.

"Nice to meet you, Alexandria Jones. I figure if we're going to keep running into each other like this, then maybe we should at least know each other's names," he said with a broad smile.

"Yeah, I guess so," she said, smiling invitingly.

"Yeah." As quickly as he had shaken off his nervousness, he found himself at a loss for words again. He had to refocus so that he wouldn't miss this opportunity to find out more about this mysterious woman.

"I assume you work downtown?" she inquired.

"I do. At Century," he said, pointing to the direction of his building.

"Oh. Okay," she said, nodding to let him know she was familiar with the bank he spoke of. "I've actually done business with you guys in the past," she added.

"Oh. Well good. Glad to have had your business. And you?" he asked.

"I actually work out of my home. I just like this place and it's a good spot to meet my clients."

"Yeah. So what is it that you do?" he asked.

"I recently started my own real estate company."

"Wow. That's great." Gabriel was sincerely impressed with the fact that she owned her own business. He admired anyone with an entrepreneurial spirit and the gusto to pursue their dreams.

"Thank you," she replied.

"Yeah, most definitely. I believe more talented sistahs need to step out and exercise their gifts. I'm sure you're going to do well."

She was already impressed with this brotha and, for some reason, she could tell he really meant what he had just said.

"Thank you for the kind words," she remarked, curious as to why he spoke with such sincerity and confidence when he really didn't know anything about her. Uneasy at how deeply moved she was by all he had said, she quickly shifted the conversation to him. "I was telling one of my friends about you," she said, surprised at the fact she had even admitted that.

"About me?" Gabriel wasn't sure if he had heard her right.

"Yeah. Just about how funny it was that we saw each other again and all."

"Oh. Yeah, that was funny," Gabriel agreed, even though he secretly knew that, unlike their initial meeting, he had deliberately planned today's encounter.

"Yeah. She thought so, too. In such a big city and all."

"Right. What *are* the chances?"

"Exactly. And here we are again." They both smiled at their awkwardness. Gabriel was desperately trying to keep the conversation going. Alexandria couldn't shake away the fact that this complete stranger was arousing emotions in her she had believed she had buried deep down inside. "What *are* the chances?"

"You don't sound like you're from here," he said, starting to feel a little more relaxed again.

"Born in Boston, but raised here pretty much," she said.

"Boston, beautiful place."

"Oh, you've been there?" she asked.

"On several occasions. Business mostly."

"And you? Are you from here?" she asked.

"No. Jersey actually."

"What part?"

"Newark."

"Oh, okay. I've got some family there, too."

"And what made you move here," she inquired.

"College. Scholarship. And plus I have family here, too."

"Oh, okay."

Suddenly changing the subject, he said, "Look. I hope this doesn't sound too forward and, if it does, please forgive me," his voice had switched to a softer tone and a sudden boost of self-confidence empowered him, "but I'm surprised you're here having lunch alone," Gabriel said.

"Well, my one-thirty appointment canceled on me at the last minute."

"Oh."

"Yeah. But that's kinda presumptuous of you to assume I was having lunch alone," Alex replied.

Gabriel smiled, somewhat excited by her directness and corrective tone. He liked that she knew how to handle herself. He wasn't afraid to continue their conversation. In fact, he was more intrigued than ever. She was obviously not a woman to be taken lightly, and a brotha needed to choose his words carefully. Gabriel began, "Oh. I don't want you to think . . . I wasn't . . . I mean, I'm not trying to . . ." He fumbled for an explanation.

"You don't have to explain," she said, sensing his sincerity over an unintentional blunder. Alex smiled.

He continued, "Oh, okay. Well, look . . . I'm sorry to have bothered you. I just thought you might give me the honor of buying you lunch if you just happened to be free. Hopefully, with the possibility of learning more about you besides your name."

"Didn't you just do that?" she asked, her face dead serious. In the few minutes he'd been standing there, he knew her name, her occupation, and where she was from. Apparently he wanted to know more. She wasn't sure whether he had even took notice of her wedding ring.

Her reply produced a trickle of sweat on his forehead, an obvious sign her response had made him nervous, and he mumbled, "Oh, I guess I did. Ummm . . ."

"I'm just joking with you," she said. "Thank you for the offer," she added.

Gabriel stared at her, waiting for a more definite answer to his invitation. There was a deafening moment of silence, and then Gabriel began speaking in a cautious tone. "Well, is that a 'thank you, yes' or a 'thank you, no'?"

Alex flashed a half-smile at him and said, "Well, seeing that we don't know each other, ummm . . ." She was searching to remember his name, but her mind had gone blank for some reason.

Noticing her struggle, he decided to help her out, even though he was disconcerted that the impression he'd made so far hadn't been sufficient for her to remember. "Gabriel," he said, softly.

"Gerald?" she asked.

"Gabriel," he said, just a little louder than before.

"Gabriel," she repeated. "That's right." She had no idea why she hadn't been able to remember it. It was such a pleasant name. "I will have to respectfully say thank you . . . but no."

"Okay. Well, I hope to see you around again," he said, preparing to escape from a downhill situation.

"I'm sure we will." She gave him a friendly smile

before he started to leave. What would it hurt? He seemed nice. Before he moved too far away, the sound of her voice stopped him. "Maybe some tea?" she said, surprising herself with her spontaneity.

"Hmh?" He stopped, and turned back to her. He wasn't sure if he had heard her correctly.

"Maybe you could join me for some tea or something?" she asked, with a hint of uncertainty in her voice. She wasn't sure if she was doing the right thing by asking a complete stranger to join her at her table. But it was a public place and being so there was little for her to fear.

"You're sure you don't mind?" he asked, as he moved closer, cautiously placing his right hand on the chair and then pausing for her permission to be seated.

"It's okay," she replied in a disarming tone. She didn't want to appear overly-enthused by his presence, but truthfully she wasn't ready for their conversation to end and her heart fluttered at the prospect of talking with him even more.

He smiled, pulled out the vacant chair directly across from her and sat down. He placed his carryout bag carefully beside him in the unoccupied chair to his left.

"Have you placed an order yet?" he asked, his eyes sparkling.

"Not yet. I was only going to get a soup and salad. I'm not extremely hungry," she replied.

"You gonna eat your food? You don't want it to get cold."

"Yeah, I will. I'll wait until yours arrives."

They were silent only for a moment, getting a feel for one another. Then they smiled, and any awkwardness that existed gradually began to vanish.

And they sat there.

And they talked.

And it was nice.

And when the conversation opened itself to the point where it was appropriate, Gabriel, being the honest man that he was, told her his story. He mentioned the fact he was engaged. Gabriel was a rare breed. Most brothas' wouldn't have done that. Catching her off guard, Alex's body tensed when he said the word "fiancée." She was completely taken aback at her involuntary reaction to his admission. Though surprised, she nodded to let him know that she had heard him and understood, yet, inside, her heart sank when he spoke of it. Without him directly saying so, she could sense there was doubt in the journey he was embarking on with the woman he belonged to. She thought how ironic it was that here she sat, her marriage disintegrating, while this man sat across from her on the point of beginning a new life that she assumed would be filled with hope and excitement with his wife-to-be.

Alex knew he had every right to be spoken for. He was a good looking man. Her head understood completely, but in her heart she didn't want him to be engaged. She didn't want to think about the fact that she was married. So much so, that she didn't ask him any questions in regards to his engagement, not when it was or to whom, and accepted what he chose to tell her in the moment. Not questioning him about his engagement made her better able to cope with the conflict she was feeling.

Mostly, she respected his honesty because it was her husband's dishonesty that had torn their marriage apart.

The fact that Gabriel had been so open convinced her that his intentions were honorable. His honesty spoke volumes about who Gabriel Washington was. That was enough for her. He didn't have to mention another thing about his engagement because at the conclusion of this meeting, they wouldn't have done a thing wrong. There's no harm in talking. There was absolutely nothing wrong with that. In fact, it was painfully apparent to both of them they shared a common need to talk and have someone really listen. Right now, a stranger would suffice.

And so they sat there even longer.

And they talked even more.

And it was even nicer.

Before they realized it, two hours had passed and it seemed as if they were just beginning. He listened and absorbed every word she'd said, remembering every detail about Alexandria Jones—even that her birthday was June 9th. Her favorite movies were *When a Man Loves a Woman, Sleepless in Seattle,* and *Love Jones*—she loved happy endings. Her mother was a retired music teacher and her father, unfortunately, was killed in a car accident when she was a teen.

Looking away, she told him with a shaky voice, "One day he was here, and then the next he wasn't. My dad was gone. I needed him, and I didn't understand why God would take him away from me. He didn't deserve to die like that. I can still feel him give me a kiss on the cheek right before he left for work that night. He whispered I love you baby girl." Alex took a deep breath and, with glassy eyes, said, "God, I miss him."

There was a brief moment of silence between the two.

"I'm sorry you had to experience the pain of that," he said, expressing his sympathy in a heartfelt tone. He leaned forward towards her, placing his hand on the table near hers.

She mustered up a smile, and said "Thank you."

"Was he saved?" he asked.

"Yes. Why do you ask?"

"My mother always told me it makes a difference in how we remember our loved ones," he replied, with a gentle smile. "And that we shouldn't think of those we still love and hold on to as dead or gone, but transcended."

"Um-hm," she replied, attentively.

"Because we, in a sense, still keep them alive in our hearts and thoughts," he concluded. "So as long as you're here, he's still here in a way."

As time passed by, Alex found herself sharing even more intensely personal things about herself with this man. She told him she lived in Cary, loved it there. She said it was a lot quieter than Raleigh. She had a real appreciation for music, real music that is. Alex went on to tell him she was a huge Billie Holiday fan, admired her style and loved her voice more than any present artist today. When the conversation opened itself, he asked how long she'd been married and she surprised herself by sharing the details of her recent split. She mentioned who her husband was. Being a sports fan himself, Gabriel said he remembered hearing about that. Gabriel, though surprised by the facts and that this was the wife seated before him, listened as she talked about the state of her marriage and the possibility of divorce. She mentioned how she had been praying for peace and the heart to forgive. Right now, she wasn't there. Gabriel didn't ask for more. He didn't question her. He just listened.

During the time that ticked past, he told her stories that made her laugh so hard that her stomach ached. She loved the ones about his lovable know-it-all Uncle Arthur. How his sister had brought over a new boyfriend for dinner recently and how he got put through the ringer. It was comical to the point Alexandria was close to being out of breath from laughing so hard.

She found herself telling him just about everything else that she could think of about herself, including her relationship with her crazy girlfriend, Jaz. The whole conversation with Gabriel was therapeutic beyond belief for her. It was the most she'd shared with anyone since her breakup with Lionel. It was refreshing to feel like someone cared enough to not only listen, but listen without giving unwarranted advice or trying to fix her.

"Do you have any children?" he asked.

"No," she answered, losing eye contact with him for a moment as she thought about how she had longed for a huge family and how it seemed that with her marriage ending, that would be denied.

"Has it been difficult starting your own business?" he questioned, quickly changing the subject, noticing her mood shift after he had inquired about children.

"It's had its ups and downs," she answered before expanding on her anxieties about starting her real estate agency. "I was only there for a short while, but the company I left was financially good to me. But it's nothing like having your own and being your own boss. Now that I've experienced it, I wouldn't trade it for anything. I love being in control of my time."

As she told her story, Alex was keenly aware that

Gabriel never once turned his attention from her, not even to glance at patrons entering and exiting the restaurant. She took notice that he was confident, but not conceited. Relaxed, but not too sure of himself. Understanding, but not overly-sympathetic, and she just loved the way he looked directly into her eyes whenever she spoke, as if they were the only two in the restaurant . . . in the city . . . in the world.

Time was continuously slipping away.

"What is it that you do at the bank?" she asked.

Gabriel spoke softly, explaining the details of his job to her. And when he finished, she asked, "So do you enjoy what you do?"

"It's a good place to work. In this economy, I'm glad to be working. I've learned a lot and I believe I'm good at what I do there. I was recently promoted, which of course means more responsibility. I've been very blessed to be as far as I am in my career and I'm thankful for that." He added hot water to warm his tea, and then took a sip. "But, to honestly answer your question . . ." he hesitated, and then looked into her eyes, "No, I don't enjoy what I do." It was a truth Gabriel had never revealed to anyone. But now, sitting across the table from a woman he hardly knew, he felt as if he could share his innermost being without judgment. This kind of conversation usually sparked a heated argument with Tracee.

"Most people don't understand what it means to have a passion to do something that you know you've been created to do," Gabriel continued. "Most of us go through life never realizing that we've all been given a gift, and that one day we're going to have to stand before God and tell him what we did with our talents."

Alexandria nodded in agreement.

"Right," she replied.

"But it's when you finally realize what your gift is that you know it's going to happen with some hard work. It's the waiting and being patient that gets you though. That's the tough part," he said.

He told Alex about his screenplay and his hopes of having a full-time writing career.

"I'm always writing. Like in this meeting I had this morning that I should have been focused on, I was scribbling the lines of a poem that suddenly popped into my head. I get inspired at the oddest times and I just have to write."

"What was it?" she asked.

"Hmh?"

"That you wrote?"

"Oh." He smiled at her interest. "It's not finished. It was just the first few lines of something."

"I would still like to hear it."

"Really?"

"Yes, really."

"Okay," he blushed, "I promise, when it's finished though."

She held him to that promise. He talked more about his writing, spoke in detail about what his screenplay was about, the rejection letters received, and his persistence to keep at it regardless. Alex was an avid reader so the conversation was interesting to her. Surprising to him, she even offered to read it and give him her take on it if he wanted. She spoke of her interest in photography, even though hers was more of a hobby than something she wanted to make a career of.

Several times during their conversation, Gabriel slipped in compliments about her beauty. Each time, Alexandria deflected his comments, but blushed nevertheless.

"I'm making you blush."

She blushed even more.

"I'm sorry," he said, apologetically.

"No, it's okay. You don't have to apologize," she said.

"Thank you, because I'm just telling the truth."

"Thank you. You're too kind."

She could listen to him compliment her all day if he wanted to. She was becoming very fond of Gabriel Washington. His off-balance sense of humor and sarcasm made her laugh even when he wasn't trying to be funny. She couldn't help but wonder why she felt so comfortable with him in such a short amount of time. Instead of being the two strangers they really were, they both resembled old friends reunited with lots of catching up to do.

By four o'clock, Gabriel had memorized everything about Alex right down to the simplest of things. She had a small, heart-shaped birthmark on the inside of her left pinkie finger. There was a very light scar on her forehead, almost invisible, unless you were paying close attention to every detail of who she was. Her eyes *sparkled* when she was excited about something she spoke of. She toyed with her wedding ring whenever she spoke of her marriage. And she had the cutest little facial expression that she would make whenever something was said that touched her heart. And her smile, made him smile.

Deeply mesmerized by every move she made, Gabriel hadn't realized how much time had passed.

As their conversation came to a close, he thanked her for allowing him to join her. She didn't regret it. They walked out together and he escorted her to her car. They exchanged business cards and a prolonged handshake. But as they said their good-byes and Alex drove off, she glanced at his ivory card and decided not to call him. If she saw him again by chance, then maybe she could get away with a brief chat or, at most, a kind smile if he happened to be accompanied by his significant other. Given her vulnerable state, she secretly hoped this would be the end of it, regardless of how incredibly wonderful it had been. She really needed that, but he was, after all, spoken for and she had to keep repeating that to herself. She had to respect it, and the prospect of falling for an unavailable man grieved her fragile heart more than the prospect of never seeing him again. It was done.

CHAPTER TEN

Forget It

"No, I'm not going to call him, Jaz," Alex said firmly as she stepped into her laundry room with a basket full of clothes under one arm and the cordless phone pressed between her ear and her shoulder.

"Why not?" Jaz questioned.

"I already told you why." Alex wasn't quite ready to share the complete details of her newfound friend, especially of his present status of being engaged. She set the laundry basket on top of the dryer, measured a cup of Gain detergent, and turned on the washer.

Jaz chuckled and said, "You're a real trip. You know that?"

"Why I gotta be a trip because I won't do what you would do?"

Jaz could be so persistent, especially when it came to affairs of the heart. She was a hopeless romantic, always believing the impossible was possible. Not that it served her well. Jaz had been hurt more than once in a relationship doomed from the start. Alex, on the other hand, was a bit more protective of her heart. She wasn't going to take advice from someone whose track record wasn't all that great.

"I know what I'm doing, trust me," Alex said, pouring in the detergent. She pulled the colored clothes out of the basket and tossed them in piece by piece.

"You said yourself that it was good to talk to somebody, a male somebody, about what's been going on. Didn't you say it helped?"

"Yes, I did say that. And it did help, but . . ."

Jaz interrupted, "Then there's nothing wrong with being friends. And that's all I'm talkin' about here, just talking. It can be done, even with two beautiful people involved."

"No, it can't," Alexandria said, defiantly.

"It can. I've done it."

"When and with who?"

"What about me and what's his name?"

"Yeah, what is his name Jazmine?" Alex asked, knowing Jaz was really going to have to reach for this one.

"Ummm . . . the Lucas fella."

"Lucas? You gotta do better than that."

"What? All we were was good friends, remember? And he was a nice looking guy."

"Jaz, now you know you ended up sleeping with that man."

"Did I?" Jaz thought about it for a second. Realizing Alex was right, Jaz said, "I had completely forgotten about that."

"Apparently."

"But that should tell you how little it meant. It was nothing and it only happened that one time."

"Seven times," Alex corrected. "That you told me

about."

"That many? Really?"

"Yes."

"Um, I might have to give ol' Lucas a call."

"See. You seriously need Jesus in your life."

"Ain't it the truth? Pray for me, girl."

"Lord, deliver my friend," Alex prayed, then chuckled as Jaz's argument began to unravel. "Girl, you are really somethin' else. I'm gonna have to stay in constant prayer for your salvation. What is wrong with you?"

"Bad example, huh?"

"Yes." Alex lowered the washing machine lid. She headed into the den to stretch out on her sofa.

"Well, don't just use my experiences as an example. I don't claim to be the role model. Just believe me when I say it's possible. I know of others who've done it successfully."

"Like who?"

"You just had to ask that question, didn't you? Okay, let me think . . . umm . . . my Aunt Deloris and the Henry dude. What about them? Hmh?"

"Yo' Great Aunt Loris? Your Grandma Myra's sister? She's eighty-six years old. What else can she do with a man besides be a friend?"

"It's impossible for me to make my point with you," Jaz said, pretending to be offended.

"I hear ya' even though I don't understand ya'." Alex knew her friend had a big heart and was only trying to get her to see things her way out of the best intentions, but it wouldn't work today.

"I'm serious. He knows you're going through a difficult time, right?"

"Right. So?"

"So, you know yourself that you're not looking for anybody, right?"

"True." Alex picked up the television remote and channel surfed with the TV muted.

"You said he's in a committed relationship, right?"

"He is," Alex stated calmly.

"That's the perfect setup for both of you. No strings attached. No one is expecting anything from anybody, apart from companionship. Get it and go your separate ways. Now tell me what's wrong with that?"

"Jaz, I don't know," she sighed, most of the fight gone out of her. "I'm just not tryin' to cause any confusion, for him or for me."

"Right, but you're just talking. That's not a crime. I'm trying to help you heal so you can get on living."

"I know, but . . ."

Jaz interrupted again, switching the tables, "I tell you what, don't call him."

"What?" Alex was confused.

"Don't call him," Jaz repeated.

"Huh?"

"Save the number for me, I'll call him. I've got plenty of problems I need to talk to somebody about and there ain't nothing like a handsome, attentive heterosexual brotha hanging on my every word and willing to give me some free counsel. I'll take him!" Jaz shouted into the phone.

"Jaz, be serious," Alex smiled.

"I'm playing, but I'm for real. You just don't know it, girl."

"Yeah-yeah."

"Call the man," Jaz pleaded. "I'll help you make up a reason of why you called. He's in banking, so it'll be easy to make up an excuse for the phone call. And just take it from there."

"I don't know. I don't like being the first one to call."

"Girl, just pick up the phone and dial his number. We're living in new times."

Alex pondered for a second. "Okay, I'll call him," she said, but her tone sounded doubtful. "It did help. I felt so much better after talking to him, like the world had been lifted off my shoulders. Did I tell you how good I slept last night?"

"You did."

"Did I mention how funny he was?"

"A regular Chris Murphy, Eddie Tucker—yeah, you did."

"You mean Chris Tucker, Eddie Murphy, silly woman."

"What'eva."

"Did I mention he was a writer? That he had written a screenplay," Alex proudly added.

"John Singleton and Eric Jerome Dickey all rolled into one. Yeah, you mentioned it."

Alex's voice lifted in excitement. "Y'know he told me three times . . ."

"That you were beautiful," Jaz finished Alex's sentence for her. "Yes, you're beautiful. Everyone wants to be you. Now call the man."

Alex smiled. She thought for a second before suddenly coming back to her senses. "No. I changed my mind. I'm not going to call that man. Why am I listening to you?"

"Alex, you're making me crazy," Jaz shouted.

Alex and Jaz debated the issue for a few more

minutes before saying their "I love yous and good-byes." Alex hung up the phone, still thinking it over. What did she hope to accomplish by calling him? What did she want from him?

She looked at the phone.

Glanced at the time.

It was 5:45 p.m.

She picked up the phone.

His card was in her purse on the coffee table. She took it out.

She thought for a minute.

She dialed.

And just as quickly, she changed her mind before it even rang. She hit the 'off' button. *What am I doing? I'm not listening to Jaz's misguided ramblings.* Alex tossed the cordless on the chair next to her. Frustrated, she picked up a magazine from the coffee table and thumbed through the pages to try to take her mind off the whole thing. "I am not calling that man. Forget it, let it go," she muttered.

"I can't let it go," Gabriel mumbled to himself, as he stood in his office, holding the phone in one hand and Alex's business card in the other. They had both gone their separate ways sometime ago and he was still thinking about her. He paced, finally stopping in front of the Palladium window and taking in the view. He glanced at his watch. It was 5:45 p.m. He dialed her number.

He changed his mind. Hung up.

He took a deep breath.

He picked up the phone again.

He began to dial.
He changed his mind.
"Forget it," he muttered. "I'm going home."

CHAPTER ELEVEN

What Did You Just Do?

As she walked through the front door, Alex's cell phone rang. She didn't recognize the number and wondered who would be calling her this early on a Tuesday morning. She flipped it open and answered in a professional tone, "New Life Realty. This is Mrs. Jones, may I help you?"

There was a brief pause as she listened closely, then struggled to keep the shock from her voice.

"Yes. Hi. How are you? Good. Yes, I'm fine, thank you. And you? Good. No. Just surprised. No, it's okay. No, it's not a problem. Um-hm." She listened. She chuckled. Listened some more, making her way into the living room to sit down. "When? Today? Ummm . . . I don't know. I haven't even checked to see what my schedule is like for today, to be honest with you. What time were you thinking about? Oh. Well, I have a great deal of listings. Do you have any idea of what you're in the market for? Price range, location, or anything? Okay. Right." She laughed. "Um-hm. Right." She scribbled something on a notepad on the coffee table. "I'm sure I can find what you want without any problem. Yeah. Well, could you hold a second so I can check my calendar? Okay, thanks. It'll only take a sec." She placed her cellular down. There was no need to check her calendar. She already knew she had nothing scheduled for today. She just needed to think for a second before she gave a response. She stood still for a moment. Gave it all deep thought. Placing her phone to her ear again, she continued smoothly, "Sorry to keep you on hold. It looks like I'm free around one-thirty." She listened. "Sure. Yes, I know." She laughed. "No, I don't think so." She listened some more. "Okay then. Well, I guess I'll be seeing you at one-thirty then." She smiled. "You, too. Bye."

She sat on the edge of the sofa for some time, until she shook herself out of her daze and eventually stood up. She took a heavy sigh and questioned her actions.

"Alex, what did you just do?"

CHAPTER TWELVE

Completely Harmless

"Completely harmless," Alexandria muttered to herself as she took off her diamond studs and returned them to her velvet-lined jewelry box. She scanned the box again, rifling over necklaces and rings until she found a pair of small pearl earrings that Lionel had bought for her. They were a little less elegant than her initial choice. She put them on and stared at herself in the mirror: earrings, fuchsia-colored, strapless bra and matching French-cut panties. So far, so good.

She took a deep breath.

Now, what to wear? She tried on a powder-blue dress and regarded herself again in the full-length mirror. She liked the view from the front, but the rear was another story. She shimmied out of the dress and tossed it onto the bed. Next, she put on her black check trousers. "Nope," she said to herself as she turned around and examined her backside. "Now my butt looks too small." She pulled three more outfits out of the closet.

She finally selected a nice pair of slim-fit, navy trousers still in the dry-cleaning bag. She laid a white, long-sleeve shirt beside the pants and gave the outfit a quick once-over. She was exasperated with herself for making such a fuss. She hadn't quite decided if she was actually going to go through with this whole thing or not, but she reassured herself again that their meeting was completely harmless.

She slipped her feet into a pair of navy Italian calfskin mules. After a final check in the mirror, she was, at last, pleased with her choice of outfit. She looked good, but not like she was trying too hard.

Now, for makeup. Alexandria liked to look natural. A little makeup went a long way. Her favorite chocolate lip liner, a soft brown eyeliner, and a little face powder for shine control did the trick. She put on some lip gloss, smacked her lips, stood up from her chair and felt ready to face this so-called business lunch. As an afterthought, she dabbed on her favorite fragrance, Christian Dior's Dune, careful not to put on too much but just enough.

Pacing back and forth, she wondered if the perfume would give Gabriel the wrong impression. She quickly brushed the thought from her mind. After all, as far as she was concerned, this lunch was simply a business meeting—nothing more and nothing less. He was looking for a house and that was her specialty. So what did it matter if she found him attractive? It was definitely harmless and the thought of anything more developing was absolutely out of the question. Taking a deep breath and trying to curb her natural tendency to overanalyze things, she feathered her hair once more with her fingers to give it a more tousled look before heading out the door.

With one hand on the doorknob leading to her garage and the other hand tightly clutching her briefcase, she hesitated. Suddenly, her mind was riddled with doubt and confusion, and her stomach was tied in knots. She couldn't think what to make out of this whole event. Feeling overwhelmed, she headed back to the den to give herself a moment to think. She sat down on the sofa and picked up the phone. She took Gabriel's business card from her bag, hoping she would be able to catch him before he headed out to meet her. She dialed quickly, nervously anticipating his voice on the other end. But, before it could even ring, she quickly hung up and dropped her phone in her bag. She sighed heavily. "Get it together, Alex," she muttered.

Suddenly, her cell phone rang. Her first and immediate thought was that Gabriel was calling to cancel their lunch engagement, giving her a way out. She grabbed her phone from her bag, picked up, and saw Jaz's shop name and number on the display screen. She relaxed and flipped open her cell, knowing she would have to make this really quick to avoid getting entangled in a convoluted explanation that would make her late.

She answered and said, "Hey, girl. Let me call you back," before Jaz could dive into asking a million questions.

"Okay, but call me back quick. I got somethin' juicy to tell you." From the sound of her voice, Jaz obviously had some serious hot gossip to share.

"Okay," Alex promised.

She would have loved to talk to Jaz, but right now was not the time. If she had told Jaz about her lunch meeting, it would have sparked a lengthy conversation. She would tell Jaz later, way later in fact. Right now, she had to go before she lost her nerve. Her upbringing had taught her that to be on time is to be late and to be early is to be on time. Before finally heading out the door, she thought for a second and then took a breath before heading for the car.

Gabriel was already seated at a table for two near the window when she arrived at Ramona's. Her heart raced at the sight of him. He had not yet noticed her. He seemed preoccupied with his thoughts. She took advantage of the moment to observe him. He sat with an air of dignity and power, erect and sure of himself. His hair was tapered neatly on the sides and in the back as if freshly trimmed for this occasion. His suit flattered his physique, and his hands rested on the table in a prayerful position.

He looked even more handsome than the last time she'd seen him. Alex had been in the presence of handsome men before, some even more attractive than Gabriel Washington. But just the thought of sitting and talking with this man, even about business, left her nervous and unsure of her motives. In those sweet and all too brief hours she had spent talking with him, she had felt something deeper than mere physical attraction. It scared her to death to feel this way in the face of her own circumstances with Lionel. This inexplicable connection with a complete stranger threatened to send her farther into the eye of an emotional storm. She couldn't let that happen.

As she drew nearer to the table where he was seated, his attention appeared to be focused on a painting hanging on the wall. She briefly wondered what he was thinking as he looked at it. Finally sensing her presence, he looked up at her, eyes gazing directly into hers. He smiled broadly as he rose to his feet.

"Hi," he said, extending his hand.

"Hi, long time no see," she replied, jokingly.

Again, his touch induced a feeling that surged through her entire body. It compared to the sensation she experienced whenever Billie Holiday combined perfect pitch with emotional depth in her favorite song. Alex enjoyed it then and now. Gabriel pulled out her chair, made sure she was seated comfortably, then returned to his own.

"Thank you," she said. *A perfect gentleman and he smells delicious,* she thought.

"So how's your day been so far?" he asked.

"It's been fine, and yours?"

"Good, real good," he replied.

There was a brief pause.

"I was very surprised to hear from you," she said.

"Really? Why?" He looked perplexed.

"I don't know. I just was." She gave him a shy, coy smile.

In return, he flashed the beautiful, hypnotic smile she had come to appreciate and said, "I'm in the market for a new house, so . . . I thought who better else to call than the realtor I just met. Seems like perfect timing, if you ask me. I hope it's not a problem." He was trying to make her feel comfortable with him.

She seemed flustered. "No. I don't know. I mean . . ."

Gabriel interrupted, changing the subject and hoping to make her feel more at ease. "You look nice."

She blushed, glad that he had noticed. "Thank you."

"Just tellin' the truth," he said. "No need to thank me."

"So, your fiancée is okay with you conducting

business without her?" she asked, feeling the need to keep their conversation neutral. She needed to remind herself, and him, that he was already spoken for and that she was fully aware of that fact.

Without answering her question directly, he said, "There's nothing wrong with gathering information, y'know?"

Alexandria hesitated. "No. I guess there isn't," she replied.

"But I have to be candid with you."

"Okay," she said in a cautious tone.

"I just really enjoyed our conversation last time. And, for my own selfish reasons, I wanted to talk to you again—even if it was only about business."

"Okay." She smiled a little when he said that.

"So please forgive me if *this* makes you uncomfortable in any way. That's not my intention," he said sincerely. "So, I hope you're okay with *this*."

"I'm fine. Really," she reassured him, still wondering exactly what *this* meant.

He smiled and asked, "Would you like to order?"

"Water would be fine for now, thank you."

Gabriel poured them both a glass from the pitcher that was on the table.

"So, how is everything?" he asked.

"Things are well. I'm not complaining," she said.

Gabriel nodded, smiling.

She continued, "Business is well."

"Good . . . but how's Alexandria doing today?" he asked.

She smiled at his genuine concern and replied, "Alex is okay. Thank you for asking."

"Good. I'm really glad to hear that," he said.

It wasn't long before Alexandria began to relax in the face of Gabriel's own ease with the situation and his calming influence. Despite her worries, for the next hour or so she laughed and she talked with Gabriel Washington, the aspiring writer, as if all was okay in their world and that they were doing no wrong.

But, truthfully, this situation was far from okay. She thought about how she would explain this to Jaz. What language would she use to talk about Gabriel? A friend, an acquaintance, or just the guy she met at Ramona's? But none of those titles accurately described who Gabriel Washington was to her in the present moment.

How would she explain today's lunch meeting? A prospective client, an innocent follow-up to their initial conversation, or a lunch date with a nice gentleman-friend? Truth be told, this whole scenario was like an ill-timed plot in a romance novel. She was married, and he was engaged. What a mess.

They both had only a little to eat. They talked and she hung onto his every word. She noticed every little idiosyncrasy. Like the way he added the phrase "and whatnot" every so often at the end of a sentence.

After some time, he realized he was doing all the talking and Alexandria was only listening. He smiled and said, "See. I'm talking too much. Telling you everything. Now, I'm gonna be quiet and listen to you."

"No. I like listening to you. It's funny, because I did most of the talking the first time. You're the mysterious one."

"Mysterious?"

"Um-hm."

"No," he said, shaking his head. "I wouldn't say that. It just takes some time to get a feel for a person to know whether I can be myself and act silly or if I need to be serious."

"So this is not an act?" she asked.

"No, this is me," he answered.

"I hear ya," she said with a small smile. She was truly flattered that he felt comfortable being himself in her presence, sharing himself and being vulnerable with someone he hardly knew.

"I'm serious," he smiled again.

"I believe you."

"I wanna know more about you."

"What do you want to know?" she asked.

"Everything," he said softly.

"Everything, huh?"

"Yes, everything. Pick something," he said, "we'll talk about it."

She thought about it for a few seconds. Then looked at him and smiled.

"Do you know that you . . ." She stopped before finishing. "Nothing."

"What?" he asked.

"Nothing. Never mind," she said, shaking her head.

"No. What? Tell me."

"It's nothing," she replied, waving it off.

"You can't start something and not finish it."

"Oh, I can't?"

"No. Why would you do that to me? Now it'll be on my mind and I'll be thinking about it all day and whatnot. And the thing about it is, I won't even know what I'm thinking about because you never said it," Gabriel jokingly taunted her. "Tell me, please," he begged.

"Okay-okay," Alex smiled. "Do you know that you say "and whatnot" a lot?"

Gabriel chuckled. He did know that. "Was that it?" he asked.

"That was it. That's all I was gonna say, honestly. I told you it was nothing," she smiled.

"See then, that's still about me and not you."

Later in their conversation, Gabriel found out that, to his surprise, Alex was a serious basketball fanatic, as he was. He hadn't met many women who enjoyed the sport as much as he did, but Alex was a diehard fan. That led to conversation about their favorite NBA players and, even though Gabriel was all about the L.A. Lakers and a huge Kobe Bryant fan, he didn't hold it against Alex that she was all about Michael Jordan. She referred to herself as Mike's self-proclaimed number one fan and Gabriel believed that Wilt Chamberlain was the greatest that there ever was in the League.

"I mean, I'm not saying he wasn't. I respect the man's accomplishments," Alex said, "but you gotta give Mike something. The guy was awesome on the court, and when he got the ball that's all she wrote. Everybody's always known that when it's down to the last seconds of any game, that Mike was your go-to guy."

"And, yes, he's amazing, but you gotta recognize Chamberlain as basketball's most unstoppable force. I bet if you asked any basketball fan who was the greatest player ever, Wilt 'the Stilt' Chamberlain would be at the top of the list."

"Yes, along with Michael Jordan," she said.

"Michael Jordan, Michael Jordan, Michael Jordan," he repeated, the conversation becoming comically intense.

In the heat of their playful argument, Gabriel

challenged Alex to a basketball game of their own. Alex warned Gabriel that she could whoop his butt any day, anytime, on the court. "All you gotta do," she said, "is name the time and place."

To her surprise, he did.

"What about this evening, say around six?" he asked.

"Oh, you wanna get whooped that soon, huh?" she asked, not really sure if he was serious or not.

"Bring it on."

"Are you serious?"

"Yes, I'm serious."

"No, you're not."

"I am. Today. No need to wait."

"Name the time and place," Alex said, letting her competitive side show and take control.

Gabriel named the time and place.

"And don't let your fear of losing cause you to be late," he joked.

"You don't know what you're getting yourself into, but six o'clock it is then," she said before she knew what she was doing. Apparently that means they would be seeing each other again.

He liked her feistiness and tough talk. He wasn't accustomed to discussing sports laced with trash talking with a beautiful woman.

It was different.

She was different.

He liked that.

"Now, I don't play for nothing," she stated firmly.

"What? Oh, you wanna put some money on it or something?"

"Nawww, that's too easy. And I wouldn't want to take your pocket change," she joked.

"See. You're already talkin' trash. I love people who get cocky because I don't feel guilty about whooping 'em on the court. I was gonna be generous enough to at least let you score, but you done messed up now."

"Oh really?" Alexandria looked intrigued.

"Yes. Really. You just don't know it." Gabriel moved in closer towards her.

"You're a real funny dude, especially if you think you're going to beat me," Alex mocked him, as she leaned in towards him. She could feel his breath making contact with her lips while they looked at each other as if frozen in a standoff.

"And you still talkin' trash. Now, I don't even know if I'm gonna let you touch the ball. I was going to at least let you bounce it for a second or two before I took it from you, but now . . . I don't know," Gabriel teased.

"You think you're that good, huh?"

"I know it." He stared deeply into her eyes with a deliberate air of cockiness.

"Okay," she said, as she repositioned herself slightly out of his penetrating stare. She felt a bit unnerved by how quickly they had become comfortable in each other's company and how easily they could talk to one another about anything.

Gabriel, noticing Alexandria's tenser body language, moved back in his chair to give her more space. "What's the wager? Name it. It doesn't matter 'cause you're not going to win. In all fairness, I should let you know that I was MVP for two consecutive years in high school," he said proudly.

"High school?!" she chuckled.

"Yes."

"Man, you're still livin' in the past," she said,

jokingly. "I thought you were gonna say you at least played in college or something. I mean, you said high school with such conviction and all. What was that, like almost 20 years ago? They would let anybody whose mama signed a permission slip play in high school."

"Oh, you got jokes, I see," Gabriel fired back. "Tryin' to belittle a brotha's athletic accomplishments and whatnot. Demeaning my lil' trophies I got and everything."

"Naw, I'm just saying you might want to let that whole high school thing go like everyone else has. Sounds as if you like to celebrate a lot of mediocrity in your life."

"Okay, okay," he chuckled. "So it's like that, huh?" He loved her sense of humor.

"It's like that," she said.

"Okay then. This will definitely be settled on the court. It really is on now."

Remembering the Greek letters she had seen on his license plate, she continued to joke, "Besides, I know you pretty boy Kappas' can't hold a cane without dropping it at least once during a step show, so keeping hold of a basketball has gotta be a real challenge for you."

"No you didn't go there. I know you ain't talking about my frat like that." His eyes widened in mock amazement.

"What? It's the truth, ain't it?"

"No, it ain't the truth. The only thing you got right was the *pretty* part, but that's it." Gabriel blushed.

"I'm just playing," Alex reassured him. "I have a great deal of respect for the Kappas. My brother is trying to be down with you guys so I'll be quiet out of respect for him and not say anything else."

"Ohhh, is that right?" Gabriel asked. "What school is your brother at?"

"He's at Georgetown. He's going to be the family's first lawyer."

"Cool."

"Where did you attend college?" she asked.

"Duke."

"And you?"

"UNC at Chapel Hill."

"Okay, good school. Now I see why you're a big Jordan fan," he said. Noticing her half-empty glass, Gabriel filled it for her.

"Thank you." His attentiveness made her smile.

"You're welcome."

"I don't think I asked you this last time, but how long have you actually been writing?"

She lifted her glass to her lips and took a sip, looking at him over the rim.

"Well, since I was about twelve or thirteen."

"Oh."

"Writing poetry soon branched off into writing anything that I could express with words. Poetry is my first love, but as I said, I'm trying my hand at screenwriting right now, hoping something will happen. Trying to find an agent and whatnot has been the challenging part. It's a hard business to get into unless you know somebody that knows somebody. But I'm hoping that a door will open for me."

"I'm sure it will," she said, smiling, as if she knew something he didn't.

He smiled at her genuineness.

"Do you ever let others read your work?" she asked.

"I really don't tell many people about my work. Besides my boy, Eddie, who's a writer as well, I haven't met too many people that I feel I can trust to be honest with me about it. I do wish sometimes . . ."

"You should let me," she said, interrupting. I can give you an honest critique of your work."

"Hmh?" He wasn't sure whether he had heard her correctly.

"I said you should let me," she repeated.

"I'd like that," Gabriel said tentatively. "Thank you."

"You're welcome. Do you remember the first thing you ever wrote?"

"Yes. Now that brings back memories. It was this poem entitled *Where are the People?* I actually still have it."

"Sounds interesting."

"It wasn't," he said, with a smile. "It was the '70s. Most of the stuff I wrote back then was a bit militant. A lot of the revolution will not be televised, and *'boy'* is a white racist word kinda stuff."

"You were a regular ol' Michael Evans from *Good Times* then, huh?"

He laughed.

"Basically," he said. "Hey, I still love my Good Times now."

She interjected, "Eleven o'clock on channel 12. Me, too. I watch it like every episode is a new one."

He smiled.

"Now here's my thing, I really can't get into the episodes where James had left the show," he said.

"Yeah, I agree that the shows with him are definitely the better ones," she stated. "I hated it so much when they killed him off, even how they did it."

"I know, right."

"Do you have a favorite episode?" she asked, becoming excited about their conversation.

"Man," he said, thinking, "I've got a few . . . but I think any episode with Sweet Daddy Williams in it," he replied. "But especially the one where he was going to give J.J. a one man show for painting his girlfriend Savannah Morgan."

"Oh, a Sweet Daddy fan," she said. "You like that whole pimp thing, do ya?"

"No, that's not why. He was a fine actor," he said, smiling.

"Umm-hmm," she murmured, with a disbelieving look.

"Seriously," he smiled. "What's your favorite episode?"

"Mine is the one when Florida's cousin, Raymond Brown, came to town. Remember? Supposedly, he was finally getting them out of the ghetto and . . ."

"Oh yeah," Gabriel replied, obviously familiar with the particular episode, "I remember that one."

"And he had the girls come in at the beginning singing, *"Cousin Raymond's comin' at 'cha, Pookie Poo . . . he'll be here in just one second . . ."*

He smiled while she sang the short verse, remembering the episode vividly. "Oh, you can sing, too," he said.

She blushed, and then said, "A little, but I'm no Gabriel 'Donny Hathaway' Washington."

"What'eva." He blushed hard when she said that, remembering their initial crossing of paths.

Gabriel could tell Alex was feeling more comfortable

with him and that's what he wanted, but there was more. He felt a burning desire to touch her. He wondered how her hair would feel between his fingers, how it would feel to have her arms wrapped around him in a tight embrace, and how her cheek would feel pressed against his cheek. He tried to erase the thoughts from his mind. But he failed. His attraction to her was undeniable.

Gabriel wasn't the only one fighting his feelings.

Alex sensed in the man before her an authentic, true and kind human being. She wondered if his fiancée appreciated those qualities in him. Alex admired him for not being a phony brotha looking to impress a woman just to get a good time. This was the real him, she was sure, and she liked him. She liked him a little too much, and really didn't even know him. But then again, she felt as if she did.

He was interesting. Funny. A brotha that seemingly had it all together. Her mind drifted for a moment as he talked, thinking how his arms would feel around her. How her lips would react to his kiss. And how her body would respond to his touch.

We really should be going. But heaven knows I'm not ready to go, Alexandria thought. They had been talking for quite awhile now. And neither one had tried to end their time together. Just in case he was simply being a nice guy, Alexandria felt she shouldn't keep him any longer than she had already, especially since they would be seeing each other again in only a matter of hours for a friendly game of basketball. She was certain he must have more important things to get back to at the office.

She took a quick glance at her watch. "Oh my," she said in a soft, but astonished tone.

"What?" he calmly inquired.

"I didn't realize it was already three forty-five. We've been talking for over two hours," she said. "We never even got to the listings." She reached for her briefcase, pulled out a sheath of papers and pushed the stack across the table to him while she gathered the rest of her things, preparing to leave. In a rushed tone, she said, "We should go. I know you have to get back to work and all. And look at me, I'm just talking away like you don't have a thing to do besides sit here and chitchat all day with me."

There was a brief silence, until he asked, "Do you have time to go for a walk or something?" In his heart, he was praying she would say "yes."

She relaxed a bit, slowly lifted her eyes to meet his, and they both smiled at one another. She softly replied, "I do. I think I would like that very much."

Before they left, Gabriel made his way to the bathroom. As he pushed the bathroom doors open, he found himself out of breath, dizzy to a degree. He went to the sink and splashed water across his face, trying to come to grips with what he was doing here. Conflicted, he tried to pull it together, tried to answer his own questions being asked of himself while wondering if he had the situation under control. He wanted to convince himself that he wasn't doing anything wrong, but his flesh was battling with his spirit. This wasn't cheating. Was it? This woman and him were only talking, and what harm could come from that? He stared at himself for a moment, and finally convinced himself they were doing nothing wrong.

"I got this," he stated, with a deep sigh.

Alex was staring out the window at a faint reflection of herself peering back at her, as she waited for Gabriel's return. She was lost in some deep conflict of her own, trying to bring herself to understand what was happening here. "What are you doing, girl?" Is the question she kept asking herself over and over in her head. And the longer she sat there, the more she thought about the fact this man was spoken for and they had just now made plans to see each other again later. She was having doubts on whether this was smart, the right thing for them to do, and on whether it was best to back out. She had decided she was going to gather her things and leave. And just as she was about to, Gabriel's voice interrupted any abrupt motion to leave on her part.

"You ready," Gabriel asked, now back at their table from the restroom.

Alex turned to him, smiled, and nodded yes.

As they began their walk, the downtown square was noticeably quieter. It was a different place after the midday rush. There was hardly a soul in sight, which gave the two of them a moment to absorb the peaceful atmosphere. They walked in silence for a moment, both pondering the events that had ironically brought the two of them together. Gabriel was a complete stranger she had just happened to notice in traffic many months ago. And then, in another place at another time, the two had met again. Now, she was walking with this man as if they were the closest of friends.

As they silently strode together, Gabriel thought about how people are always in our lives for a purpose. Sometimes we never realize or understand that purpose until after it's done. What was her purpose in his life and his purpose in hers?

For the next thirty minutes, they talked comfortably, still as if they had known each other for years. It was so nice. They didn't seem to run out of things to say, things to ask, things to wonder about.

When they finally reached her car, she turned to him and said, "Thank you."

He looked at her, smiled and asked, "For what?"

"For nothing . . . and everything," she replied.

CHAPTER THIRTEEN

Love Being with Her

It was exactly 6:02 p.m. when Gabriel stepped out of his car and into the gym parking lot, carrying a basketball under his left arm and his leather gym bag strapped over his right shoulder. He was casually dressed in a pair of white shorts, a sleeveless white T-shirt exposing his muscular arms and a pair of Nikes. Alex had arrived only moments before, and when she stepped out of her car, Gabriel closed the door behind her.

"Heyyyy," she said, giving him a subtle glance from head-to-toe. "You already changed."

"Yeah, I left work a little early to run home and grab my gym bag. I went ahead and slipped into my gear," he explained.

"Hmm," she murmured.

"What?" he asked, looking down at his clothes.

She shook her head and, with a sly grin, said, "Nothing." She tried to look innocent as if she had no idea why he was paranoid.

"No. C'mon. Why did you look at me like that?" he

asked, feeling slightly self-conscious.

She admitted, "It's nothing. It's just that the few times I've seen you you've always had a suit on, that's all."

"Oh," he smiled, relaxing.

She nodded and said, "I like this look on you, too."

"You sure?" He quickly looked himself over again, still feeling uncertain.

At his request, Alex checked him out again. "Yeah, I'm sure," she said in a flirtatious manner.

"Okay. I'll take your word for it," he said glancing at her profile as they walked towards the entrance of the gym.

"Something's different about your hair," he remarked, being extremely careful how he phrased the comment. He knew how sensitive women could be about their hair.

It was too late though. The question had unleashed Alexandria's insecurities. She had only had her hair up, instead of down like last time.

"What? What's wrong with it?" she asked, brushing her hand briefly over her hair.

"Nothing's wrong with it. It's beautiful," Gabriel said sincerely.

"Are you clownin' me?" She stared at him to see if he was trying to hide his real thoughts.

"No. I'm for real," he said, as they reached the door. He held it open for her.

Alex was so preoccupied with her thoughts that she didn't hear his next question.

"What?" she asked.

"I asked if I could touch it," he repeated.

"Touch what?" Alex was taken aback by his question

simply because she had missed what 'it' referred to.

"Your hair," he said.

"My hair?" She seemed confused.

"Um-hm."

Feeling totally insecure, she wondered why in the world he wanted to do that, but responded by saying, "Uhh, yeah . . . I guess so. If you want to."

"I do."

Stopping in the lobby area of the gymnasium, he took a moment to touch a loose strand of her hair, slowly placing it behind her ear. She caught herself closing her eyes for a second, enjoying the therapeutic effects of his caressing fingertips near her earlobe. His touch was stimulating right down to the essence of her womanhood. The young lady at the front desk admired the beautiful couple for a moment before turning away.

"It's all real if that's what you're trying to figure out," she joked.

"No, that's not it. I just wanted to touch it. That's all. Honestly."

"Umm-hmm."

He smiled and said, "Honestly."

"Okay, if you say so," she said, secretly hoping he would ask again.

Once inside, they headed to separate locker rooms. Gabriel took a deep breath as he entered. His thoughts about her were running wild. He had to get himself under control, but he was losing out to his emotions.

Within fifteen minutes of Gabriel stepping out of the locker room, Alex was already waiting for him. She was wearing navy blue shorts, a cut-off white T-shirt that exposed a hint of her navy blue sports bra, and a

Polo cap turned backwards. Gabriel couldn't help but to admire how tight her body was. And those legs and calves of hers looked as if she was a runner.

As he moved towards her, Alex took note of the blue bandanna that encircled his head, making him look like a ballplayer from the streets.

"Look at you, looking like you're ready for a serious game and whatnot," Gabriel said to Alex, checking out her athletic gear.

"I am." Glancing at his shirt, she said, "But look at *you*. Come here a sec."

"What?" he was confused as he moved towards her.

"Your tag is sticking up out of the back of your shirt."

"Oh." He stooped down a bit so she could reach his shirt and place his tag back inside.

"There you go," she said, giving him a friendly pat on the back.

"Thank you."

"You're welcome. Now you can get your butt whooped with a little bit of dignity," she joked.

"There you go. Still jawjackin'. You don't quit, do you?" He smiled.

Gabriel decided they would use the outdoor court for their game since the weather was nice and, for some reason, there were more people playing inside than out today. He didn't feel like sharing Alex with anyone, especially with the fellas that would, undoubtedly, be checking her out. He wanted her all to himself.

As they headed to the courts, both continued talking trash about how bad they were going to beat the other in their ruthless game of one on one. Alex said she would give him the honor of having first ball.

He asked if she was sure about that. She said it was only fair.

She warmed up first with stretches. Gabriel stood by and watched, chuckling a few times at how seriously she was really taking their game. After a good two-minute warm up, she was ready. Giving him her game face, along with a steely seriousness in her voice, she said, "Let's play."

"Let's." He tossed her the ball. "Check."

"I'm telling you right now, I'm not an easy win so stay on your toes," she said, tossing the ball back to him.

"What'eva." He playfully brushed her comment off, and then he drove around her and to the hoop, scoring his first shot with no problem. "One to nothing," he said. "I bet you wish you hadn't given me that first ball now, huh?"

"Games just beginning, pretty boy." She tossed him the ball back. "All part of my strategy."

He stared at her as he dribbled towards her. She stared back. Stepping up her game, she stayed with him, covering him tight. He dribbled through his legs, then faked a right, and went left. He did a fancy move before he shot it up on a short jumper. The ball bounced on the rim . . . and didn't go in. They battled for the loose ball. She then grabbed it, gripping it tight. Gabriel was on her as close as humanly possible. She dribbled, maneuvering around him. She took it strong to the hoop. She put it up, but missed the lay up. She grabbed her own rebound. Gabriel tried to stop her. He was too late. She was too quick. She scored.

Gabriel would later swat two of the six shots that she attempted to put up from behind the arc. Alex would have two astonishing steals. She would catch Gabriel off guard by shooting over him once. He would make two shots on a short jumper, and then later sink three shots from behind the arc. She would get the lead on a rebound shot after the game had been tied three times. Gabriel would dunk twice. She would throw up one brick. He would toss up two air balls. And, after pounding the pavement and playing for an intense forty-five minutes, Alex was only one shot from claiming victory. Both were drenched with sweat from playing under the beat of the sun. She was dribbling and shooting like someone who had played pro ball.

She now had the ball and Gabriel remained close, guarding and trying to block her attempt to make a final shot. Their bodies touched occasionally and a sexual tension mounted. They both felt it.

"What'cha gon' do? You know you ain't got nothing." Gabriel guarded her tightly as she dribbled, while talking trash the entire time to distract her.

"Oh, I ain't got nothing, huh? I told you not to underestimate my game. Don't sleep," she said, now with her hips backed into him.

"Where did you learn how to play, prison?" he joked, his hands across her chest as he guarded her.

"Ha-ha."

"You makin' me dizzy with all this dribbling," he teased. "When are you gonna at least try to shoot?"

"Oh, you dizzy now?" she said, now facing him. "A few minutes ago you were cryin' about not being able to breathe. I thought you were about to have an asthma attack on me or something. What's going to be your next excuse, cramps?" she laughed.

"Funny," he said. "You're not going to make this

shot," he warned, chuckling. "You might as well just forfeit this game. But if you're going to shoot, at least try to before it turns into a new day."

"I'm not going to feel bad about whooping your butt at all. Okay, Mr. Funny Man. I see I'm going to have to shut you up."

"Show me what'cha got." He held his hands high.

"Let me tell you exactly what I'm going to do," she said. "First, I'm gonna fake left, then right, and back left—leaving you even more dazed and confused than you already are. You won't even know whether you're comin' or goin' by the time I'm finished with you."

"Oh really?"

"Yes, really. But that's not all. It gets better. Then I'm going to bounce the ball off your forehead, giving you a mild concussion right before I knock you to the ground, because you keep gettin' in my way. And that's when it's possible that I may use your back as a springboard to put up my dunk, depending on how I'm feeling at the time. I was tryin' to show you some mercy, but you keep right on talkin' that smack."

"I'm scared of you," he said, laughing.

"Okay, keep laughing."

"As long as you keep telling jokes like that, I will."

"Laugh at this." Alex's dribbling intensified as she attempted to get around him. Trying to head to the basket, it was almost impossible to move his tall, muscular frame. He was utilizing his strength and size to shadow her every move like a NBA player guarding the opposition's leading scorer. "Move now," she playfully told him, dribbling hard and fast while pressing her shoulder firmly in his stomach.

"Put it up."

"I can if you get out my . . ." All of a sudden, she faked an outside shot. He fell for it. Driving around him, she accidentally knocked him down onto the hot asphalt. She took the shot and called it before the ball even hit. It was all net, making a quiet, but ever so sweet, swish sound.

"That was a foul," Gabriel said, trying to regain his composure as he sat frozen in shock on the pavement.

"No ma'am, that was game. You gotta live with that."

He shook his head, laughed in defeat. He actually thought it was quite cute as he struggled playfully to stand up while she did a little victory dance all around him, still talking trash about her win.

"Gabriel got beat by a *girl,* and I'm gon' tell *everybody*," she sang, teasingly.

"You just gon' rub it in, aren't you?"

"That's right. I did it—it needed to be done. Every now and then I gotta shut some people up. Let 'em know they're a visitor on my court."

"I can't believe I just got beat like that." He shook his head to himself. "And you're such a modest winner," he added, sarcastically.

"Don't be a hater now. You don't wear it well." She smiled and extended her hand to help him up. "You okay?" she asked, in a baby voice.

"No," he replied, the smile still on his face.

"It's just your pride that's hurting, that's all. C'mon, big baby. Get up before somebody sees you."

He took her hand. There was that electric feeling again.

"I'll admit you got a lil' game and everything. You

caught me off guard with that. But see, I think I could've beat you if my leg wasn't actin' up on me all on the right side and whatnot," Gabriel said, as he rose to his feet and brushed his shirt off.

"Yeah and whatnot," she mocked, shaking her head in doubt. "Oh now it's the leg? Let me guess, an old high school injury from '85, right?"

"See."

"No, but seriously, you played a good game and whatnot. You're at least some competition. But I think you would have given me more of a run for my money if you had concentrated more on your defense, and less on putting up every shot regardless of where you were positioned on the court. You had a few air balls out there," she said, sounding like a coach counseling a new rookie.

"Um-hm," he murmured, squinting his eyes at her unsolicited tips.

"I mean, you were throwin up shots trying to hit threes just about every time your hands touched the ball. It became too predictable. I mapped out your entire game within the first ten minutes. Let's just say I know why you're a Kobe fan. You should work on your strategy of laying it up more, instead of taking the long shots. You left me open quite a bit out there too, never underestimate your opponent. And you missed a few easy shots when I was nowhere near you. It was all yours. Just a few things to think about for *our* next game."

"Thanks, coach," he muttered.

"No problem," she said with a broad, confident smile.

"I didn't know anyone could be so informative after

winning by only one shot," Gabriel said, matter-of-factly.

She tossed him the ball. "After you treat me to a well-deserved cold drink, I'll give you another chance to get your pride back. How 'bout that, big baby?"

Gabriel smiled, shook his head to himself, and accepted her challenge. "Sure."

She teased him while he purchased two Gatorades from the vending machine. They walked over and sat on one of the benches at the edge of the court, watching some kids race one another on the outdoor playground.

With her towel, Alex dabbed the sweat from her forehead.

She then offered her towel to Gabriel.

He took it and wiped the sweat from his forehead.

She turned to him and asked, "I know you asked me this, but I don't think I asked you. Do you have any kids?"

"Noooo," he said. "I'm not quite ready to throw a baby seat in the ride just yet, but definitely one day," he said, taking a swallow of his Gatorade.

"Does your fiancée want kids?" As soon as she had asked the question, Alex wasn't sure if she had crossed the line by asking such an intimate question that was really none of her business. She stared at Gabriel's profile as he looked straight ahead. There was a long, awkward moment before he turned to face her.

"Well," he said in a low-key, calm tone as if she had given him something to think about, "to be quite honest with you, I really don't know the answer to that question."

Alex, sensing his discomfort, decided to immediately change topics. Although she was curious as to why he didn't know the answer to such an important question, particularly for two individuals with plans to spend their lives together.

Abruptly changing the subject, she asked, "Is your car a five-speed or an automatic?" His car had caught her attention as they sat facing the parking lot.

"A five-speed," he confirmed, still thinking about her previous question.

"A friend-girl of mine has a car similar to yours, but hers is an automatic."

"Do you know how to drive a five-speed?" he asked.

"A little."

"So that basically means 'no', right?" he chuckled.

"Basically," Alexandria chuckled at herself.

"I've never had anyone with the patience to teach me. My brother, Omar, tried teaching me a long time ago, but he said I was killing his transmission or something—giving him whiplash from jerking the car so much."

Gabriel chuckled. "It's not that difficult. I could teach you in an hour."

"And I'd probably wreck your car in the first fifteen minutes."

"No, you wouldn't. I have that much faith in my ability as a teacher."

"I don't know, Gabriel."

He smiled when she said his name. "What did you say?"

"I said, I don't know, Gabriel." This time she noticed his smile. "What?" she asked, smiling at his smile.

"Nothing."

"No. What?"

"I just like the way you say my name, that's all. Most

people just call me Gabe after they get to know me."

She blushed and said, "Really? I don't know why anyone would shorten such a dignified, not to mention, biblical name."

He smiled big, and enjoyed a silent moment between the two of them. Turning to her, he said, "Okay, if you wanna learn how to drive a five-speed then I'm willing to teach. It'll be just like learning to ride a bike, I promise."

"I hope not. That was a bad experience for me, too. I won't even begin to tell you how many times I ran into the side of our house just trying to learn how to use the brakes."

"I'll be patient with you, you've got my word on that."

"It's your repair bill. But if you say so."

"I do."

"Just don't get mad at me if I mess up your car and you find yourself riding a ten-speed to work from now on."

"I promise I won't get mad at you," he said. "Well, let's do it."

"Right now?"

"Right now. No time like the present."

"I really don't know about this, Gabriel," she hesitated, realizing he was for real.

"I got you. It'll be easy, I promise," he said, reassuringly.

"Okay."

Finally convincing her, they headed towards his car for a quick driving lesson. "I'm gonna start with the basics, so some of this stuff you may already know from your brother going over it with you." Gabriel opened the passenger side door for her. She stepped in. He moved around to the driver's side and got in, putting on his seatbelt. "See. The first step is to watch the teacher do it." He placed the key in the ignition. "And then see how easy it is."

"Okay."

"Are you ready?"

"I'm ready. Are *you* ready is the real question," she replied, giving him a second chance to back out of his offer.

"I'm ready. First thing you wanna do is press the clutch down like so."

She watched his foot press down the clutch, but specifically the muscles in his legs.

"Make sure the car is in neutral or it'll jump ahead," he warned, wiggling the gearshift slightly to demonstrate what he was saying as he started the engine.

"Okay," she said with a nod as she put on her seatbelt, continuing to watch him closely.

"Release the clutch and let the car warm up."

"Right," she said, watching his every move closely like an anxious first-time driver.

"If you put your hand on top of mine, you'll feel how I change gears," he said.

She did as he instructed, just as if it were the natural thing to do. Her eyes never left her handsome instructor as he shifted gears while pressing and releasing the clutch simultaneously. She could see the muscles in his thigh flexing as he depressed the clutch. He spoke slowly in a nurturing voice. He was a wonderful teacher. Alex wasn't sure which she enjoyed more, his company and the long drive or being told what to do by such a gentle voice.

As she drifted in thought, she was jarred back to reality as Gabriel pulled over to the edge of the road and parked.

"Okay, your turn."

"Oh boy." She was a little nervous.

He stepped out and, with a grace all his own, walked around the front of the car while smiling at her the entire time. He opened her door. She stepped out and moved around to the driver's side. They looked at one another, peering over the roof of the car before stepping back inside.

"You okay?" he asked.

"I guess," she replied, a hint of uncertainty in her tone.

"Don't worry, I got you."

Alex repositioned the side and rearview mirrors to her liking and settled herself in the driver's seat. She took a deep breath. Gabriel gave her a reassuring nod.

"Don't be nervous. You can do it," he said, patting her hand.

Just like he had shown her, Alex first made sure the gear was in neutral before she pressed the clutch. "Like this, right?"

"Right," he said, smiling inside at her innocence.

She started the car.

"Make sure you don't . . ." Alex took her foot off the clutch too soon and the car jerked forward and stalled, "come off the clutch too quickly," he added, belatedly.

"Sorry." She fanned herself with her hand. "Okay, I'm getting hot now because I'm nervous. I'm telling you I'm goin' to kill us."

"Please don't do that. I've got things to do tomorrow," he joked. "But seriously, it's okay. It happens to everyone. Try again."

She started the car again. This time she was

successful. She couldn't help but be pleased with his patience about the whole thing, particularly because he was teaching her in such an expensive vehicle. She was nervous, but knew she was in good hands. Taking a deep breath, she checked to make sure nothing was coming, then pressed the gas and the car slowly glided onto the road. Her heart was beating fast, but she eventually got the hang of it.

"Can I open my eyes now?" he kidded her.

She laughed. "Don't play. I have to concentrate."

"Make a right here," he said, motioning with his hand.

"Okay."

She right signaled, successfully turning while tightly gripping the steering wheel with both hands. She bit down on her bottom lip when she saw an eighteen-wheeler coming up behind them. She didn't want to let her nervousness show.

Gabriel smiled when he noticed how her forehead wrinkled from being overly tensed. "You look cute when you're stressing," he said.

She smiled at his compliment, but her focus was straight ahead.

The truck passed and moved in front of them.

She took a deep breath and relaxed her grip.

"You know this car can go faster than 35mph," he joked, noticing how slow she was creeping along in the 65mph zone.

"Ha-ha."

She changed gears and, without warning, the car gunned abruptly forward. She had mistakenly changed from fourth to third gear instead of shifting from fourth to fifth gear. "Oops! I'm sorry. What did I do?"

He placed his hand on top of hers. "It's okay. You

just tried to go from fourth to third. Just push in the clutch and take it back to fourth, then go up to fifth." He guided her hand. "Like this," he said.

"Okay."

"There you go. Just relax. Listen to the engine and you'll know when to change gears."

She did.

"You hear it?" he asked.

"Um-hm."

"It revs up when it's hungry for a higher gear. You have to find that sweet spot so it's a smooth transition," Gabriel said, like a driving instructor who took his job seriously, "and you don't want to be rough because that puts a lot of wear and tear on your clutch."

"Is that what they taught you in Driver's Ed, find the sweet spot?"

"Well, that wasn't exactly how Mr. Roberts put it, but it's close enough."

"Umm-hmm." She shot him a quick, disbelieving stare. "How am I doing?"

"You're doing great. I think I'll take a nap now. Let me know when we get back," he kidded.

"I'm getting the hang of it, but don't you dare go to sleep on me. I need you."

He looked at her, appreciative of what she had said, even if it was only about the driving lesson. It felt good to be needed. Gabriel didn't hear those words very often, if ever, from Tracee.

"You want some music?" he asked.

"What'cha got?"

He reached for his CD case in the backseat. "I've got a bunch of old school stuff, that's all I really ever listen to."

"My kinda music," she replied.

He flipped through his selection.

"Let's see. I've got *LTD.*"

"*Every time I turn around, back in love again,*" she hummed.

Gabriel smiled.

"*Earth, Wind, and Fire.*"

"*Reasons. The reasons that we're here,*" she sang.

Gabriel smiled.

"*The Gap Band,*" he said.

"*Outstanding, girl you knock me out,*" she sang softly.

Gabriel smiled harder. He liked her impromptu medley.

"*Cameo.*"

"*Just like candy,*" she sang.

She continued to make Gabriel smile.

"*Kool and the Gang,*" he said.

"*Joanna, I love you. You're the one, the one for me.*"

Her voice was so angelic to his ears. Gabriel held his smile even longer. She was so much fun to be with.

"*The Temptations.*"

"Ohhhh, put in *The Temptations,*" she said.

"You are not a *Temptations* fan," he said in anticipation of her answer. He was a huge fan and loved anyone else who appreciated and respected the group's timeless sound as musch as he did.

"Like the biggest. *The Temptations* is one of my all-time favorite groups," she said, in an excited tone. "Oh, and if you haven't seen the movie, you gotta see it."

"See it. I own it on DVD."

"Is that not the best?"

"It is. I completely had a newfound respect for

them after I saw that movie. It's one thing to appreciate their music, but to understand the struggles they went through to make it happen is a whole different story."

Their voices had a hint of childlike excitement as they talked about details from the movie.

"Y'know who my favorite group member was, though?"

"Who?" he asked.

"Paul," she said.

"Yeah. Paul was cool. The boy could dance his tail off like nobody's business," Gabriel said.

"I know. But I was so brokenhearted from that scene when he killed himself," Alex said in a sad voice as if she had personally known him.

"He tried to keep it together. They should've just been with him twenty-four seven like ol' boy, Cornbread, suggested. Y'know? At least until he kicked that bottle. That alcohol had him."

Alexandria agreed.

Gabriel slid the CD into the player.

"Forward it to "Just My Imagination" if you don't mind," she requested. "That's one of my favorite cuts."

He slid the CD in and the song began to play. They listened. And, unable to resist the urge, she began to hum to the words. By the second stanza, Gabriel had eventually joined in with her, murmuring the words. All the while he was thinking how he didn't want their time together to end. As he listened to her humming in unison with his husky voice, he thought about how absolutely perfect she was and how he wished they'd met before she was married and he was about to be married. Her voice, her personality, her smile, her gentle spirit, and everything about her made him want to walk away from the life he knew. He was falling in love with her. And, although he still loved Tracee, he couldn't accept the thought of never seeing Alex again, never hearing her sing.

They drove around for a long while with no destination in mind, listening to more CDs, from Stevie Wonder's Greatest Hits to Shalamar's *'Second Time Around'*. They sang their hearts out, Gabriel doing Howard Hewitt and Alex doing Jody Watley.

"I know you come a long way, baby.
But you don't need that heart of stone, no
You proved that you could do it, do it, baby.
You could make it on your own.
But you can't keep runnin' away from love
'cause the first one let you down, no, no, no.
And though others try to satisfy you, baby.
With me true love can still be found.
Love can still be found.
(The second time around)
Ooh, the second time is so much better, baby.
(The second time around)
And I'll make it better than the first time."

This song somehow had meaning for both. It all felt so natural, not at all forced. They laughed, acted like high-schoolers who were cruising the town just before curfew.

When they finally returned to the gym parking lot, they talked awhile more as they stood outside their cars. They agreed to a rain check for their next game of b-ball since the sun had now completely set.

Gazing into her eyes, Gabriel touched Alex's cheek

and brushed a stray strand of hair behind her ear and asked, "So, would it be okay if I called you later? You know, just to say goodnight."

She smiled at his attentiveness and nodded "yes."

"Okay, then," he said.

"Okay."

"Well, I guess we'll talk later," he said, sounding like a nervous teenager who needed to make sure this wasn't the last time he'd be able to talk to her.

"I guess so," she said, with an innocent look.

Nneena Freelon's "If I Had You" played smoothly in the background, echoing throughout the bathroom and vibrating quietly against the walls while Alexandria stood over the bathtub, naked. She unscrewed the cap on a bottle of her favorite bubble bath and inhaled deeply. *Ahh, Plumeria. Smells good.* She slowly poured her bubble bath under the running water, creating a covering of satin-like bubbles. She lit the candles surrounding her garden tub, sprinkled in bath beads. Lit a few ginger peach incense sticks. For Alexandria, a bath was the one moment in her hectic daily schedule when she could reflect, relax, and listen to her inner voice. She stood in front of the mirror and studied her reflection. She touched her face. Her hand slipped down over her breasts, across her tummy, and then down to her thighs. She now liked the woman she was looking at. Staring at her reflection, she felt *special* tonight. Not because of who she saw in the mirror, but because Gabriel Washington had made her feel that way. The way he had looked at her, touched her hair, sang with her, and admired her. All of this left her warm all over. It was a sensation she hadn't felt in a very long time. Gabriel was the first and only man she'd considered allowing into her life since her breakup, even as a friend. And now, standing in front of the mirror, looking through his eyes, she loved what she saw in herself. She turned the water off and carefully stepped into her warm bath. She eased herself down and her body sank under the bubbles until it disappeared, feeling her tensions immediately melt away upon contact with the silky water. She exhaled. Relaxed. It felt good, really good. She closed her eyes in delight. After a moment, she opened them. She sighed. She blushed. She smiled even harder, embarrassed over a stray thought. She closed her eyes, allowing herself to drift deeply into a daydream about the infinite possibilities of it all. *I love being with him*, she thought, giddy.

Gabriel turned on the shower, letting it steam the glass enclosure before he stepped in. He immediately yielded to the force of the spray as it pounded against his athletic frame. *Feels good. Just what I need*, he thought. Humming Stevie Wonder's "All I Do" playing softly from the stereo, he reached for the bottle of skin cleanser. Moving his body smoothly to the beat, he placed a small amount in his hands and then massaged it all over his face and neck. He adjusted the water temperature to a cooler setting as he stepped back and closed his eyes, allowing the warm spray to hit him directly on his face. He took a white cloth and gently dried his forehead, cheeks, eyes and nose. He soaped his body from his chest down to his feet. Feeling clean, he rinsed off and began shampooing his hair. *That feels good*, he thought. He took a deep breath. Adjusted the water temperature again. Steam filled the room. He began to reminisce about Alexandria, still humming quietly to himself. He smiled as his eyes glazed over, consumed by thoughts of her. Suddenly, he remembered something she had said earlier. He thought it was funny. He smiled. Then he chuckled quietly to himself. *Man, I love being with her*, he thought absentmindedly.

Later that night, a simple phone call to say goodnight somehow evolved into a lengthy conversation about everything from favorite foods to good books to world issues. Soon after, they relaxed and found themselves imitating characters from their favorite black movies. They could not stop laughing, and their conversation wasn't even close to coming to an end.

"Okay. Here's one. If you don't get this one then we're tied." Alex cleared her throat, getting into character. "*Knock knock . . .*" she said in a seductive, yet baby-talk voice.

"Who's there?" he answered, slightly confused by her imitation at this point.

She was good at this.

Alex raised her voice an octave higher and said, "*A scared little boy named Marcus and he wants to come out. He's been hurt, hasn't he? Tell me about him. Tell me all about Marcus.*"

Gabriel laughed, now recognizing her imitation from the movie *Boomerang,* even though he couldn't think of the female actress who had played the part in the movie.

"Ummm . . . it's on the tip of my tongue . . . man."

"C'mon now. It's an easy one," Alex said. "You got that it was Boomerang, but who was the actress who played the role?"

He thought for a second more, before finally giving

up. "Okay, I don't know. My mind is blank. Lisa something."

"Lela Rochon," she said.

"That's right. Shoot, I missed an easy one like that."

"You'll be okay."

"Well, see if you can figure out which movie this is from," he said.

"Okay, go ahead." Alex sat up in her bed, listening attentively.

Gabriel cleared his throat, and then began talking fast, almost stuttering, "*Everybody got problems. Now-now, I don' gave up that there narcotic. I'm dealin' wit mine.*"

She chuckled. "Okay, crazy Ike Turner. Laurence Fishburne from *What's Love Got To Do With It?*"

"I made that one too easy," he said.

"Yes, you did. It was a good imitation, though." She smiled big.

Their game of "movie trivia" went on for an hour. Back and forth they went, imitating characters from popular black movies and challenging their memory of famous lines. Their conversation mimicked that of two teenagers having one of their many phone calls about absolutely nothing, and yet about absolutely everything.

Eventually changing the topic of conversation, Gabriel said, "Ohh, it's eleven o'clock. You're gonna watch *Good Times* with me, right?"

"Sure. I didn't realize it was eleven o'clock already." Alex checked the television guide on her screen to see what tonight's episode was about. She read the episode title to Gabriel, "Tonight's show is entitled 'The Rent Party'." She then read the episode synopsis aloud. "The Evans' neighbor, Wanda, is in danger of being evicted for failure to pay back-rent. The Evans' decide to throw a party and variety show for which they charge admission."

"That's a good one. That's the one when Michael sings "When You're Young and in Love," Gabriel hummed off-key. "I like that song."

She snickered and said, "Before hearing your rendition, I did too. That must be your own remix version that you're singing because that song doesn't sound anything like what you just attempted to sing," she playfully replied, still giggling like a love-struck teenager.

"Don't hate a brotha because he got gifts and gotta use 'em," he joked.

"Stick to writing," she said.

As they watched television together, they made small talk about the trademarks of the different characters. How Thelma was always quoting statistics. How James and Florida had such chemistry that they really seemed as if they were married. How Willona wore more wigs than any wig shop ever had. And in the midst of their discussion, Alex, trying to stifle the sound, yawned quietly.

Gabriel, having heard her, asked, "Are you sleepy?"

"No. I'm a little tired, but I'm not ready to go to sleep. I'm okay," she assured him. She didn't want to hang up. It had been a long time since she had a late night conversation with anyone apart from Jaz. Her body was tired, but her heart was willing and fully engaged. Feeling cozy, with the help of a light rain that tapped softly against her bedroom window, she repositioned herself in bed and continued to enjoy talking with Gabriel. Her eyes were becoming heavy, but she was holding on to his every word, subconsciously determined that this night would never end.

"What can I do to help you stay awake?" he asked in a deep, sultry voice.

"What can you do to help me stay awake?" she repeated and then said, "I don't know." She thought about it for a second. "How 'bout you read me one of your poems or something?"

He laughed softly and asked, "Are you serious?"

"Yes, I'm serious. What makes you think I'm not serious?"

"You really want me to read you a poem?"

"Yes, I really want you to read me a poem."

"Okay," he smiled.

"Did you ever finish the one you were working on?" she asked.

She was feeling more awake at the thought of listening to him read his work and hearing his voice massaging her ears.

"Actually, I did. If you would hold on a sec, I'll go and get it."

"Of course."

He stepped away from the phone while she patiently held the phone awaiting his return.

When Gabriel came back to the phone, he said, "Okay, I'm back." You still here?"

"I am."

"I titled it *True Beauty*."

"I like that. *True Beauty*," she said, taking a deep breath in anticipation of listening to words written from his heart.

"It's kinda long. Hopefully, it won't make you any sleepier than you already are," he said. "Are you ready?"

"I'm ready. Waiting on you," she said attentively.

He started to read in a husky-sounding, midnight voice.

"True beauty is when she looks at me looking at her, and how it overwhelms me completely to see that she is truly and surely the quality of everything that is perfect and pure as well as holy to me."

Gabriel continued reading for about three minutes more, holding her attention. And after he finished, a dead silence rang loudly in his ears as he waited for Alex's response. Finally, she spoke slowly and said, "You wrote that?"

He wanted to tell her that she was the inspiration behind those words. He cleared his throat and answered, "I did."

Another long moment of silence occurred.

Just as Gabriel's insecurities reached critical mass with thoughts that she may have not liked it, he heard her angelic voice whisper, "It's the most glorious thing I've ever heard." There was another moment of quietness. Finally, Alex began to speak again. "Forgive me, but I have never been so overtaken like that before. I am moved."

For the first time, Gabriel had shared a piece of himself with someone through his poetry and, unexpectedly, touched something inside of another human being. Listening to her talk about how beautifully his words flowed together and how the hairs over her entire body stood to attention as he read them, left him speechless . . . and in love.

"So what else is there that I don't know about you, Gabriel Washington?" she quietly asked.

"What is it that you wanna know?"

"Just tell me everything," she requested.

And tell her just about everything is what he did. They asked each other a hundred and one questions. They gave each other a hundred and one answers.

And, at 4:17 a.m., with telephone receivers still pressed against their ears, and like two high school sweethearts unwilling and afraid to hang up, Alexandria and Gabriel both fell asleep for the first time—together.

CHAPTER FOURTEEN

A Hug?

The roaring sound of a vacuum broke the early Wednesday morning stillness as Alex stood in the middle of her bedroom, meticulously going over every corner. The opened curtains revealed the grand view, a professionally landscaped backyard enclosed by evergreen trees with an occasional fawn or rabbit passing through. Suddenly, she stopped what she was doing. She thought she heard her cell ringing. She propped the vacuum cleaner handle in an upright position, turning it off. Muting the television, she could now clearly hear that the phone was ringing. She grabbed her phone off the dresser without first looking at the caller ID, as she usually did.

"Hello?" she quickly answered, fearing she may have missed the last ring.

"Hey you," the voice said.

Now familiar with his voice, she didn't have to guess. Her heart skipped at the mere sound of his husky, yet gentle-sounding voice.

Sounding even more elated than the last time they

talked, she answered, "Heyyy you." The words fell from her lips as if she had hummed them.

"What'cha doing?" Gabriel asked.

"Just doing a little housework before I head to Cameron Village. I've got this 'thing' that I really don't wanna go to this weekend, but I need an outfit for it," she said, as she caught her breath.

"Oh, okay," he replied.

"Why?" she asked, as she sat on the end of her bed.

"Because I was comin' to pick you up," he answered.

"Huh?"

"I was comin' to pick you up," he repeated. "I wanted to spend the day with you."

"Where are you? I thought you had to work today," Alex said.

"I'm taking some time off," he said. It was true. He had the next two weeks off for his wedding and honeymoon.

"Oh," she replied. "You don't even know where I live."

"I know it's in Cary somewhere, so I thought I would just drive around until I found you. Maybe knock on every door until I got the right one," he joked.

Without asking where they would be going, she answered, "Okay."

"Okay?"

"Yes, okay. Come get me."

"Well, I can go shopping with you if you like," he replied. "Do you mind my company?"

"Of course not," she quickly replied.

"And after that, I'm open for anything else. I'm free for the entire day. So it's whatever you feel like doing," he said.

She was elated by his desire to spend the day with

her. "Umm, where are you now?" she asked, nervously twisting a strand of hair around her finger.

"I'm over by Blue Ridge Road right now."

"Oh—you're about twenty-five minutes away then."

"So you'll spend the *entire* day with me?" he asked.

"I will."

"Maybe we can grab a bite to eat later."

"Okay," she said, blushing at the thought of spending more time with this man she so immensely enjoyed being with.

"Okay. Well, I guess I'll see you in about twenty-five minutes then," he said.

"Okay. Sounds good."

"Cool."

They were just about to hang up when he suddenly remembered he didn't have directions to her house. "Whoa, Alex," he called, hoping she hadn't hung up.

Alex, hearing his voice again, placed the receiver back to her ear. "Yes?"

"I forgot to get your address," he said.

She gave him her address. "But, if you do happen to get lost or turned around," she said, "just call me and I'll take care of you."

"I like the way that sounds," he replied in his best Barry White voice. "I'm plugging your address into my GPS now. But I'll definitely call you if I find myself being taken in a direction that doesn't feel right."

As soon as Alex hung up the phone she thought about something that neither she nor Gabriel had considered. *Cameron Village? A public place? That's totally different than us just sitting in Ramona's talking. Could definitely be a mistake.* She immediately hit *69, calling him back.

"Hello," he answered.

"Hi, it's Alex."

"I know who you are," he said, smiling through the phone. He was hoping she hadn't called back with a change of mind. "What's up?"

"I was just thinking that maybe the Cameron Village-thing might not be such a good place to go, y'know?"

"Oh," he replied, waiting for her to finish her thought. He understood why she might think that.

"I just wanted to let you know that there's no pressure if you don't think it's a good idea. We can do something else. I mean, I can go shopping anytime. It's really no big deal," she assured him.

Without any hesitation, he said, "Alex, I'll do whatever you're comfortable with. Don't feel like you need to protect me from anything. It's your call."

She smiled and said, "It works for me."

"Okay. "Well, I guess I'll see you in a few then," he said, confidently.

After hanging up, Alex contemplated Gabriel's words. *Was this right?* No time to think about it now. She needed to get dressed in a hurry before he arrived. Going through her closet, she picked out a semi-casual, two-piece she had only worn once since buying it from Lord & Taylor, a beige, princess-seamed shell and a pair of chocolate-colored slacks. She slipped into a pair of opened-toed sandals. Pleased with her appearance so far, she then touched up her hair, breathing deeply as she tried to find the right style for her unexpected date.

Up? No—he's seen it in an upsweep do before.

Down? Definitely down. Yeah.

No, up? He liked it up. Or was it down?

Deciding to go with it up, she sat at her vanity table powdering her nose. Added a little blush to her cheeks, just enough to highlight her cheekbones. After about fifteen minutes, she headed out of the bedroom, feeling almost giddy with excitement. Halfway down the stairs, her house phone rang again. She rushed downstairs and made her way to the kitchen, hurriedly grabbing the phone.

"Don't tell me you're lost," she answered.

There was a brief period of silence.

"Alex?"

The voice on the other end was familiar. Her heart raced. She froze and didn't say another word.

"Hello?" the gruff voice called.

Alex let out an audible sigh, signifying to the caller that she was still there. Finally, with eyes closed, she asked, "How did you get this number?" She had changed the number and requested a non-published listing.

"Can we talk? Please. It's important."

"Lionel, I don't have a thing to say to you. Deal with my lawyer and stop calling me, please. It'll save me the trouble of having the number changed again."

She hung up without giving him the chance to say another word. Just as she was about to walk away from the phone, it rang again. She picked up the receiver and quickly hung up. She stood over the kitchen counter, holding the phone in one hand and resting her forehead in her other hand. Her mind was reeling from hearing Lionel's voice. What did he want from her? What part of *over* did he not understand? She thought she had made things perfectly clear.

Suddenly, the phone rang again. *Not him, again,* she thought to herself. In a harsh, unfriendly tone, she answered, "What?"

"What's up, chick? Why you hangin' up on me?"

Alex smiled in relief at the sound of Jaz's usual, upbeat voice. "Hey, girl. I'm sorry. What's up?"

"You tell me. I'm wondering why I called you and haven't heard back from you since. And then when I call, you pick up the phone like something is wrong. You okay?"

"I'm sorry, girl. My fault. I've been so busy the last couple of days. Got a lot goin' on."

"Umm-hmm. I bet you do," Jaz responded, a hint of suspicion in her voice.

"What's goin' on with you?" Alex asked.

"Nothing. We're still on for lunch today, right?"

"Today?"

"Yes, today. Like every Wednesday."

"Jaz, it totally slipped my mind. I'm actually about to head out the door."

"You standin' me up? What's goin' on, Alex? Inquiring minds want to know."

"Nothing's going on. I just need to run some personal errands, that's all. Are you gonna be home later on?"

"Yeah," Jaz said, sensing something was up and Alex wasn't telling her the whole story.

"I'll call you back and we'll talk, I promise," Alex said, feeling guilty about standing up her best friend for a man she'd only met a few days ago.

"Okay. But everything's fine, right?" Jaz asked.

"Everything's fine. Why?"

"You're just acting different, suspicious-like. You're hiding something." Jaz knew from experience that whenever Alex was being discreet and aloof, she was holding back critical information.

"No I'm not, silly. What are you talkin' about?"

"Alex, I know you too well. Out with it."

"Jaz, it's nothing . . . I'm tellin' you." The broad smile on Alexandria's face was evident in her voice.

"Well, *nothin'* has you smiling through the phone like you've been to third heaven. Out with it. What is it? Or who is it?" Jaz demanded.

"Who's who?" Trying to sound innocent, she played along with Jaz's interrogation.

"Who's who," Jaz mocked, "Whoever's occupying your time, causing you to forget our standing girlfriend lunch meeting, that's who!"

"Girl, what time is it? I have to get ready to get outta here and I know you probably got some heads to do." Alex attempted to wrap up their conversation.

"Alex . . . what's goin' on? I'm not hangin' up til you tell me."

"Nothing. Work is keeping me occupied, Jaz. Business is picking up, everything's goin' good, and . . ."

Jaz interjected and said, "And who is he?"

"Jaz, I know how you are."

"How am I?"

"You turn *nothing* into *something*. And then turn *something* into *something* sexual. Let's just talk about it later, okay?"

"Now how you gon' try to play me like that? 'Fess up." Jaz was hoping to wear Alex down.

"Nobody's playing you."

"Are you and Lionel working things out?" Jaz asked in a hushed tone.

"Girl, no. But I don't wanna get into that right now. I'm going to have a good day."

"Then what?"

Alex started to blush. "Okay. But don't blow it out of proportion like you usually do. Promise?"

"Of course. I promise."

"He's just a friend. It's nothing serious. It's the guy I was telling you about."

"Ahhh, now I see. I thought you said you weren't going to call him."

"I didn't. He called me."

"Ohhh, okay. I'm listening." Jaz waited anxiously on the other end for the rest of the story.

"We met for lunch, talked a few times over the phone, that's it. He's a real nice brotha and whatnot. We talk, and that's it."

"Talk, huh?"

"Yes. Talk. That's it."

"Umm-hmm. Well, tell me more about him."

"There's nothin' else to tell."

"There's always somethin' else," Jaz said.

"He's just a guy . . . I don't know."

"Got it."

"And I really enjoy his conversation." Alex seemed to lose herself as she talked about him. "He makes me laugh . . . even when he's not trying to be funny. I like him. To be honest with you, we don't even know each other. But then we do. There's such a spiritual connection. I just met him. Already everything is moving so fast."

Jaz listened quietly without saying a word.

"He calls me and we talk . . . like we've known each other forever or something. Like we've been best friends as long as either of us could remember. It's nice. And it doesn't seem forced, y'know?"

Finally, Jaz asked, "Alex, do you know what you're doing?"

Suddenly, Alex realized she was saying way too much about her new gentleman friend. "Honestly . . . I don't," she answered. "But for once, I'm okay with just going with the flow of things."

The doorbell rang. "I've gotta go," Alex told Jaz. They said quick goodbyes, with Alex again promising to call her later.

When Alex reached the door, she was trying to catch her breath. With one hand on the doorknob, she hesitated. *Alex, what are you doing?* The doorbell rang a second, then third time. She opened the door. Gabriel stepped in and the two exchanged quick, awkward hugs.

"How are you?" he asked, standing back to look at her.

"Good," she replied, nervously. "I'm glad you didn't get lost."

"No problem at all," he said, flashing a sincere and charming smile. "These are for you," he said, presenting her with a bouquet of roses.

Her eyes widened in surprise. "Thank you. They're lovely, but you shouldn't have," she replied, modestly.

"I wanted to."

She accepted the beautiful yellow roses, and invited Gabriel to make himself comfortable while she searched for a vase. He complimented her on her beautifully decorated home as he quickly scanned the room. While she was in the kitchen, he studied some of the framed photos in the living room. They were mostly of her, her family and friends, but not one of her husband.

When she walked back into the living room, she noticed Gabriel was observing an abstract piece of artwork hanging above her fireplace.

"You like that?" she asked.

"I do. David Tyre, right?"

"Yes."

"I thought so."

"You're familiar with his work?" she asked, somewhat surprised that he recognized the work of this up-and-coming African-American painter.

"I am. He's an incredible artist. But this piece you have is exquisite. See here," he motioned with his hand, "the use of colors and lines. Outstanding. His passion is evident in everything he does. You can tell the brotha's heart is definitely in his work. That's becoming rare these days with a lot of new artists."

"I agree," she said, nodding.

Gabriel turned his attention from the painting to Alex as she grabbed her handbag and checked her purse for her house keys. "Are you ready?" she asked, smiling.

"Sure," he said, still staring at her without as much as a blink.

"What?" she said, noticing his stare.

"Nothing. I'm just glad to see you, that's all."

She smiled big.

"I'm glad to see you, too," she replied.

The short drive gave them a chance to talk along the way. The past few days had flown by as they shared childhood stories, funny moments, things they loved to do, and things they had never done but wanted to.

Arriving at Cameron Village, they leisurely window shopped together, resembling newlyweds as they moved about the plaza. After searching the music store with no success for Billie Holiday's *Lady Day* CD for Alex, they headed into a few clothing stores. Gabriel stood alongside all the other husbands and boyfriends, while she scanned racks and racks of clothing. Noting his rigid stance, she respectfully asked if he would mind if she quickly tried on a few items.

"I won't be but a minute, I promise," she said.

"Sure. Go ahead. I'm fine."

Gabriel patiently took a seat outside the fitting room until the moment she walked out in bare feet wearing flat-front khaki trousers and a cotton tee. She lifted her shirt up slightly to get the full view of the pants and to get a feel for how much room she had in the waist. She turned towards him. He nodded his approval.

"I like it," he said.

Gabriel's cell phone rang, as Alex smiled and headed back into the fitting room. Gabriel flipped open his cell phone and heard a troubled, yet familiar voice on the other end. Tracee. Calling to ask where he was and to rant about the latest drama with the wedding planner.

"Just calm down, Tracee. Everything will be fine. I'll be there Friday and I'll help you with whatever needs to be done, okay? Exactly. There's no need to get stressed. Right. Good. No, I'm fine—just out doing a little shopping. Yeah. No. I thought maybe cufflinks or something for them. Trust the fellas will be happy with that. Right. Ummm . . ."

Gabriel nervously stood up. He didn't want this phone call to interrupt what was otherwise starting out as the beginning of a perfect day. He also knew that this moment couldn't last forever. There was someone else in his life, and right now, she was on the phone and reminded him that there was. Moreover, if Tracee heard a woman's voice in the background it would surely arouse a million and one questions, something he wasn't prepared to deal with. He tried to listen attentively to Tracee's wedding woes.

"Did you ask your mom?" Gabriel questioned Tracee.

Alex, stepping out of the dressing room again, looked over at Gabriel at the sound of his voice, catching only the last word of what he had just said. Noticing him on the phone and hearing him say the word 'mom' led her to assume he was on the phone with his mother perhaps from the little bit she caught. She didn't think too much into it.

As Tracee continued, Gabriel was distracted by Alex, who was now standing in the mirror examining herself in a mauve-colored halter dress. Gabriel kept his eyes on her while she carefully studied her reflection. In the mirror, she could see him watching her every move. His stares made her feel beautiful, sexy. She raised the dress above her knees for a different look.

Covering up the mouth of his phone, Gabriel mouthed to Alex, "I'll be off in just a sec."

She nodded okay.

Tracee rambled on. With Alex standing so close and looking so dangerously fine, it was impossible for Gabriel to concentrate fully on his phone conversation. Struggling to seem interested, Gabriel purposefully changed the subject, "Umm . . . so what's on your agenda for the rest of the day?"

As Tracee spoke about her to-do list, Gabriel watched Alex, now trying on a straw hat. She placed the hat on top of her head with strands of her long, auburn-tinted hair peeking from underneath. With the dress and hat together, she looked like a tropical goddess. She waited for his approval. He gave her a wide-eyed look and nodded, giving her a 'thumbs up' sign. Still with his cell phone pressed to his ear and the sound of his fiancée's voice ringing in his head, he moved closer to Alex.

"Yeah, I know," he replied in a monotone voice as he reached out with his free hand and adjusted the hat slightly on Alex's head, moving a strand of loose hair behind her ear. She liked his touch, enjoyed it more each time. She longed for it. She turned towards the mirror, and smiled at their reflection.

"Right," he replied into the phone, while standing directly behind her as she continued looking at them both in the mirror. He was standing so close to her that any noise from her would leave him with some serious explaining to do. But Alex was quiet, but not because Gabriel had said to be.

She took the hat off her head and put it on Gabriel's while he continued on the phone. As he stood motionless, she shaped the hat in several styles that she found humorous. She laughed quietly. In the process, her hand brushed against his face. It felt so good to feel her touch that he wished she'd do it again. And then she did. She went and removed another dress from the rack. Instead of trying it on herself, she placed it against him to get a visual for how it would look. She shook her head "no." He shook his head. She found another one. She raised her index finger, quietly signaling him to "wait one second." She grabbed her handbag from the floor to add to the dress that now hung on the front of his shirt. She came back and, amusingly, placed her bag in his hand. And there he stood, with a woman's dress hanging in front of him, a lady's handbag in hand, and a straw hat atop of his head. Alex nodded, as if to say "that's it," while he smiled at her crazy antics.

While removing the articles of clothing and

accessories from him, Alex stared deeply into Gabriel's eyes. They swapped a silent, loving smile. As she turned to go, he reached for her hand and held it inside his in the way a man does when he loves a woman. In a little over forty-eight hours, Gabriel Washington had come to care deeply for this woman. He had heard of love at first sight, read about it in books, had seen it occur in movies, but had never experienced it himself . . . until now.

Gabriel had no idea what Tracee was saying at this point. His mind only registered how perfectly Alex's hand fit inside his. Suddenly he heard Tracee shrieking his name repeatedly on the other end as she realized he hadn't been listening.

"Huh?" he shook his head as Alex smiled and headed back into the dressing room. "No, I'm listening. Nothing. Yes. Finish what you were saying."

In the middle of her rambling, Tracee got another call and placed Gabriel on hold. But when three minutes had passed and Tracee still hadn't returned, Gabriel flipped his phone closed.

Alex stepped out of the fitting room with both outfits in hand.

"Everything okay?" she asked.

"Everything's fine," he said. "You looked absolutely stunning in those outfits."

"So did you," she said, trying to hold back her laughter.

As they headed to the register, Gabriel tried to process what was happening. He knew she was married and he was about to be married, but the more he knew about her the more he wanted to know. But, the call from Tracee had forced him to deal with the reality of his situation. He had one woman who was waiting to marry him, and, here he stood, desiring another. This wasn't as innocent nor as simple as he'd rationalized earlier to himself. Now he knew it. He wondered if Alex knew it, too.

The clock on the dashboard read 11:42 p.m. when they pulled up in front of Alex's house. It was where their perfectly unplanned day together began, and where it would end. Now with a full moon illuminating their faces, the two sat reminiscing about the day. The roller-skating excursion and Gabriel's lack of coordination. Their stroll in the park interrupted by a photographer wanting to take their picture. And to seal a perfect evening, they had dinner at "Chauncey's"—an intimate candle-lit nightspot with a live jazz band. After warning Gabriel about the restaurant's abbreviated weekday hours, she was totally surprised when they arrived at 9:15 p.m. and the maitre d' immediately greeted Gabriel by name. Only as Alex walked to their table did she realize they were the only patrons in the entire restaurant. While the band played quietly, they talked. They laughed. They danced. And they fell even more in love without ever saying the words to one another. They felt it.

As they sat in his car, Alex wanted Gabriel Washington more than ever. He made her feel whole again.

"Well, I'm very glad you allowed me to spend the day with you, but I've got an idea for next time," Gabriel said, giving her hand a soft squeeze.

Alex replied, "What's that?" She felt a bit uneasy

about what he might suggest.

He gave her a radiant grin and said, "I'll cook for you."

"Do you know how?" she joked, feeling more at ease and flattered by his offer. No other man had ever cooked for her except Lionel. She tried not to appear overly excited. "Cause y'know cookin' and microwavin' are two different things," she added, in a playful manner.

"I can cook," he said, with an air of self-assuredness.

"But can you burn?" she asked.

"Just tell me what you wanna eat. I've got it covered."

"Maybe I should be askin' what can you cook?"

"Anything. I cook all the time," he replied.

"Is that right?" A look of intrigue appeared on her face. She was truly impressed with Gabriel's versatility.

"Yes. And I'm good, too." He stared seductively into her eyes. He looked confident and ready to take on the world. She liked that about him.

"Okay, then I'll let you surprise me," Alex yielded.

"Okay."

"So, Chef Boyardee, when are you going to cook this so-called gourmet dinner?" she asked. "Of warm me up some canned spaghetti," she joked.

"Funny." He smiled. "How 'bout tomorrow?"

"Tomorrow?"

"I'll go by the market to pick up a few things and . . ."

"So let me get this straight," she interjected. "You cook all the time, but you don't have any food? What's wrong with that picture?" she playfully remarked.

"Hey, Funny Lady, I just haven't been shopping this week," he defended. "It's all cooked up."

"Okay," she replied.

"Plus you're special, so I gotta do something a little out of the box for you," he said with a sly grin.

He looked at her and smiled. Inside, he was nervous about what he was doing—spending the day together and making plans to cook a meal for just the two of them. He was leaving for Maryland on Friday, a mere two days away. But, there was something about this woman that made him need to be around her as much as possible. It had become as important to him as breathing. He was elated about the prospect of preparing a scrumptious meal for her pleasure. He knew that she was the type of woman who would appreciate his efforts, but her jokes inspired him to prove to her his ability to 'burn' in the kitchen.

He had planned to whip out his specialty, pasta primavera with grilled chicken and his own secret saucc.

"I also want to talk to you about something," he added, in a serious tone. We'll talk tomorrow, over dinner." He stared intently to see if she looked nervous or anxious about the delayed conversation between the two of them.

"Okay," she said, smiling to break the tension.

She frantically began thinking over all the things he might have to tell her. But the troubling thoughts invaded her mind as quickly as she pushed them away. She studied him closely as he talked, trying to find some physical flaw in him. She found none.

She was shaken from her thoughts when Gabriel asked, "What is it that you look for in a man?"

"What do I look for in a man?" she repeated.

"Um-hm," he murmured.

She smiled, looked at him in his eyes, and, giving him a serious look, she answered, "Everything. More than anything, someone I can grow with."

She went into even more details. He listened, taking mental notes.

They sat there in his car talking, listening to love songs on the radio. Hours slipped by. At 2:37 a.m., the serenading sounds of Stevie Wonder's "If It's Magic" left them vulnerable to their soaring emotions and ready to yield to their fleshly desires. Their hands rested inside of each other's.

He gently massaged her fingers. Even though she didn't want him to leave, she reluctantly said, "It's gettin' late. I'd better let you go."

He smiled at her as he watched her hastily searching for her keys with her free hand. He knew he should let her go. The reality of his situation was screaming at him. He needed to take a cold shower and forget this fantasy. He knew he just needed to walk her to the door and say goodnight, letting that be the very end of it all.

But Gabriel couldn't do it. Instead, he asked, "Would it be too much to ask for a hug?"

She blushed, and replied without hesitating, "I think I can definitely do that." She needed a hug just as much as he did.

They leaned closer to each other and, just as he was about to take her into his arms, his cell phone rang. It caught them both off guard. They slowly moved away from each other. Without saying a word, Alex prepared to leave, assuming the call must be important given the late hour.

Refusing to let go of her hand and never taking his eyes off her, he reached for the phone, without looking to see who was calling. This moment with Alex was too important. He pressed the button to turn it off.

"I apologize," he told her.

He looked deeply into her eyes, and then guided her towards him. A sweet awkwardness washed over them in anticipation of this intimate moment that had been building inside of them both since their day together began. She moved towards him, placing her arms around his neck, bodies touching like they'd been fused together over a burning flame. And they held each other as if their lives depended on one another. The moment was an explosion of confused emotions, incomprehensible to either of them.

"You smell wonderful," he told her, his arms molded to the curvatures of her body.

"So do you," she whispered in his ear.

She could feel his heart beating faster, racing to catch up with hers. Both waited for the other to be the first to let go. Neither moved. He felt so strong to her. His powerful arms created an impenetrable barrier from the world. She belonged in his arms. She knew it. He knew it. Their heated bodies were inseparable. There was no space, no air, no time between them. They rested their cheeks against each other's and took deep breaths. And they continued to hold each other. The sexual tension was intensifying.

After several minutes, Alex tried to suppress a yawn, but Gabriel felt it. He could tell she was getting sleepy. They had a long day together. He smiled and said, "I'd better get ready to go."

She didn't say anything, but her thoughts were racing. She didn't want him to let her go. Not now, not ever.

"Would it be okay if I called you when I got home,

just to say good night?" he asked.

"Of course it's okay. You can call me anytime you want," she said, resting her face against his neck.

She slowly ran her fingers through his hair and down the side of his face.

By 2:58 a.m., Gabriel and Alex were still lying in each other's arms. Her head was on his chest. Patti Labelle's "If You Asked Me To" played quietly on the radio.

"Alex?" His tone sounded as if something serious was about to follow him saying her name.

"Hmh?"

"Would you mind if I used your bathroom?"

She laughed softly at his poor sense of timing.

"Sure."

"I think I drank too much tea at dinner," he explained, as they both reluctantly released each other.

As they entered the house, Alex pointed down the hall and said, "Second door on the left."

"Thank you," he replied, placing her shopping bags in a nearby chair before heading towards the bathroom.

"You're welcome," she said, watching him as he moved down the hallway to the bathroom. She went into her family room, took a seat on the couch and waited patiently for his return. She picked up the television remote from the coffee table and turned the TV on. Nothing much was on at this time of the morning.

Channel surfing, she finally landed on Nick at Nite's airing of *The Jeffersons* marathon. She relaxed, struggling to keep her eyes open. It had been a long while since she'd been out this late.

She glanced at the clock on the wall. It was 3:10 a.m. She yawned quietly again. Her eyes were getting heavier. Resting her head back against the couch, it was becoming harder to stay awake, almost impossible to fight the heaviness of sleep weighing upon her. "Gabriel," she sighed dreamily to herself, then closed her eyes, willfully submitting.

When Gabriel stepped out of the bathroom, he found Alex fast asleep. Looking at her, he hated to wake her. Instead, he knelt beside her and took a moment to simply watch her, memorizing details again. He ran his fingers carefully over her hair. Kissed her softly on the forehead. Then smiled at her.

"Alex, I'm getting ready to go," he whispered in her ear.

"Hmh?" She was half out of it.

"I said I'm getting ready to go, okay?"

"No. Don't go," she murmured.

"Hmh?"

"Stay with me, please," she said, asleep within a matter of seconds.

Her request was an easy one to accommodate. Gabriel seated himself directly across from her in an oversized armchair. Her simple, yet magnetic beauty mesmerized him. So much so, that there he sat like a protector, observing her as she slept and watching her chest rise and fall with every breath. It was one of the most peaceful visions he'd ever seen. And he watched her until, finally, a hint of early morning sunlight crept through the windows as the birds chirped happily outside, welcoming in the new day.

It was 6:42 a.m., Thursday morning.

What are We Doing?

Melodious jazz played in the background while Gabriel busily diced and chopped vegetables to accompany the main course, pasta primavera with lemon chicken. He tasted a pasta noodle to make sure it was al denté. "Ah, perfect," he said as he began to sauté his vegetable medley.

He had just placed a loaf of Italian bread in the oven to warm, and the scent of garlic and rosemary permeated the kitchen. The dinner salads were ready with a choice of light vinaigrette dressing or his all-time favorite, lemon tahini.

Looking around to make sure everything was in order, he shifted his attention to the dining room. The floral arrangement looked slightly off balance. Out of his desire to have everything perfect, he repositioned it for what seemed like the hundredth time. He looked at it again. Frowned. He moved it again. Better.

He headed into the living room to turn down the music just a notch. There were a few pictures of him and Tracee scattered about the room. He didn't want Alex to feel uncomfortable and, as wrong as it may be, he put them inside a cabinet in his entertainment center. He hesitated. He had every intention of putting them back after Alex left, and that made him feel the deception a bit more deeply. On the other hand, it felt like the right thing to do in the moment.

When he made it back into the kitchen, he was unaware that he had started to hum a song he'd heard earlier in the day that seemed to describe his relationship with Tracee. The song reminded him that where he should be and where he wanted to be were two entirely different places. Knowing he would be leaving in the morning for Baltimore made him realize how quickly the week had flown by. His mind suddenly flooded with visions of standing at the altar on Saturday saying "I do" when his heart was now elsewhere.

As he began to mentally unravel his relationship with Tracee, he reasoned that maybe the two of them were in love with the Gabriel and Tracee from their college days. They had both become different people since then though. Their relationship at times appeared to be one of convenience because of the years they've known one another. They both had been there for one another through some tough times, from the loss of a parent, health issues, the car accident, and all the woes that draw couples close together.

Gabriel wasn't fully convinced if he was even the Gabriel that Tracee wanted to marry. Or was he just the Gabriel everyone expected her to marry because they had been together for so long? He knew she had this picture-perfect plan that included him, but he missed that feeling of being in love. Of being head-over-heels for someone who accepted him unconditionally with no desire to mold him into someone else. He missed being in love with Tracee. But standing there, he wasn't really sure if real, unconditional love had ever truly existed between them.

The doorbell rang.

As he headed to the door, he stopped briefly to give himself a quick once-over in the hall mirror. He brushed his hand across his hair. Checked his teeth. He flashed a reassuring smile at his reflection.

Alex rang the doorbell a second time. Thoughts about whether this was the right thing to do had plagued her the entire drive over. Since she agreed to have dinner with him, she'd had second thoughts, but only had to envisage Gabriel's reassuring look and that made her okay with everything. He told her she had nothing to worry about coming here tonight. She believed him. She trusted him. Removing her wedding ring from her finger for the first time and slipping it into her handbag, she smiled at the thought of just how much she had entrusted herself to him.

He opened the door.

"Hi," he said with a pearly grin.

"Hey you," she replied, smiling back.

"You look nice," he said.

Alex was wearing a simple pair of black slacks and a fitted sleeveless knit top, her favorite coral blue-colored one that made her skin glow.

"Thank you."

"Come on in. Any problems finding the place?"

She stepped inside and said, "No. I had no problem at all." Her eyes ewandered around the living room. "Nice place you have here," she added, as she slowly strolled through the living room admiring the artwork hanging on the warm walls.

"Thank you so much. Look around. Make yourself

comfortable."

"Thanks." Noticing his baby grand piano, she asked, "So do you play or is it just for decoration?"

"I play a little," he said.

Again, she was impressed.

"Oh, I've got a little something for you on the coffee table over there, too," he said, motioning with his hand.

"What?" she asked, wide-eyed.

"Check it out." He gave her a meaningful smile as she moved towards the small gift bag sitting on the table.

She examined what was inside. "Billie Holiday's *Lady Day*! You found it. Awww, thank you," she said, warmly. "You didn't have to do that. This is so sweet of you."

"Not a problem. I knew you said you had been searchin' for it for awhile, so . . ."

"Where did you find it? I called just about every music store in town and no one had it in stock."

"I picked it up from this little hidden spot downtown where I get all of my stuff from," he said, proudly.

"Thank you again." After looking at it for a few seconds more, she slipped the gift inside her handbag. She was still smiling.

It pleased him to see her happy. "Well, dinner's almost ready so please make yourself at home."

"It smells good. You need any help in the kitchen?"

"No, I'm good. Thank you. You can relax."

"I don't mind," she said, as she followed him into the kitchen.

"Everything's basically done except I haven't set the table yet."

"Let me do that," she insisted. "Where are your

plates?"

Gabriel smiled at how easily her persistence and subtle charm defeated him. "In the top cabinet over there," he said, pointing at a pair of tall oak cabinets with glass doors.

Placing her handbag on the countertop, she said, "Oh, I meant to tell you that I finished reading your script. I have it with me." She carefully removed two plates.

"How much did you read before you got bored?" he asked, sarcastically.

"Oh you silly, modest man. I read the whole thing and thoroughly enjoyed it."

"You read the whole thing?"

She took out two wineglasses. "Yes, I read the whole thing. I told you I would. Why does that surprise you?"

"I don't know. I just thought you would read like the first couple of pages or something."

"No. It was only one hundred twenty pages. I've read four hundred-page books on a rainy day before, so your script was no problem. Plus, it was really good. Once I started reading, I got excited about the ending," she said.

"Really?" He smiled. "Thank you very much for reading it. It means a lot."

"You're welcome. I hope you didn't mind, but . . . I jotted down some ideas and suggestions that I'll give you. It's nothing major."

Alex mentioned a few ideas about the characters and the plot, but Gabriel, still mroved by the fact that she had actually read the entire script found it hard to focus on the details. Many times, he'd offered to share his work with Tracee, but she was too busy or just not interested. He always said it didn't bother him, but it did.

She moved about the kitchen and dining room as if she belonged there, and Gabriel noticed.

"I think you're going to provide the world with some movie masterpieces," Alex told him. "Your work is different. I get so tired of seeing the same thing all the time. I'll scream if I read or see another baby-mama-drama anything or a gay brother and his lover hell-bound romance. There's more out there than that, y'know? Like what you're writing about . . . black love. Why don't people write good love stories anymore?"

Gabriel stopped what he was doing at the stove to listen intently. He was in awe of how her mind worked.

Noticing his attention, she apologized. "I'm sorry. I'm just rambling on and on."

"It's okay," he said, taking a deep sigh.

"You're going to do well. Don't ever doubt that. You've got a gift."

"Thank you."

"And plus, I prayed for you today."

"For me?" Gabriel quietly asked, slightly taken aback.

"Yes—that God will allow you to fulfill your dreams, and grant you the desires of your heart."

He had to repeat the words 'she prayed for me' mentally to himself.

"Thank you," he said warmly, still staring at her as she moved between the kitchen and the dining room. That last statement of hers had moved something deep within him.

"For what?" she asked, looking in his direction.

"For nothing . . . and everything," he said.

Gabriel felt reaffirmed as a writer. Her words, her interest, her attention was exactly what he needed. Having an intelligent, cultured woman applaud, as well as critique, his writing was music to his soul. His confidence in his future as a writer had wavered lately, especially as he had yet to receive any type of response from agents or entertainment companies regarding his script. But, in a matter of minutes, Alex had laid the foundation and begun rebuilding his confidence. Tracee was wrong. His writing wasn't just a hobby. He *was* a writer. Alexandria confirmed it. And, at that moment, he silently thanked God for her presence.

Alex was seated in Gabriel's sitting room. The open floor plan gave her a clear view of him as he worked in the kitchen as he put the finishing touches on dinner. Before she forgot, she removed his script from her bag and placed it on the coffee table. She touched the top of it with her fingertips as if she were touching something extremely special. She thought about what a wonderful man he was. At the thought, her heart began beating at an irregular pace. Right then, she knew beyond a shadow of a doubt that there was nothing she could do to stop *this*. This man had her. She was falling hard for him. With her eyes fixed on Gabriel's every move, she was reminded of Lionel's love for cooking gourmet dishes. She felt guilty about thinking of Lionel in Gabriel's presence. And after realizing she had, she promised herself she would not do it again. The sound of Gabriel's voice captured her undivided attention.

"You gotta busy day tomorrow?" Gabriel inquired.

"Um, not really. Nothing in the morning, just one appointment in the afternoon at one-thirty. I try to keep my Friday's light."

"That's smart."

"My meeting is actually downtown. I'll be at Ramona's. I don't know what your day is looking like, but are you free for lunch?" She was hoping he could possibly carve out some time for them.

"Um . . ."

Gabriel had plans of telling Alex about his pending wedding taking place this weekend and his scheduled flight to leave in the morning. He had been waiting for the right moment. And when she asked about his plans tomorrow, it opened the door to have that conversation. Before he could respond fully, Alex glanced over at the meal he was preparing.

"That looks as good as it smells," she said, admiring the meal laid out in the kitchen.

"You wanna taste?" he asked.

"Sure," she said. She stood and walked towards him.

"It's still a little hot." He fed her from the tip of his fork, and then said, "Be honest."

There was a brief moment while she took in the taste.

"Mmmm . . ." was the only sound that came out of her mouth when the food landed on her tongue. "Oh-my-goodness." She closed her eyes for a moment. "This is really good."

"See. I told you that you were underestimating a brotha's know-how and whatnot."

"My bad. I give props when props are due. It is good."

"All a brotha wants is a lil' recognition, that's all," he joked.

"Okay, I'm impressed," she said, shaking her head at his boyish pride.

"Well, everything's almost ready. The garlic bread's in the toaster oven, and I say about another fifteen minutes we can eat. I have a DVD library in the other room," he motioned, "if you wanna watch a little TV before we eat. Or we can see if a game is on or something."

"Okay. Sounds good," she replied.

Gabriel reached for her hand to lead her into another room. As they entered, a familiar, warm feeling came over Alex and she stopped. Gabriel looked back at her, and what he saw when he searched her eyes lifted his heart almost from his chest. There, together and alone, they stood lit only by a soft glow from a lamp in the corner. In the background, Will Downing's "Stop, Look, Listen (To Your Heart)" played. They stood face-to-face, staring into the windows of each other's souls. At first, neither of them spoke a word. They just quietly stared at one another.

Gabriel moved closer to her, and when he reached her, his lips eventually found their way to hers, tongues began to dance while they slowly made attempts to dissolve into one another. Their kissing intensified. The heat between them both was now revved and they were willing to submit to wherever the flow might take them. It was like something they both had been wanting and now it was finally here. Even so, every touch became an explosion of complicated emotions that left them at the will of their intimate desires.

Gabriel ran his breath over Alex's neck, through her

hair, and across her lips. Images raced through both of their minds, envisioning what this moment of foreplay might lend itself to in the next few minutes. Their unspoken thoughts only intensified the burning desires between them, as their faces began to trickle beads of sweat.

There were more thoughts.

There was more touching, more kissing, more heavy breathing.

Suddenly, the insistent sound of the oven timer quietly beeping in the background gradually brought them back to some form of their senses. The realization of what was about to take place here had dawned upon them. They stopped moving, stopped tearing into each other. Alex was shaking slightly. She was breathing like a person just revived back to life.

There was a long silence between the two. They held each other for a bit. Alex rested her head on his chest, arms wrapped around him tightly as if he belonged to her.

"I'm sorry," Gabriel said, being the first to speak.

Gabriel held her closer, her head still resting on him.

"I don't think I can do this," he continued. "Not like this. You're still marr . . ."

"Shhh . . ." she softly replied. "I understand. You don't have to explain."

Finally, Gabriel whispered in her ear, "What are we doing?"

It was something they knew would have to be discussed, a conversation they both had avoided since their first meeting. Since these feelings they both shared had come upon them.

"I don't know," she replied. She took another deep breath, relaxing in his embrace. She felt vulnerable, but alive, in his arms.

"I can't get enough of you," he said.

Pleasant chills ran over her entire body as she felt an arctic-like breeze traveling across her neck as Gabriel spoke. She smiled, and then quietly asked, "Are you sure about that?"

"Without a doubt," he said in a muffled voice, his lips now pressed against her forehead.

"Then I guess we feel the same way about each other," she replied.

She felt him smile when she said that.

"I guess we do. Look at us. What has it been, like three or four days now?"

"Yeah, something like that." She smiled, and then asked, "How is it that we feel this way about each other in such a short amount of time? It's crazy."

"I don't know. But when I think of you, I realize what's been missing," he whispered.

"I know that feeling," she replied.

"It's like I can't wait to see you, talk to you," Gabriel continued. "You make me smile on the inside, just thinking about you. I had forgotten what that feeling even felt like until you came along. Where do you want to go from here? You tell me, and I'm there with you. I won't have any regrets, so don't worry."

Slowly shaking her head, Alex said, "We're thinking with our hearts, and we couldn't expect anyone else to understand *this*, Gabriel. I could tell you I want you for me, but I haven't figured out my own situation yet. I can't ask you to undo your life for me. Right now, we've done nothing that I have regrets about, and I don't want any regrets when it comes to you."

Gabriel hugged her tightly and whispered in her ear, "I know. But everything in me tells me that I need you. That this is where I belong."

He could feel her smile before she said, "And I need you, too, Gabriel."

They were both slightly nervous. This was the first time they had openly admitted true feelings for one another.

"I don't want to let you go." His tone was serious and unyielding. He felt a tear fall from Alex's cheek and onto him.

She cleared her throat and slowly began to speak. "I've never fallen for someone so quickly. In these past few days, you've shown me how to love myself again. It was something I had forgotten how to do. I never thought I would feel this way about another man. I keep wondering where you came from. Wondering why are we here at this stage of our lives. You've changed me and given me so much in such a short space in time. Whatever it is that has been created between us has truly become bigger than I could have imagined, and it's consuming me."

"And me, too," he said.

"Bottom line is, I have to let you decide what you want to do about us, but I can't tell you what to do. I can never do that. Even though every fiber of my being feels for you, I'm too weak to fight any more battles. You decide what's best for Gabriel, and I'll follow your lead. Honestly."

Gabriel slowly pulled away, looked into her eyes and whispered, "Only you, me, and the heavens could ever understand this *thing* that we've created between us. I want to be with you, I don't need any time to think about that. But, first, there's something I need to tell you because I want to be completely truthful with you about everything. I have to. There are things I should have told you in the beginning, but . . ." He took a deep breath to steady his nerves, "I never expected things to get out of my control like this."

"I'm listening," she said, watching his lips closely. "You're a beautiful man, you know that?"

He kissed her lightly on the forehead. "You're beautiful. Just perfect. You're everything, I mean everything, that a man could want in a woman. This is all that matters right now to me, y'know?"

"I know," she said, smiling. "Me, too."

"I want you to know that I would never do anything to purposely hurt you."

"I know."

Just as he was about to continue, she placed her fingers over his lips to silence him, and then guided his face towards her lips. "Hold that thought," she said seductively.

They kissed softly, tongues dancing passionately in unison again. Gabriel closed his eyes and wished that this moment would never end. She was so soft, so warm, and her skin felt like satin.

Through their kisses, Gabriel managed to mumble, "Alex?"

"Hmh?" she answered, as she continued kissing him softly all over his face.

"Please. It's important. I really need to tell you this." Gabriel could barely keep his mind focused on what he needed to say to her. Each kiss to his face melted him just a little bit more inside.

"Okay," she whispered.

But her wet lips left him dizzy and confused, unable to capture his fleeting thoughts. "It's just . . ." Gabriel struggled to put his words together.

She interjected and said, "Gabriel?" Her voice suddenly became serious.

"Um-hm?" he murmured, kissing her on the neck.

"Would you . . ." She kissed him again, losing her own train of thought.

"Um-hm?" he murmured.

Another kiss.

"Mind telling me . . ."

Another kiss.

"Um-hm?"

Another kiss.

"Whatever you have to tell me . . ."

Another kiss.

"Yes?" Gabriel was lost in her affection.

"After I use the bathroom?" she asked, with a hint of embarrassment in her voice.

Her request for a bathroom break broke the tension surrounding the pending discussion that needed to take place. It was important.

Gabriel chuckled, reminded of his own need for a bathroom break the night before.

"That's fine," he said, determined to tell her everything after collecting himself and gathering his senses. "You can use the one in my bedroom upstairs. I'm having trouble with the one down here. Third room on the left, you can't miss it."

"We probably should pull ourselves together," she said.

Gabriel made a playful sad face.

"You sure?" he asked.

"No. But it's the right thing to do," she replied.

"Boooo," he playfully responded.

They smiled at each other, giving each other another once over with seductive eyes.

"I'll be right back, I promise. And you'll have my undivided attention. And we'll finish talking about us, with no distractions."

"I'm looking forward to that," he said.

Alex grabbed his face with both hands and kissed him on the nose. Like a giddy schoolgirl, knowing his eyes were still on her, she dashed upstairs with quick, light footsteps, and headed to his bedroom.

He then yelled upstairs and said, "I'm gonna run out to my car a sec! I'll be right back!" He wasn't quite sure if she had heard him, but he planned to be back inside before she came back downstairs. He grabbed his keys and headed out the door.

When Alex walked into the master bedroom, she quickly glanced around the enormous, beautifully decorated area. She was keenly aware of his cologne lingering in the air as she passed by his walk-in closet where she could see a long row of designer suits and starched dress shirts. Standing in front of his dresser mirror, she smiled at her reflection, and then worked on getting herself back together, hair and all. She was happy. Love was all over her.

All of a sudden, her smile began to fade. It was like the sun had immediately and unexpectedly disappeared behind some clouds. One would think she was still looking at herself, but she was not. Her eyes had fell upon a framed photo that now had her attention, a picture which she had not initially noticed. Alexandria blinked furiously, not really sure if what she was actually seeing was just a trick on her eyes. Disbelief clouded her mind, and then a steady stream of panicked thoughts rushed in. Everything now seemed to be moving in slow motion.

With her hand covering her mouth and realization beginning to quickly settle in her mind, she mumbled, "Oh my God."

Attempting to fight back the desire to unravel emotionally, she found herself succumbing to it willingly.

Suddenly, her breathing became erratic.

Her mind raced.

Her heart leaped from her chest.

She mouthed the other woman's name to herself, while focused entirely on the image of Gabriel and her pictured together as a couple.

Gabriel was back in the house and searching through DVDs when he heard her coming down. "That was fast," he said. He hadn't looked up yet, so he didn't notice her tortured expression. "So what do you think you're in the mood to watch?"

There was no answer.

It took him a moment, but the silence eventually made him look up for some kind of response. When he did, he saw a troubled look in Alex's eyes. She was standing there, almost frozen, holding her bag.

"You okay?" he asked, standing to his feet.

She didn't answer.

"Alex?" He began walking slowly towards her out of concern.

"I have to go," she said, without looking at him directly.

"What's up?" he asked.

"Nothing. I really have to go." She still didn't make

eye contact with him, but there was an obvious sadness consuming her face.

"Are you not feeling well," he asked.

"Something like that," she replied.

He followed closely behind her as she headed towards the front door.

"Do you need me to take you to the hospital or something?"

"No, I'll be fine," Alex said sharply. Her eyes were beginning to well up, as she fumbled to unlock his front door.

"You got me worried." He attempted to search her face for some hint of an explanation, but she wouldn't look at him.

"Don't be. It was very nice meeting you, Gabriel." Her eyes were positioned only on the front door, purposely avoiding any eye contact with him for fear he might see her tear-filled eyes.

"Huh?"

"I really need to go, please. Just let me go."

"Okay." As he reached to unlock the door, he added, "At least let me walk you out to your car."

"Thank you, but I'll be fine," she replied, making her way out the front door and to her car without looking back.

Gabriel followed in an attempt to get some answers, but she was moving so fast that he couldn't catch her. Besides, he didn't want to upset her anymore than she already was.

"Was my bathroom not clean or something?" he shouted to her, hoping a desperate joke would stall her, giving him a chance to figure out what had suddenly upset her.

She didn't respond.

Confused, he stood back in an attempt to calm her by keeping his distance. "Can we talk about what's wrong?" he pleaded.

Again, Alex didn't answer. She was so desperately trying not to break down in front of him. All she wanted was to get in her car before she dissolved into a sobbing mess.

Finally, she realized she was inserting her house key into her car lock. Locating the correct key, she jammed it into the door. She jumped into the car and revved the engine into life. As she drove off, she glanced in her rearview mirror and saw him standing at the curb with his hands atop of his head, watching her car until it disappeared from view. She still couldn't believe it. This could not be real. Her mind continued assembling the facts, putting pieces of this life-size puzzle together. There were still parts of it missing though.

Gabriel called repeatedly to make sure she was well. She let voicemail pick up every message. On his last attempt, he said, "Alex, this is Gabriel again. I don't know what happened here, but if I did something—anything wrong, then I'm sorry. Just let me know. Please give me a call so I won't worry, okay? It doesn't matter how late. Just call me, please."

He hung up the phone and stared aimlessly at the floor with a blank expression on his face. He wondered exactly what had happened. Into the early hours of the morning he sat, replaying everything back in his mind, but there was nothing that stuck out as strange or unusual. He had been so far gone that he hadn't even noticed his script lying on the coffee table. It was only when he stood to his feet to head upstairs that he did see it. When picking up his script, a business card fell from inside. Retrieving it from off the floor, he looked at the handwriting scribbled on the back that read:

Told my cousin Stephanie about your script. She loved the plot and would like to review it. She'll be waiting to hear from you. May God richly bless the works of your hands and intentions of your heart!

Alex

Her cousin? he pondered. Confused, he flipped the business card over and it read:

Stephanie Robertson-Edwards, President
Edwards Entertainment Group, Inc.
230 West 57th Street, Ste. 2345
New York, NY 10107

Before the revelation of what this business card in hand truly meant and could fully settle in for him, the phone rang. He quickly picked it up, hoping it was her. "Hello, Al . . ."

He was about to say Alex's name, but quickly caught himself.

"Hey. Did I wake you?" a soft voice asked.

"Hey. No," he replied, still in awe as he looked at the business card.

"You're still up?" Tracee asked in a hushed tone.

"Yeah, I'm still up. Just about to hit the bed though." Gabriel managed to mask his disappointment that it wasn't Alex calling. "How's everything going?"

"I'm okay. I just wanted to call and tell you 'I love

you' before I fell asleep."

"Oh. Thanks. You sound funny, are you okay?"

"Yeah. Why?"

"Your voice sounds muffled. I can hardly hear you," Gabriel said.

"Oh. I'm okay. Everybody here at my parents is already asleep, so I'm just trying not to disturb anyone," she explained in a fast, nervous voice.

"Oh. Okay."

"I didn't call to keep you up. I know you have an early flight in the morning. I just needed to hear your voice before I fell asleep."

"I appreciate that."

"Are any of the groomsmen flying out with you?"

"No. Eddie is taking me to the airport, but then he and the rest of the fellas will be flying out later."

"Okay. Well, make sure they know that rehearsal starts promptly at seven."

"They know."

"Well, I'll let you get some rest."

"Okay, I'll see you in the morning."

"Okay, good night," she replied.

"Good night."

"Gabriel?" she called before he could hang up.

"Yes?"

"I love you."

There was a beat of silence.

"Me, too." Gabriel rubbed his forehead in frustration as he spoke. He was confused, but not as much as he was torn on the inside.

Seemingly satisfied to hear his voice, Tracee hung up her cell phone. She stared at her image in the dresser mirror, seemingly lost in thought. She was thinking that she would soon be a married woman and ever since she had said "yes" to Gabriel's proposal, the days had done nothing but fly by. Her train of thought was suddenly broken by a male voice from across the room.

"I'm done in the bathroom, Tracee. You gonna take a shower?"

It was the voice of David Williams, an old fling from her college days that she really never let go of, even when she started dating Gabriel. David stood in the middle of his bedroom in front of a full-length mirror, bare-chested with a white cotton Polo towel around his waist and smiling with pride at her conquered nakedness. He had just stepped out of the shower, drying remnants of water from his frame. Tracee looked up at him with a funny feeling in her stomach—maybe it was pangs of guilt from the inferno of unwedded, animalistic lovemaking that had just occurred between the two of them so close to her wedding day. But this half-naked, six-three, dark chocolate Zeus with a body sculpted like an African masterpiece had always held her heart in one hand and strummed her sexual cords with the other. David had a special hold on her. It was a hold that if Gabriel ever knew of it was crush him to the core, being that there was history between the two.

David was in his mid-thirties, worked in pharmaceutical sales, and was seemingly the perfect package. He would be the ideal man if he weren't such a womanizer. David passionately loved two things, himself and what a woman could give up to him. Tracee's chief complaint with him was that he just couldn't keep his 'thang' in his pants. He was the kinda guy that could sleep with her, and just as soon as she left, have another woman in his bed within the hour. Like a hummingbird, he went from flower to flower withdrawing just the right amount of sweetness from each female to satisfy his selfish desires. And knowing that, Tracee was still foolish when it came to him. His bad boy persona kept her coming back whenever she got the opportunity. He was a familiar body to help relieve stress whenever she happened to be in town or vice versa. No matter how much time passed, he maintained his prowess in bed, and the physical chemistry they shared from the past still existed. Tracee fell into David's welcoming arms for wild, unbridled sex that always had an unpredictable conclusion. Yet, in all their encounters, there was actually never an end to their noncommittal lovemaking. Each time they'd pick up where they had left off—in the bed, bodies tossing and pounding against each other.

Watching him wipe down his nude body in front of her, she shook her head in shame, realizing this was only a physical thing between them that she would eventually have to force herself to let go of. Sad thing is, she couldn't keep falling prey to the temptation of something that had been an off again and on again type of thing since her college days.

Glancing at the clock, it was now 2:45 a.m. and officially Friday morning. She thought about the fact she would be a married woman tomorrow. She shook her head in disbelief, pondering on the fact that a woman in love with the man she is due to marry would not be doing such a thing as she is right now the night before.

"You don't wanna take a shower?" David asked, mistaken her head shaking as response to his question.

"Hmh? What?" she mumbled, lost in a daze.

"I asked if you wanted to take a shower. I placed some clean towels in the bathroom for you," he motioned with his hand.

"Yes. Thank you, David," she said with a forced smile. "In a minute."

"Are you okay?"

She wasn't. Far from it.

"I'm okay," she quietly responded, while biting the bottom corner of her lip, something she did occasionally whenever she lied. As she did, she told herself that this was the last time. Promise.

Unbelievable

With her hair in disarray and still wearing her outfit from last evening, now wrinkled by a night of tossing and turning in her attempts to sleep, Alex slipped out of bed. Disoriented, she fumbled her way to the bathroom. Last night's discovery had taken a toll on her, not just emotionally, but physically as well. Not having eaten anything, she had woken with a pounding migraine and she felt unusually warm all over as if she might be coming down with something.

Moving hesitantly across the bedroom floor, she surveyed the disheveled bedcovers and bits of tissues, and felt a growing hole in her stomach. It was like the numbness she had experienced after Lionel. With Lionel, there had been something specific to grieve over—the loss of her future with the man she had loved most. With Gabriel, there was no formal relationship to speak of. He had someone else in his life. It wasn't his fault that she never asked to whom he was engaged. And she could not hold him accountable for how she was feeling. She totally blamed herself for that. She was so blinded by her emotions that she couldn't put the puzzle together. It now seemed that there were so many clues she overlooked. Even so, why did her heart feel shattered into a million pieces?

What started as a harmless friendship, was now something far more complicated, an undefined relationship with a lose-lose outcome for everyone involved. She knew his friendship had helped her to deal with the whole Lionel thing. She felt that he was sent to help her heal by opening up to someone about her pain. What else could it be? Why else would God send an unavailable man into her life if not for that purpose and that purpose alone? Falling for one another was all their doing.

Making her way downstairs and turning on the coffeemaker, she shook her head as she thought it all through again. She didn't have the strength to return Gabriel's calls. She didn't know what she could say to make any of *this* better. She couldn't call him back. She wasn't going to call him back. This was just one of those *things* she had to let go of for the good of everyone.

She then reached in the cabinet for her favorite cobalt coffee mug. Without warning, a hidden rage surfaced and she tossed the mug across the room against the kitchen wall. It shattered, falling to the floor in pieces. Angry with herself, she made her way into the family room and nestled herself in her oversized sofa, pulled her knees to her chest, and wrapped her arms tightly around a pillow. Resisting the urge to sob uncontrollably, she rocked back and forth. How had things gotten to this point?

At the sound of the doorbell she attempted to pull herself together. Who in their right mind would be ringing her doorbell at 7 a.m.? In her haste last night she had parked her car out front instead of in the garage, so she knew any attempts to pretend she was not at home were futile. She pulled herself together even more and slowly headed towards the front door. She took her time in the hope that whoever was there would give up and leave. The doorbell rang again, more insistently this time. She was irritated now and wished the world would go away and let her work out a way to deal with things.

She padded across the tile foyer. Suddenly, she became paralyzed at the thought that it could be Gabriel, who had rushed over at the first opportunity to get answers about why she had bolted last night. She felt so bad about doing that. She knew she owed him some kind of explanation. With a barrage of thoughts flooding her mind, she looked through the peephole. Wiping the tears from her eyes with a quick sweep of her hand, Alex opened the door and there standing across the threshold was the one person who always showed up at the right time.

Over morning coffee, Jaz and Alex began to unravel her saga. The two were seated on Alex's patio underneath a pristine white umbrella overlooking a plush green lawn. It had just started to rain, going from light to heavy in a matter of seconds. In the midst of their silence, as Jaz searched for something to say, the wind chimes rang softly in the light breeze.

"I can't get him out of my heart," Alex began. "He's all I've thought about, every day since we met. What's wrong with me? We don't even know each other, but then we do. Know what I mean? I don't even know if I can let him go. I don't know if I want to let him go.

Should I even care about her? I don't really know her. He said he felt the same as me. I believe him. Things are just so complicated. Why does it have to be so complicated? Oh God, what am I doing? What am I thinking? What in the world am I saying?"

Jaz sat silent, something she rarely did. She was shaking her head in disbelief, overwhelmed by all the information gushing out of her friend. She had no idea so much had been going on with Alex this week. But now, in one seemingly endless long breath, she softly whispered to Jaz everything about this man who had captured her heart. What they had done. What they had shared. How he made her feel. How she thought certain feelings had disappeared, until she met him. How when she wasn't with him, she wished they were together. And then, finally, the moment she had found out whom he was engaged to.

Jaz began, still in utter disbelief. "Wow. Tracee Andrews? And you're sure it was her?"

"Yes," Alex replied without looking at her friend, taking a sip of her coffee to steady her nerves. She was embarrassed that Jaz was finding out everything this way.

"This is unbelievable." Jaz shook her head again. "And you didn't know?"

"Of course not."

"How . . . but . . . I mean . . ."

"I don't know," she stated in a shaky, barely audible voice, "Jaz, what am I going to do?"

"This is wild. This is like somethin' you see on *Lifetime*. Stuff like *this* just does not happen to real people."

"I know. But it did. And it happened to me. Oh

God, I'm a *Lifetime* story."

"No, you're not."

"Yes I am," Alex wailed.

"And you're sure he never said anything that even hinted as to who she was?"

"Nothing. I would have remembered. But I never asked him her name either."

"Um-hm," Jaz murmured.

"I never asked him anything about her. I guess I really didn't want to know. It was easier for me if I didn't know, y'know? I guess it was selfish, but . . ."

"Does he know that you know her?"

"No. I don't think so."

"So what are you gonna do, girlfriend?"

"There's nothing I can do. I can't see him anymore, right?"

"Right," Jaz replied, uncertainly. "But . . ."

"It's not right, right? This is really horrible. I'm such a bad person." Alex placed her face in her hands.

"Right," Jaz said.

Alex lifted her face to look at Jaz.

"What?" she asked, not sure if she had heard Jaz correctly.

"I meant *wrong*. Definitely *wrong*." She placed her hand on top of Alex's to offer some form of comfort and then moved closer to put her arms around her in a hug.

"I just don't know what to do, Jaz. Why am I going through this? I've fallen for a man just a day from being married to another woman. Maybe I should have told him why I left last night, but I honestly felt like I was goin' crazy or something after finding out. My mind was running in a thousand different directions. I couldn't think of anything else to do, but get outta there."

"Don't worry about last night right now, sweetie."

Jaz rocked Alex tightly in her arms. Once again, at another traumatic turn in her girlfriend's life, Jaz found it difficult to find just the right words to comfort her dearest friend.

"It's gonna be okay. What's meant to be will be."

It was true.

CHAPTER SEVENTEEN

Letting Our Hearts Lead Us

Gabriel Washington fervently and secretly wished that the weather was bad enough to halt all outgoing flights at RDU, but it was not. The rain pelting against the large glass windows of the airport made the mood even gloomier. He wished he could be anywhere but here.

After his confession to his best man, Gabriel excused himself for some time alone. Heading in the direction of the restroom, he wasn't sure if he had done the right thing by telling Eddie what was on his mind, in his heart.

In the men's room, he suddenly felt out of breath, almost dizzy. Standing in front of the mirror, he stared at his reflection, perplexed. He ran cold water in the sink and splashed it twice over his face.

Minutes passed as he gazed aimlessly at the image before him. The sudden inclination to try calling her one final time came over him. He needed to gauge how she was feeling towards him, even though her voicemail was the only contact he'd had with her since she had ran out last night.

After drying his face, he quickly flipped open his cell phone and anxiously dialed her number, one he now dialed without effort. With his cell phone battery completely dead, there was no use in trying to get a call to go through. Stepping out of the restroom, he quickly headed in the direction of the airport pay phones.

Alex was just stepping out of the shower when she heard the phone ringing. She walked quickly over to the nightstand, drying her naked body in the process. She glanced at the caller ID that read "Unknown Name, Unknown Number" on the display. *Telemarketers*, she thought, disregarding the ringing phone as she headed back into the bathroom. When it stopped ringing, she could hear the sound of rain pelting against her windowpane, then the phone suddenly started ringing again. She stopped halfway to the bathroom, letting out an exhausted sigh.

"Alex, you want me to get that," Jaz yelled from downstairs.

"No, I'll get it Jaz," she yelled back.

She sighed heavily and decided to answer it. It was the same "Unknown Name, Unknown Number" caller again. She was fully prepared to tell whatever telemarketer it was to remove her from their list and never call again.

She picked up the phone and sternly answered, "Hello."

There was a beat of silence.

"Hey . . . Hello?"

Something inside her leapt at the sound of Gabriel's voice. She had missed it in just these few short hours.

"Hi," she replied in a somber tone.

Two people who had never had so much as a quiet moment together since they met, were now silent over the phone, both not sure what to say next. Gabriel was unprepared for the fact that she might actually answer the phone rather than leave him to relay his thoughts into her voicemail. He had prepared himself to deal with a machine, little chance of rejection there. If she hated him for whatever unknown reason, he would never have to know.

What was left to say? she thought. One last conversation wasn't going to change anything . . . the fact that he was engaged to be married . . . the fact he just happened to be engaged to a woman she somewhat knew . . . nor the fact they would never have a chance to fully experience the *thing* that had developed between the two of them. It all grieved her heart and she didn't know what to say to him. If she had known he was the "Unknown" caller, she would have fought back the desire to pick up.

But that hadn't happened.

Instead, there Gabriel stood in an airport silently holding a pay phone, unsure where this conversation might lead while wondering whether this could really be the end. And right now the silence seemed endless. He took a deep breath and mumbled in the receiver, "How are you?"

"I guess I'm fine." She fought back the emotions bubbling inside her and tried to keep her voice from shaking.

"I was hoping you would call me, and . . . I'm sorry. I didn't even ask if you were busy," he said.

"No, I'm okay."

"Okay."

"Where are you?" she asked.

"At the airport."

"Oh." Her voice dropped. She didn't have to ask why he was there. She knew.

"I just wanted to call and say 'thank you'."

"For what?"

"For everything. The positive words. Your prayers. Everything. You've really changed my life. There's not too many people I can say that about after four days."

"Noooo, I've done nothing but complicate it."

"You haven't."

"Gabriel."

"I'm sorry," he softly blurted out, voice shaking.

"For what?" she asked.

"I don't know. For anything I did. I'm just sorry."

"Everything will be okay. Really."

"No." He was searching for the right words, something to make things right between them. "Maybe I was pushing you too fast. I don't know. I didn't mean to rush you with all that talk I was talking and . . ."

She half-smiled to herself and said quietly, "You don't have to apologize for anything. You didn't do a thing wrong. It's okay, Gabriel. Really it is."

There it was again, that beautiful way she had of saying his name.

"It doesn't feel like it's okay. I thought . . ."

"It really is, or at least it will be," she interjected. But deep down everything wasn't okay. She had deep feelings for this man, but she had to resist each and every one of them at all cost.

There was another brief silence as they both stood holding their receivers.

Gabriel then asked, "Can I come and see you?"

"No," she replied quickly, even though her whole body screamed "yes, come and get me."

"Alex . . . please. If we could just see each other, I know it'll make it all better—whatever's wrong." His eyes began to well up.

"I can't. We can't. You know that."

"We just need to talk. Is there anything wrong with that?"

"Yes. Gabriel . . . don't. Please. Don't do this to me."

"Please tell me what's wrong?" he pleaded.

"*This*," she said.

"What?" he questioned, completely clueless to what *this* referred to at this point. He waited, palpably excited to finally hear what had caused things to fall apart between them. But there was silence once again.

"Gabriel . . . please," Alex began.

"Look, just . . . just talk to me," he begged. "Tell me what's wrong. Whatever it is, I can make it right. Just give me the chance to make it right."

Taking a deep breath, she said, "You and me. *This*. Us and this, and this *thing* we've been calling ourselves doing. It's not right and I'm being punished for it." Her voice began to tremble as tears filled her eyes. She quickly wiped them away.

"I'm not understanding."

"I'm sorry, Gabriel," she said in a small whisper.

"You can talk to me. I'm here for you. You know that, right?"

"Yes, but Gabriel . . ."

Tightly gripping the pay phone in desperation, he said, "Please just tell me what I can do to make *this* right."

"There's nothing that can be done. We just can't do *this*."

"Do what?" he pleaded. He needed to know what

she was thinking. He felt like a man dying from thirst while someone dangled a water bottle directly in front of him, tantalizingly out of reach.

"I just can't see you anymore. It's not right."

"Alex, don't say that. What's wrong? Please tell me *something*. I'm going crazy. Don't do this."

"You're getting married, I'm still married, and that's what's wrong. I think somewhere along the way we tried to pretend differently."

Realizing she was right, he dropped his head and said, "I know, but . . ."

She continued, "And I've allowed myself to fall for an unavailable man. How is that possible? I've only known you for a few days."

"I know it seems crazy, but it's not. You know how I feel about you."

She was struggling to hold back her emotions and keep her voice steady. "But you're already obligated to someone. We shouldn't have let *this* happen. I don't know what we were doing. What *were* we doing?"

"We *were* letting our *hearts* lead us," he answered.

Alex continued, speaking as if she hadn't heard his reply, "We were making plans and pretending, fooling ourselves—that's what we were doing."

"Alex?"

She suddenly burst out in a soft cry, "Oh God, I'm so sorry."

Gabriel could hear her quiet sobs and ached to reach out and hold her, to comfort her. It was killing him not to be there with her, holding her in his arms through this. "Alex, please don't cry. What have I done? Alex?"

She didn't answer, but he knew she was still there.

"Alex, do you need me? I can leave here right now

and be there if you need me," he said.

"No." That one short word took all her strength.

"I can be there. Look. Nothing else matters."

"Don't say that."

"It's true. I haven't even begun to show you how I feel," he said.

Shaking her head, she whispered, "No. Please don't say that."

"But it's true."

"Take care, Gabriel. Okay?" she sighed.

With tears now streaming down his cheeks, he wasn't ready to hang up or give up on what they had created between them. Somehow things had to work out between them and Gabriel knew he needed to see her to make it right.

"Alex?"

"Good-bye, Gabriel. Thank you for calling. I wish you the best, okay?"

She continued listening to his voice as he murmured her name over and over. Persistence was one of the things that had first attracted her to him and it was that same unwavering characteristic that now made it hard for her to let go. Yet she stood strong. She felt a deep ache inside, but still she resisted. She had no choice. The emotional wall that she had built after Lionel was still there protecting her and stopping her from completely surrendering to her feelings.

"Alex, please don't hang up on me."

"I'll miss you," she softly whispered.

"Nooo. Don't hang up."

Her name from his lips were the last words Alex heard him say into the phone before she hung up, eyes studded with tears, struggling to convince herself that she had done the right thing. She sat motionless, not knowing what else to do.

Suddenly, the phone began to ring endlessly.

After several times and no answer on her part, it finally stopped.

And then, it rang again.

It stopped.

It rang again.

It finally stopped.

She was lost. Somehow or another, Gabriel held onto a glimmer of hope for the two of them. But how could he? She couldn't see it. They both knew the situation, although he wasn't completely aware of just how much she knew. They had landed in the midst of an impossible scenario where nothing made sense. She knew she was going to hate herself for refusing to even give him a chance, but of course that would be the price she would have to pay in order to do what she felt was right. On second thought, maybe *this* was kismet—destiny. Right now, she refused to submit, to surrender, and to accept the fact that she cared for this man more deeply than he would ever know. She didn't know what to make of these feelings. She hesitated to make any sort of move. And then there was his innocent fiancée. Alex was sure she loved him. How could she not? She didn't understand why she had fallen so hard so quickly. She hated herself for hesitating when it came to going after what she wanted.

And what she wanted right now . . . was Gabriel.

CHAPTER EIGHTEEN

Something Feels Wrong

"Sorry I'm late," Tracee said, breaking Gabriel's hypnotic stare at the carousel while he waited for his luggage to make an appearance.

Exchanging an awkward and quick hug with Tracee, he mumbled, "Hey. No problem."

"Traffic is just terrible at this time of the day," she rambled, unable to look him directly in the eyes for more than two seconds. The guilt of the previous night still lingered.

"You look nice," he said, commenting on the two-piece periwinkle suit with a sheer ivory-colored blouse that she was wearing.

"Thanks," she replied, shifting her weight from one foot to the other. Finally glancing at him, she noticed a distant, perplexed expression on his face. "You okay?" she inquired.

He gave a weak nod and said, "Just exhausted, that's all. I'm okay."

"Well, it's good to see you," she said, cuddling close to him. "This had to be the longest week, don't you agree? It seemed like it took forever for this weekend to get here."

"Um-hm," he murmured. "You look nice," he said again, dazed, not even looking at her.

She gave him an odd stare.

"Yes, you just told me. But thank you again."

Sensing Gabriel's distant mood, she looked at him again for a clue. It was truly unusual to see him this way. Regardless, she was determined not to allow anything to distract them from her 'to do' list.

"Okay," Tracee said, as Gabriel claimed his bags. "Well, let's get outta here so we won't be late." She took his tuxedo bag from him.

"Late for what?" he asked.

Whipping out her list, she went over their schedule for the entire day. "First," she informed him, "Reverend Allen wants to meet with us for lunch to have one more informal premarital counseling session. We have about thirty-five minutes to get to the restaurant." Without noticing Gabriel's annoyed expression, she looked at her watch and continued, "We'll have to hurry."

Listening to her demanding voice, Gabriel was reminded how much he disliked being told things at the last minute. He's also told Tracee time and again to stop planning things without giving him ample heads up, yet she persisted.

"Tracee, why didn't you tell me this when I talked to you earlier?" Gabriel asked in a subdued tone, trying to control his frustration as they made their way to exit the airport.

Noticing that he had called her *Tracee* instead of *Tracee*, something he did whenever he became frustrated with her, she innocently replied, "I honestly thought I had mentioned it. Sorry. Don't get your panties in such a bunch over nothing."

Gabriel took a deep breath, struggling to maintain his composure. Making plans without giving him an opportunity to weigh in was Tracee's way of controlling and manipulating their relationship. Gabriel knew it. So did she.

He gently caught her arm, stopping her from walking any further. Looking directly in her eyes, speaking to her slowly and deliberately as if reprimanding a child, he said, "Tracee, we both know you didn't tell me about this appointment, otherwise we wouldn't be having this conversation. I talked to you twice yesterday and several times this morning and you didn't say a word about this."

"Okay, I'm sorry. Geez. I didn't think it was that big of a deal." She gently pulled her arm from his grasp. "What's up with you?"

"Look at me," he said, glancing himself over. "I'm wearing jeans and a polo shirt. And I have flip flops on."

"You look okay," she said flatly.

"Maybe to go to a movie, but we're meeting this man at a restaurant. Look at you. You're wearing a freakin' business suit."

"Okay, okay, then change. Don't have a stroke about it. Let's just go, please. I really don't see what the big deal is."

"Of course you don't."

Glancing at her watch, she began walking again. Gabriel followed closely behind. He was starting to feel queasy. His unfinished business with Alex, the early morning flight, and now having to face a day-long, event-filled schedule was beginning to weigh on him. Coming to the conclusion that his behavior had more to do with something he had not yet admitted, Gabriel took another deep breath.

Suddenly coming to a complete stop, his bags slipped from his hands and his legs stood motionless as if his feet were bolted to the floor. He couldn't move if he wanted to. Tracee continued walking, completely unaware that he was no longer by her side. When she finally realized he was not responding to her commentary, she paused. Looked around. There, standing twenty feet away in the middle of the airport was Gabriel.

"Gabriel?" Tracee called, as she slowly walked towards him. "Are you okay?"

He didn't answer.

"Gabriel?" she called a second time, only steps away from him now.

When she finally was close enough, he pulled her closer and took a heavy breath. He whispered in her ear, "I'm sorry."

Those two words confused her. Here stood her fiancé, seemingly having a nervous breakdown of some sorts in the middle of the airport and saying he was sorry. Sorry for what? She had no idea what he was talking about.

"What are you apologizing for?" she asked, with a look of concern.

A deafening silence fell between them.

He then said, "You know that I love you, don't you?"

Nervous, she wasn't sure whether she should answer that question or not.

"Of course. Now we're going to be late, sweetie. We need to go," she said, pulling his arm to get him moving again.

He didn't budge.

He continued, "And that I would never do anything to purposely hurt you?"

"Yes. Now what is it? We really need to go if you're going to change."

Gabriel's eyes dropped to the floor as he searched for a way to explain.

"Tracee . . ."

"I apologize for not telling you about this *thing* with Reverend Allen."

"It's okay. It's not just that."

"Then what?" Tracee, still confused, was becoming noticeably agitated. She looked around, checking to see if people were watching them. "Let's go sit down for a minute," she suggested, attempting to pull him towards a seat. "People are starting to stare."

Still, he didn't budge.

"What's going on?" he asked.

"We're standing in the middle of the airport like fools, that's what's going on," she replied.

"No. I mean with us?"

"What are you talking about? Everything's fine with us. Right?"

Gabriel didn't answer immediately.

"I don't know. There's this emptiness inside of me that I can't seem to shake. Like there's a hole inside of me or something." He rested his forehead in his right hand. "Something just feels wrong."

"Wrong?"

"Yes. Don't you feel it?"

She removed his hand from his face. "Will you please tell me what you're talking about? And why are you acting so strange? You've been like this since I talked to you earlier. I don't know what else to tell you.

Nothing's wrong."

"Do you really love me?" he asked her.

"We're getting married, what kind of question is that? And why are you talking like this? You're making me feel really uneasy." Still unsure about where this was headed, she searched his face quizzically.

Gabriel took a deep breath, and then said, "I've changed."

"Okay. And?"

"And I'm not the same person I was before you left."

"Left where? To come here? Maryland?" She was looking at him now like he was losing his mind.

"Yes."

"Okay. Then who are you?" she asked, confused.

"We're making a mistake."

Her eyes dropped to the floor as she tried to comprehend what he had just said to her. There was deafening silence between them, until Tracee finally responded.

"What are you saying?"

He sighed heavily.

"I think we've been forcing this. I can't say us getting married is the right thing for us to do. I'd rather tell you now than a year from now. My heart isn't in it."

It took Tracee a moment. She finally looked into Gabriel's eyes for further understanding of what had just been relayed to her.

"You are not doing this to me the day before my wedding. I know not."

"Tracee?"

She looked off, in disbelief. The more Gabriel tried to explain how he was feeling, the more Tracee wasn't hearing it. He continued, but was literally talking to himself. All Tracee could think about was the possibility of the wedding being off and how embarrassing it would be. There was a beat of silence between the two, as Gabriel waited for a response.

Finally, it came.

Not showing just how livid she was, Tracee gave him a half-crazed smile. She stood back and just stared at him for a moment.

"You know this is really messed up," she said.

"I'm sorry."

"You're sorry?" She gritted her teeth. "Don't you do this to me."

"I can't."

There was a beat of deafening silence.

Suddenly, Tracee hauled off and smacked Gabriel hard and loud.

"Who do you think you are?! How dare you!!"

"Tracee."

"You can go to hell, Gabriel. I mean it."

His bag purposely slipped from her hands and to the floor. Just as she began to turn away, Gabriel reached, and quietly called, "Tracee?"

"Don't touch me! Get off me!" she shouted, pulling away from his grasp, pushing him back, and then walking away. "Don't you ever touch me again!"

People paused briefly in their stride to see what the commotion was about.

"Tracee . . ." he called again, in a hushed tone, prepared to go after her, but his legs wouldn't carry him a step closer.

He quietly called her name again, but this time it was so softly that he could hardly hear himself. He watched her as she kept walking. Her stride was easy and smooth, almost calculated. *He really needs to be reminded of what he has*, she thought, as if walking away would bring him to his senses of what he was about to lose. She began counting in her head, estimating by the time she reached ten he would be on his hands and knees behind her. She wanted to turn around to see the fearful expression on his face, but she didn't. She kept walking, giving him a few more seconds, waiting to feel his presence behind her. After he came crawling, she was going to use this lapse in good judgment to her advantage. Nothing was going to interfere with her picture-perfect plan—no *thing* with David on her part or Gabriel having cold feet. She was determined to marry the prince, just as everyone expected, and live happily ever after. Period.

After a few seconds, Tracee felt a presence behind her. She slowed her pace. She grinned and thought how well she knew him, running behind her like a puppy dog. *I'm Tracee Andrews. You don't do this to me,* she said in her mind.

Taking two final steps, she ended her countdown on five, four, three . . . and then turned. To her amazement, there was no one behind her—only a steady stream of airport commuters brushing up against her in their hurriedness. What?

Confused, she frantically searched the crowd for Gabriel's face. He was no longer standing where she had left him. He had vanished in a sea of strangers. And, for the first time, Tracee didn't know what to think. Gabriel's predictable good nature and willingness to go the extra mile to please her was something she could count on in any disagreement.

But, suddenly, Gabriel was gone and Tracee didn't understand.

CHAPTER NINETEEN

Really Messed Up

After Jaz had left, Alex took a long drive to try to clear her head before her afternoon meeting. With the rain steadily pounding on her windshield, she drove along the winding road leading to her house, noticing neither scenery nor passing vehicles. Finally pulling into the driveway of her home, she sat in her car attempting to summon the strength to go in. She looked through the rain-stained windshield into the distance. What she saw was a male figure walking down the steps of her porch.

Gabriel? The thought had crossed her mind.

Her heart raced at the thought. But then it slowed when she realized it was not Gabriel. It was Lionel, with a bouquet of flowers in hand. She hadn't even noticed his Denali parked on the street when she pulled in. She'd not seen him since she moved back to North Carolina. Seeing him standing there only brought back vivid memories of their exchange of words that still echoed clearly in her head.

"I SAID GET OUT!" she had screamed at the top of her lungs, furious.

"At least let me explain," Lionel pleaded while following closely behind Alex in desperation, like a man about to lose everything sacred to him.

"No! You have to go! Right now!" she insisted, pointing to the front door, not wanting to hear any of it. "I can't believe you even thought you could come back here."

"Alex, don't . . ."

"I'm not going to tell you again to get out," she asserted angrily, interrupting. "If you don't leave now I'll have the police escort you out. Try me. I am dead serious."

"What? How can you say that to me like you don't even know me? I'm your husband. This is my house, too." Lionel's facial expression was one of genuine confusion and bewilderment.

"After something like this, I don't know you," she uttered coldly.

"Don't say that," he murmured, shaking his head.

Pacing heavily, she said, "It's the truth. But liars don't know anything about the truth. You're a liar, Lionel. I never thought I would say that about you, but you're a liar. I can't trust you, in or out of my sight. And I can't be with you."

"Sweetie, please. Can you stop for a minute so we can talk about this?" he begged. "It's not what it seems. You gotta believe me."

"I don't want to hear anything you have to say. And what do you think you could possibly tell me that would be worth listening to? Huh? More lies, Lionel? Is that what you want to tell me? I already know the truth. I know what you did. Everyone knows what you did, who you are. It's in the paper. On TV. The radio. How could you?"

He dropped his head in shame, realizing he had

failed. The pain in her eyes was so evident, and hurting her was hurting him. After a brief moment, he said, "I'm sorry."

"Yes, you are," she smirked, in disgust. "About the sorriest I've ever seen. And sad. You're not the man I thought I was marrying."

Lionel let out a heavy sigh.

"I really messed up, I know it," he added, as if he was confessing to something.

"You're right, you did," she said sharply. "I was good to you, Lionel. I've never given you a reason to do something like this to me. Never. I don't deserve this. If you weren't happy at home, then . . ."

"It's not that."

"What is wrong with you? And with a tra . . ."

He interrupted before she could finish, and said, "I don't know. I mean, nothing. It's not like that. I'm not like that."

"You need to go. You're sick." Her face was serious. "And the more I think about it, it's making me sick. I literally feel like I'm going to throw up."

"Oh God, help me. Babe. Please. I don't want to lose you," Lionel said.

"Don't you get it . . . you already have. I can't be with you." Her facial expression displayed pure disgust when she said the words. "And honestly, it's taking everything in me not to put a bullet in your behind right now. That's the place you've taken me to."

Lionel suddenly realized she was serious. Never having seen her like this, the look in her eyes had him cautious.

"I'm really hating myself right now."

"Not more than I am towards you," Alex replied.

She took a breath. "Why won't you just leave? Why are you still standing here? Do you want me to shoot you?"

Lionel's departure was Alexandria's only concern at this point. She needed him out of this house and out of her life before she did something she would regret. But he didn't move. It was like he thought he was going to change things.

"You know what . . . keep standing there," Alex said.

She brushed by him, seething with rage as she bolted from one room to another looking for where she had placed her cordless phone. "I'm calling the police. They're real sympathetic to black men in domestic situations, especially ones with an already pending case for something else."

"Don't do this to us. Please," he begged, walking right on her heels.

Now with phone in hand, she quickly turned around to him enraged. Pointing her index finger directly in his face, she said sternly, "You did this! Don't you dare try to turn this around on me! Don't you dare. So just stop it. I'm tired and I don't have the strength to do this with you anymore. Do you realize what you've done?! You can't fix this. There's no fixing it. No matter what you say, or try to do, you can't. Your lawyers might be able to make it go away, but your money can't fix us. I just don't want you anymore. I shouldn't have married you. You are the worst mistake of my life!"

"Please," he continued to beg, his voice even more pitiful than before.

"I thought you were different. You're not. You're worse."

"Babe?"

Lionel attempted to reach out to embrace Alexandria. Before he could succeed, she turned on him in a fury. "Boy, don't touch me!" she yelled and, before she knew it, she had hit him hard against the side of his head with the phone, missing her intended aim for his face.

Lionel was frozen in surprise, eyes blinking repeatedly from the unexpected blow. It was obvious the hit hurt like hell from the explicit word that fell from his mouth. Then, before he could utter a word, and for good measure, Alexandria hit him a second time, this one landing across the right side of his face – hindering any form of composure on his part. Lionel looked at her directly in her eyes, his eyes almost to the point of welling up. He was now standing there as if he was asking to be hit if it would make her feel any better.

"You deserve much worse, and you know it," she said coldly.

"I'm ashamed."

"You're pathetic," she said, looking him directly in his eyes.

The longer he stood there, and the more he tried to explain how he was innocent and that he was set up, the clearer it became that he was lying.

She couldn't help but to recall when she found out. Preparing dinner in the kitchen and hearing the words of the CNN reporter saying her husband's name, demanded her to stop what she was doing and direct her focus. Looking at a mug shot of her husband pop up on the television screen and the caption below it had her complete attention. She stood in disbelief.

"Lionel 'LJ' Jones, the former right fielder for the Mets, and at one time the leagues most feared sluggers, was arrested early Thursday morning in Tampa, Florida. He has been charged with soliciting sex from a transsexual prostitute. According to authorities, Jones paid $300, but denies any sexual activity occurred. According to police reports, he has stated he did not know the individual was a transsexual. During the arrest, a small amount of cocaine was also found in his possession. If convicted, he faces a maximum of one year in prison on the solicitation charge, a misdemeanor. And up to 2 years for the drug charge. He is out of jail tonight after posting $25,000 bail. Jones currently heads up one of the most sought after sports management companies around, representing some of the biggest athletes today. He resides in Dallas with his wife."

Wait a minute. Arrested? Soliciting? Transsexual? Prostitution? Cocaine? What the . . . ?!

Weak in the knees, Alex was mortified by the time they had finished the story. Shaking her head, she was so angry and completely disgusted by the thought of it all. She had stood by this man through the good and bad, been nothing less than the faithful wife she had vowed to be. And now this! She physically started to throw up. She was sick.

Sitting in her car right now, she thought about how much she hated him that day. But right now, to her surprise, she discovered she felt more at peace with herself if nothing else. What was done was done. He was the one that had to pay for his mistakes. Even though she was still hurt by his betrayal, she didn't hate him anymore. She did hate what he had done and who he had become. She wished she had seen it coming. She would have been better prepared to handle the blow.

She stepped out of her car and, not realizing she had placed her cell phone in her lap while driving, when she stood it fell and hit the concrete pretty hard. She sighed in frustration as she picked it up, not sure of the damage that had been done. It was pretty banged up. She tossed the phone in her bag, and would have to deal with the matter of whether it was still functional or not later.

She made her way up the driveway. Her facial expression was neutral, giving Lionel no clues about how she was feeling at the sight of him. Her heart was tired and she didn't have the energy. She didn't want to argue. She didn't want to talk. She didn't want to see him. Didn't want to ask how he found her. It was still early, but it had been such a long day already. She definitely didn't have any emotional resources for this and was determined to end it smoothly without confrontation.

"Hi," Lionel said.

She said nothing, steadily walking to the front door without breaking her stride. Walking pass him as if he wasn't there, she purposely avoided eye contact with him. Even though it hurt her to see him again, she felt she was in the presence of a stranger. With all that had occurred between them, she could not deny she often thought of the love they once shared. It had been, at one time, a one-of-a-kind love, or so she had thought. Now, she felt dead on the inside even being this close to him.

She made her way up the steps of the front porch and keyed herself inside the house. When she opened the door, Lionel was behind her, quietly calling out her name in hopes of having a minute of her time. Without looking back, Alex closed the door gently behind her, leaving Lionel standing alone and bewildered on the doorstep. He looked like a pure fool.

CHAPTER TWENTY

I'll Miss You

Alexandria's voicemail immediately picked up, without so much as a ring.

"Alex, this is Gabriel. Ummm . . . will you please give me a call on my cell as soon as you get this message? I've got about one bar left on my phone, so I'm hoping I'll hear from you before my phone goes completely dead. I'm back in town, just leaving my house. I really need to see you." He glanced at his watch. "It's almost two o'clock now. I remember you said you had a meeting at one-thirty today. If you would hang around until I got there then I'll explain everything. But I'd rather see you face-to-face to do that. I don't want to do it over the phone. I'm on my way towards downtown right now." Gabriel spoke quickly, hoping his phone wouldn't cut him off before he could complete his message. "And I should be there in the next thirty . . ."

His phone went dead before he could complete his final sentence. He made his way off the exit ramp and into the thick of traffic. He hoped she would check her messages soon and that she wouldn't leave until they really had a chance to talk. Nervously tapping his fingertips on the steering wheel, he drifted from lane to lane occasionally, unconsciously cutting off other drivers in his path.

It only took him twenty minutes to reach downtown and another five to arrive at Ramona's. As he was searching for a parking space, he saw Alex's car parked in one of the available spaces. He smiled to himself as he took the parking spot of a car that was just pulling off. He threw the car in park and jumped out and into a steady rain, forgetting his umbrella. He made his way across the street, and as he did, his eyes shifted to the window of the restaurant. He immediately froze in his tracks when his feet made contact with the sidewalk. He blinked several times. His heart soared a bit. From outside looking in, he could see Alex already seated at a table. She was alone.

Before moving another step forward, Gabriel took advantage of the fact Alex hadn't yet noticed him. Flashbacks of the time they had spent together in this very place suddenly raced through his mind. It brought a huge smile across his face. With his heart beating even faster, he started inside, but hesitated just a second at the sight of her seemingly wiping tears from her cheek. He hoped it wasn't because of him.

As Gabriel stepped into the restaurant, he started in Alex's direction. He was almost to her, but the sight of another man heading in the direction of her table as well brought an immediate air of confusion over him. Gabriel knew he had seen this face before, but he couldn't immediately remember where or when. He slowed his pace, and kept looking and trying to recall. Suddenly it hit him like a ton of bricks.

"Lionel," he mumbled the name to himself, remembering his face from his days of playing with the Mets. Trying to comprehend the situation, the two men's eyes met briefly as Gabriel watched Lionel beat him to Alexandria's table before he could get there himself. Lionel took the seat directly across from her.

Unseen by Alex, Gabriel slowly grabbed an unoccupied table not too far away from the two and slid into the seat. He tried to make sense of what might be happening here. He thought Alex was waiting on his arrival, but apparently not. In an earshot of the two, Gabriel was able to make out their conversation. Their talk began as just casual conversation. After awhile, Gabriel overheard Lionel speaking on his recent prognosis of doctor's discovering he had colon cancer and that he would have to undergo chemotherapy. He admitted he was scared.

While speaking to Lionel, Alex's voice remained soft and understanding. If she was angry for what had occurred in their past, she didn't let it show now. There was no anger in her tone. She expressed to him how deeply sadden she was to hear that. It was evident that she still cared about his well-being.

From his seat, Gabriel couldn't see Lionel's face, but he could hear his voice trembling as he spoke about his current health crisis. There was a long pause in their conversation. Gabriel's imagination took over and he envisioned Alex holding Lionel's hand to comfort him during their silent moment. He dared not look over his shoulder for fear he might somehow be discovered, although he was sitting with his back to Alexandria's. It was obvious to Gabriel that she understood.

After further conversation, and even Alex saying

a short prayer for him and his health while they sat—Lionel eventually shifted things.

"I have to let you know that this entire situation has only made me realize just how much I really need you, Alex. That I shouldn't take the ones who mean the most to me for granted. I made a foolish mistake that I'm still paying for. I'm grateful that you're even willing to be here for me right now, just sitting here. But it kills me everyday that we're not together. I believe that will take me out quicker than the cancer would. I didn't mean to hurt you, hurt us—and destroy what we built together. I know it wasn't right. The things that I did weren't me. I wasn't myself. I was stupid. I thought I could find the answers in the drugs, that it would somehow make all I was dealing with go away. I don't expect an 'I'm sorry' to undo the pain I've caused you, but you must know that I'm not a horrible person. I'm not the monster the media has made me out to be. I'm still the same Lionel you fell in love with. But somewhere along the way I lost myself, my way. I've given my life to God, going to church now, trying to do the right thing."

"Good for you, you need God," she calmly interjected.

He took a deep sigh as if he was displeased with himself. "I do. I know it," he said. "I just hate I lost you before I found Him."

"I've never been as disappointed in another human-being as I am you," she said, slowly shaking her head at him. "I still don't understand. Were you not getting something you needed at home? Why did you feel the need to do something like that?"

Lionel dropped his head. He was still ashamed. Alex's words cut him deeply and, with his head bowed, he mumbled, "It wasn't that. You are everything I need."

"Then what?"

"I don't have an answer. It was just stupid."

"Foolish," Alex corrected.

"Yes," he sighed. "But, for the record, I'm not gay. I'm not into that."

"I know you're not," she replied.

"I honestly had no idea that she was a . . ."

"I know you didn't know. I believe that."

"I had never, and I promise you, did anything like that in my life."

"I can't say I believe that," she replied, looking him dead in his eyes.

"It's the truth."

"I guess you're the only one that knows for sure."

"I don't expect you to forget the pain I've caused both of us. I'm willing to accept that this all is going to take more time, and that's what I've been trying to give you. And that's why I've stayed away, kept my distance—because it's a lot to ask, I know, without some healing involved. And I realize it's not going to be a quick fix, but I want to save our marriage. I'm willing to do what it takes. I'm clean. I'm done with that," he said, sincerely. "Whatever needs to be done to make us *right* again, I'll do it."

She replied, "I stood by you so many times. I believed in you when no one else did. When I think of all the lies and everything I thought . . ."

Lionel gently interrupted, "I know, and there's no excuse for what I've done. None at all. And as God is my witness, if you would just give us another chance to start fresh, I will show you what you mean to me. No more lies. No secrets. Nothing."

Alex looked at him, remaining silent for a moment. She looked nauseous.

"I'm getting sick even talking about this again," she said, with her head resting in her hand as if a migraine was on the horizon.

Gabriel could hear Lionel's voice shaking as he spoke, his mind visualizing the man's anguished facial expression. Gabriel rubbed his forehead as he sat hunched over, listening intently. He wanted to get up right now and carry Alex out of this place, far away from Lionel's pleas. If only he could make her aware of his feelings before Lionel confused her. His heart was racing as he sat tensely on the edge of his chair, readying himself to jump up and declare his need for her. But, he remained fixed in his seat, listening to their conversation. He needed to know more about what Alex was feeling before he intervened. His mind was filled with unanswered questions. Did she still love this man as she did before? Was he being sincere? Was their marriage salvageable?

Gabriel waited and listened.

Lionel continued, now talking about the past and how much fun they used to have. He asked Alex did she remember this and did she remember that. He brought up the trips they took to Europe, Hawaii, and the Virgin Islands. They laughed privately about their shared moments, things they only knew. The memories he spoke of were ones that couldn't possibly be erased. From the way Lionel spoke, Gabriel could sense that this man was sincere in his plea to win her back, which frightened Gabriel to the core. Possibilities existed, but they seemed to be more related to Lionel actually winning her heart again—not for her and Gabriel. After all, it wasn't as if Lionel had just stopped loving her. He had made a horrific mistake, done the unthinkable, and he was apparently still paying a huge price, especially when it involved losing Alex.

Realizing this, Gabriel was prepared to walk out and away from Alex if he sensed there was a possibility she and Lionel might reunite. With that—he was willing, but not wanting, to say good-bye and walk away quietly as much as it would pain him. He cared for her enough to sacrifice his own happiness for hers. Maybe that's why she ran out last night. Maybe she realized her marriage was more important than this undefined "thing" that existed between them. That had to be it, he reasoned. It was all starting to make sense to him now. Echoing in his head were the words she had once said to him about her marriage always meaning more to her than anything. Gabriel had to consider that she and Lionel were still legally married. Alex was Lionel's wife, and Gabriel couldn't change that.

Gabriel considered that possibly leaving now was for the best. He certainly didn't want her to know he was here, eavesdropping on their conversation. He didn't want to cause her any more pain. The acute anguish of being so close, yet so distant, was overtaking him and slowly killing him inside. He needed to leave now. His feelings were much stronger than he had realized which was making this even harder. He heard the voice of his Uncle Arthur saying, "Listen to your *heart*. Let your *soul* confirm what you hear." Right now, his heart was telling him that he didn't want to be without her. It was telling him he needed to stand up right now and declare his feelings openly for this woman. He wanted to let her know that he had come back for her. His soul was confirming that's exactly the thing he needed to do.

Coming to his senses, he realized that his own selfish needs were not as important as what was best for Alex. Humbled, Gabriel sat immobile, waiting for a defining moment to confirm whether he should leave or stay. Within, he already knew the answer.

Suddenly he heard Lionel ask, "Do you still love me?"

There was a long moment of silence between Alexandria and Lionel.

Alex finally answered, "Yes. I still love you, Lionel."

Gabriel envisioned Lionel smiling big when Alexandria replied with the words *Yes. I still love you.* Gabriel felt an overwhelming sadness settle inside him. It was the kind that makes you feel hollow.

"So, then what does that mean for us?" Lionel asked.

Alex's response to Lionel's question had physically drained Gabriel, to the point he appeared deflated. She still loved Lionel. What else was there to say? What else did Gabriel need to hear? It was now clear to him that this was the defining moment that he had been waiting for. It was time to go.

Rising from his table, and without turning around, Gabriel moved slowly towards the door. He was willing to be the noble one here if that guaranteed Alexandria's happiness. It was seemingly over for him and her.

As he placed his hand on the doorknob, he froze for a moment as if he had second thoughts about leaving. He resisted the overwhelming urge to take one final look at her. Doing so would hurt even more. He took a deep and heavy sigh, his heart extremely heavy. Was this right? Or had it been wrong from the beginning?

Then, just before he stepped out of this place, Gabriel whispered a few final words, as if Alexandria could somehow hear them.

"I'll miss you, Alex," he said.

" . . . I'm really going to miss you," Alex replied, her facial expression one that appeared perplexed, as if saying the very words aloud pained her heart.

There was a moment of pure quietness. The noise of Ramona's had somehow halted all of a sudden, and all movement that was had quickly become no more.

Alexandria closed her eyes, as if she had finally let go of something that once was truly special to her. The feeling resulted in a sigh of relief.

She reopened her eyes at the sound of Lionel's voice.

"What?" Lionel wasn't sure what she meant. Alex had just said she still loved him. Thinking she hadn't fully understood what he had asked, Lionel repeated himself.

"I asked you what does that mean for us? You know I still love you, too."

There was a beat.

Alex slowly repeated herself from her earlier statement to him just moments before.

"I said, it only means that . . . *I'm really going to miss you, Lionel.*"

"Hm?"

"Nothing more," she added.

After a few final words between the two of them, and Alex letting Lionel know that the chances of them reconciling were not possible, she assured him that she would be there to support him through his chemo if she was needed. She reiterated a final time on her stand of moving on without him, but cared enough to be there for him during his health crisis. With that, she slowly rose from their table, said her good-bye, and then headed towards the exit.

As she did, she felt a sense of peace and optimism immediately return unto her spirit. She was going to be fine. She walked out of Ramona's filled with promise and possibilities. Life awaited her and she was certain true love would be just around the corner, finding her in the most unexpected place and at the most unexpected time.

As Lionel watched her leave this place, his eyes displayed his hurt as they followed her outside. He couldn't accept what was taking place here. He had to get her back, wasn't going to live without her. As she opened her umbrella and eventually became lost in the mix of people moving about under the pouring rain, Lionel's cell phone abruptly interrupted his trance on the third ring.

Looking down at who was calling and recognizing the number, he eventually answered, "Yes."

"I got something. I've been following her like you asked and there was nothing . . . until just this week."

"Go ahead," Lionel replied.

"I'm sending the pictures to your phone now so you can see for yourself," the voice on the other end stated.

Lionel took a heavy sigh, preparing himself for what was about to come, and replied, "Okay."

After a few seconds of waiting, the images came to his mobile. They were of Alex and a male stranger. Lionel took a moment to study the unfamiliar face of this man with his wife, finger-swiping through several images of the two of them together – some that appeared to be in this very place. In this moment, a crazed type of jealousy that had been buried deep was slowly resurfacing inside of him – one that had been hidden well over the years.

When Lionel was done, he took a heavy swallow and then placed the phone back to his ear and asked, "Who is he?"

"His name is Gabriel. Gabriel Washington," the voice replied.

For more information on
Edward Dean Arnold,
visit him online at
www.edwarddeanarnold.com